this
adventure
ends

Henry Holt and Company · New York

this
adventure
ends

emma mills

Henry Holt and Company
Publishers since 1866
175 Fifth Avenue, New York, New York 10010
fiercereads.com

Library of Congress Cataloging-in-Publication Data

Names: Mills, Emma, 1989- author.
Title: This adventure ends / Emma Mills.
Description: First edition. | New York : Henry Holt and Company, 2016. |
    Summary: "Sloane isn't expecting to fall in with a group of friends when
    she moves from New York to Florida especially not a group of friends so intense,
    so in love, so all-consuming"— Provided by publisher.
Identifiers: LCCN 2016001536 (print) | LCCN 2016027354 (ebook) | ISBN
    9781627799355 (hardback) | ISBN 9781627799362 (Ebook)
Subjects: | CYAC: Moving, Household—Fiction. | Friendship—Fiction. | Dating
    (Social customs)—Fiction. | High schools—Fiction. | Schools—Fiction. |
    Florida—Fiction. | BISAC: JUVENILE FICTION / Social Issues / Friendship.
    | JUVENILE FICTION / Love & Romance. | JUVENILE FICTION / Family / General
    (see also headings under Social Issues).
Classification: LCC PZ7.1.M6 Th 2016 (print) | LCC PZ7.1.M6 (ebook) | DDC
    [Fic]—dc23
LC record available at https://lccn.loc.gov/2016001536

Our books may be purchased in bulk for promotional, educational,
or business use. Please contact your local bookseller or the Macmillan Corporate and
Premium Sales Department at (800) 221-7945 ext. 5442
or by e-mail at MacmillanSpecialMarkets@macmillan.com.

Epigraph reprinted with the permission of Atheneum Books for Young Readers,
an imprint of Simon & Schuster Children's Publishing Division from FROM THE
MIXED-UP FILES OF MRS. BASIL E. FRANKWEILER by E.L. Konigsburg.
Copyright 1967 E.L. Konigsburg; copyright renewed © 1995 E.L. Konigsburg.

Book design by Liz Dresner

First Edition—2016

Printed in the United States of America by
R. R. Donnelley & Sons Company, Harrisonburg, Virginia

1   3   5   7   9   10   8   6   4   2

For the greatest papa (my papa)

The adventure is over. Everything gets over, and nothing is ever enough. Except the part you carry with you.

—E. L. KONIGSBURG,
From the Mixed-up Files of Mrs. Basil E. Frankweiler

one

My immediate priority is air.

Bree has dragged me to a house party, and the place is too warm. Everything is a little too close.

I don't like being in a stranger's house at the best of times. Seeing the pictures on someone else's fridge, the knickknacks on their mantel, whether or not their toilet-paper roll goes over or under . . . that stuff is personal. To be so outside of it, and yet still privy to it, feels like some kind of a violation.

I can't say this to Bree. So I just listen in on one more conversation about whether Jen and Asher from calculus are finally "official" ("Do they need to be notarized?" I ask, and no one laughs), and then I make my way to the kitchen to escape out the back door.

Unfortunately, escape is barred.

"It's not a big deal," this kid is saying, pitching his voice over the thrum of the room. Clearly it is a big deal, because a ring of onlookers has formed around him. It's that sort of Shakespearean chorus that pops up at parties like this, to observe and cast judgment and report back to the masses later.

I'm only three weeks in at Grove County High School, but I recognize the speaker from my AP biology class. His name is Mason, and he sits at the lab bench in front of mine.

I also recognize him from the pages of my father's novels. In a few short years, Mason could be the sheriff's son who backhands the preacher's daughter, or the ex–high school quarterback hell-bent on avenging some romantic slight. Guys like him were a dime a dozen in Everett Finch's world, and they usually died in a fire.

"She doesn't want to talk to you," the guy standing directly across from Mason says.

"And how the hell do you know that? Twin magic? When she's hit on, you feel it, too?"

The guy doesn't reply, but there is this look in his eyes, a quiet rage that I wouldn't have messed with had I been Mason.

"Really, you should be thanking me," Mason continues. "I don't think she's a lost cause. I could help her turn shit around."

Mason steps into the other guy's space, eliciting a quiet but firm "Don't."

"Or what?"

The guy doesn't respond.

"Or what?" Mason repeats, and steps even closer. In different circumstances, they'd look for all the world like they were about to kiss. Mason's lips curve upward into a smile. "Is this getting to you? Are you wired wrong, too?"

"Don't" is all he says again.

"Come on, it's not like you're going to hit me. You want to know how I know?" When the guy doesn't answer, Mason reaches out and puts his hands on either side of the guy's head, forcing it up and down in a nod. "Yes, Mason, I want to know." And then he moves one hand to the guy's face, smushing his cheeks between his thumb and forefinger. "'Cause you're a *nice fucking guy, Fuller.*" He squeezes with each word.

The guy still doesn't move, and maybe Mason is right—maybe he won't hit him. Maybe he's too solid to respond.

But I'm not.

"Sorry," I say, angling through the people in front of me. "I'm sorry. So sorry. Don't mean to interrupt. It's just . . . are you for fucking serious?"

Mason looks at me, his hand still grasping the guy's face. Surprise cuts through his smirk. *A girl is volunteering to talk to him*, I think, and in that moment, I know which tack to use.

So I tamp down the outrage and manage something like a smile as I reach out and close my fingers loosely around Mason's wrist. A soft touch. He lets me guide his hand away without protest.

"I mean . . . these hands aren't really meant for that kind of thing, are they?"

His eyes track me as I lace my fingers together with his.

"These hands are for . . . for caressing," I continue. "For stroking, even."

"Oh yeah?" Mason says with a dumb little smile. His target just stands there, altogether forgotten.

"Yeah," I say. "Yourself. In front of the TV. Alone. Every night."

Mason doesn't get it right away, but there's a hoot from the crowd and a few barely suppressed guffaws.

"If nothing else, you can at least use them to grasp for intelligence, or like, some semblance of human decency."

The crowd reaction amps up, like a sitcom soundtrack. Mason wrenches his hand out of mine.

"What's your problem?" he says.

3

"Your face," I reply, because that's what my sister, Laney, would say.

"Fuck you," he says, but he's lost control of the room. The chorus is already buzzing. "Fuck this." He smiles with too much teeth. "Got yourself a guard dog, huh, Fuller? Emphasis on *dog*." Like this will somehow hurt my feelings. But that's assuming I have them in the first place.

When I don't react, Mason shakes his head and retreats, the chorus folding in around us. I look back to where the guy had been standing, but he's already headed out the back door.

Bree appears at my elbow, clutching a plastic cup. Her cheeks are red, and she is grinning. "Geez. That was—was that a New York thing? Do they teach you that kind of stuff there?"

Yes. Here is your MetroCard, and this is how you publicly dismantle insufferable dicks.

"It was a person thing. That guy was an ass."

She shakes her head, still grinning. "Geez."

"What?"

"Gabe Fuller." She gestures in the direction of the guy's retreat. "You stepped in for freaking Gabe Fuller."

"Yeah," I say, because I don't how to respond to that.

A kid I vaguely recognize from my lit class comes up then, holding his hand up for a high five.

"That was hilarious," he says.

I slap his palm, but suddenly it's too close in there again, too much, so I excuse myself and make my way to the door.

It's quieter outside. There's just the low hum of crickets and the soft smack of a couple making out on the porch swing. The chains attaching the swing to the ceiling rattle as she adjusts, he adjusts. One of them sighs, a soft little sound.

I ignore them, bracing my hands against the railing. The night air hangs thick with late-summer humidity, but a few deep breaths still put me right.

Some scraggly trees populate the backyard, and there's an attempt at a garden—a trellis hung with vines, a couple of thorny-looking bushes. The ground is a study in that patchy North Florida grass, which is mostly just sand and a thick coating of live oak leaves. The leaves shine in the light from the motion-sensor bulb on the garage. That same light throws two figures at the end of the yard into stark relief.

I can't hear them from where I stand. Rationally, I know it's none of my business. But I step off the porch anyway and move across the yard toward them.

"I told you we shouldn't have gone to a non-Frank-sanctioned party," the girl is saying as I near. I'm shielded a bit by the shadow of the trellis.

"Why were you even talking to him?"

"He talked to me first. I'm not just going to ignore another human being. We can't all stare through people, Gabe."

"Yeah, well, try. Look at them, and instead of seeing them, see whatever's behind them. And then ignore that, too."

"Yeah, that's a super healthy approach. Super great social skills."

"Mason Pierce doesn't deserve your social skills. He doesn't deserve the hair in your shower drain."

"Who does deserve the hair in my shower drain? Should I start mailing it to Tash? Do you want me to save you some?"

"I swear to God—"

The end of that oath never comes, because it's then they realize I'm there.

5

Somehow at the sight of me, the guy—Gabe—looks angrier than before. It's not that quiet-rage burn, but more of an outward hostility.

The girl, on the other hand, smiles wide. It lights up her face. "Hey. It's you."

It's such a strange thing to say—like somehow I was expected—that all I can do is nod. "It's me."

"I didn't need you to do that," Gabe says.

"Thank you," the girl amends, "is what he's trying to say."

"I didn't need you to do that," he repeats, and for some reason, his irritation irks me. I did a thing. Stepped in. Dismantled a bully. I could've gone on and done nothing, like the rest of fucking Solo Cup nation in there. "I didn't need anyone's help. Everything was under control."

"So the part where he plied your face like Play-Doh was a critical step in your plan?"

The girl snorts, and Gabe shoots her a glare.

"I was fine," he says tightly. "Next time, don't help."

I nod. "Okay. Sure." But I am incapable of leaving it at that. "'Cause if this world needs anything, it's more passive witnesses to injustice, right? The U.N. should adopt that model. Amnesty International. Forget the barbed-wire candle—their symbol should just be like a guy leaning against a wall with his arms folded and a speech bubble that says 'Want to help? Next time, don't.' Someone should really get the number for the Gates Foundation and let them know."

"That's not what I'm—" Gabe begins, but once I start, it's kind of hard to stop.

"Hey, I know scientists are super busy trying to find cures for diseases and stuff, but maybe at this point in time they should just try *not* doing that—"

"I didn't say—"

"Humanitarian aid workers," I call out, like the yard is full of them. "Lay down your instruments of change, because 'Don't help' is the societal model we're going with now—"

"Okay," he says loudly. "Okay, fine, yes, I'm sorry. Thank you. For helping. Thanks. Please just stop."

The girl bursts out laughing. Gabe glares at her.

"Sorry," she says. "Just . . . your face. God. So good." She points at me. "You're great. You're staying. We're keeping you."

Gabe looks at her and then at me, and for a second I think he might laugh, too. His lips twitch, at least, and the corners of his eyes crinkle up a little as he looks away. It's almost as if something has been defused inside him. Like the right wire has been cut.

"Who are you again?" he says.

"Sloane," I reply. "Who are you?"

"Gabe. Fuller. This is Vera." He waves a hand at the girl. Framed in the light from the garage, I can see they favor each other—similar in the line of the nose and the curve of the lips. *Twin magic*, Mason had said. Two pairs of dark eyes look out from under thick lashes, framed by the kind of eyebrows that are equal parts impressive and intimidating.

"Nice to meet you," Vera says, and nudges Gabe. "Isn't it?"

"Yeah," he says. And then to Vera: "I'm going to go. Are you going to ride with Aubrey, or . . ."

"No, I'll go with you. Do you want a ride, Sloane?"

"That's okay, I drove somebody."

"Okay. Well." Vera looks to Gabe, who is now staring in the direction of the garage. "Thanks again."

"No problem. I'm here all week."

"You're vacationing?" She looks mildly alarmed.

"No. No, it's just . . . one of those things comedians say? 'I'm here all week' . . . 'Tip your waitress.'"

Vera grins. "I get it. You're funny." She glances at Gabe again, but he doesn't give confirmation. His jaw is firmly set once more. "See you at school, I guess?"

"Sure. I'll be the one who looks like me."

She laughs, and it's weirdly gratifying. I haven't had such a receptive audience in a long time. Laney's only nine, but she knows all my dumb jokes by now.

Casting one last smile at me, Vera grabs Gabe's arm and leads him toward the house, and I am alone once more.

Except for the couple making out on the porch swing, I think, until I look back and see that they, too, have left. Maybe they fled during my humanitarian-aid-workers speech.

I return to the porch and settle down on the vacated swing. It creaks as I rock back and forth. The chains look like they probably won't withstand many more vigorous make-out sessions.

I check my phone. Nine thirty-four. I think my mom will be satisfied if I stay until ten.

You should go! she had said, when I mentioned tonight's party. *Get to know some new people! Do something fun!*

Just different shades of the same things she would say to me back home. So I gave my standard response: *These things are always boring.*

You won't know unless you try, she replied. *Maybe it'll be different here.*

She had a point. Maybe it would. That's sort of what I'm counting on, after all.

8

two

Saturday mornings are for my voice lessons, two hours away on the Florida State University campus in Tallahassee. My mom drives me, despite my protests of *I can go by myself.*

You're not familiar with the roads here, she said simply when this argument first came about.

Yeah, you never know what you might encounter out there that we never had back home, my dad chipped in.

Like what? I said. *Roads are roads.*

Gators, Dad said simply.

I want to see a gator! was Laney's contribution.

Now that's the kind of enthusiasm I'm here for, Dad said. *You know, Jill, if we stay long enough, Laney might get an accent. Develop herself a fine Southern drawwwl. I might adopt one, too. I might get one of those Colonel Sanders suits.*

God help us all, Mom replied.

"Sloane?"

"Hmm?"

"I said, do you mind stopping? Laney wants one of those Floopy toys, from the movie. Think you can choke down a Happy Meal?"

I turn the corner down on the page in my book—even though it's completely pointless, as it's the very first page—and close it. "I'm willing to take one for the team."

Happy Meals acquired, we head back toward the highway. "Did you have fun last night?" Mom says as we merge back on. "You were out pretty late."

"Ten o'clock, wow. Should we throw a parade?"

"Hey, it's the odd night when you're not putting PJs on by seven."

"Maybe I sneak out and go to clubs where PJs are required."

"If there's a club where PJs are required, I'm pretty sure they wouldn't be the kind you wear."

I don't know, maybe I could charm the bouncer with my SpongeBob pants and my dad's old SUNY sweatshirt.

"How was the party?" Mom says, before I can get out a rejoinder.

"It was fine."

"Bree seems nice."

Bree is nice. One of the first things she told me about herself was that Kim Kardashian replied to her once on Twitter. I didn't know the proper way to respond to that. Like whether some kind of congratulations were in order.

Bree is my lab partner, the first person I met at Grove County High School, and arguably my only friend here. Not that we've done much else together besides AP bio worksheets and last night's party, and that was only because *You haven't been to one yet? Gosh, Sloane, you have to get out eventually!* No wonder my mom liked Bree; they were cut from the same cloth.

"Uh-huh," I say, and shove some fries in my mouth.

"Anything fun happen?"

I don't know if I would call dismantling Mason Pierce *fun*, particularly, but there was a certain satisfaction to it. Nor was meeting Vera and Gabe fun, per se, but it was . . . well, it was something different.

I just shrug. "Not really."

"How was your lesson? You didn't say."

"I did say."

"You said 'fine.' Can we expound on 'fine' a little bit? As the passenger, it's your obligation to keep the driver entertained."

This is something my dad says all the time. I think she realizes that, because she goes on quickly: "You're liking Eileen?"

My new voice teacher. I don't dislike her. But, "I miss Paula."

She glances over at me, and it's my turn to go on quickly: "But I mean, Eileen is good, too. Nice to . . . get an outside take, I guess?"

"Got to get you in shape for auditions."

My mom is approximately sixteen times more excited for college auditions than I am.

"It's still really early" is all I reply. I just sent in my prescreens before we moved. I would be learning new material with Eileen, as well as maintaining the audition pieces I started with Paula.

It's quiet as we eat. My mom has her own bag in her lap, occasionally pulling out a fry or taking a pull from her Diet Coke.

"You want me to read to you?" I say when I'm done eating.

"I thought you finished your book on the way in."

"Got another. One of Dad's." I hold up the cover for reference, but her eyes don't leave the road.

Her expression doesn't change, but her voice hardens just

a smidge: "Maybe I'll just see what's on," and she clicks on the radio. NPR, *Fresh Air*.

I read anyway. The radio is easy to tune out, even easier when traveling familiar territory. I've read all my dad's books at least once. *Some would argue that if you've read one, you've read them all*, he's said before. It's true, in a sense—there are definitely some standout Everett Finch tropes. Small coastal towns. Love as a means of salvation. Dead pets. It was rare that an entire cast of characters made it out of a book alive, but at the very least, the dog would bite it. Faithful old Rufus met his maker in *Heaven Sent*. Max the stray is cut down in *Summer Burn*. And Avery, the ten-week-old puppy, kicks the bucket in my current read, *Sand on Our Beach*.

I asked my dad once why the puppy had to die. He said simply, "Tragic irony."

Despite that, *Sand on Our Beach* is still my favorite one. It tells the story of Sarah, a twentysomething living in the shadow of a terminal diagnosis, who moves to a small beach town to live out her final days in peace. She writes her memoirs (*I know it sounds stupid, but young people can write memoirs*, Sarah declares in chapter two. *Just because you have fewer years doesn't mean they were any less meaningful*) and reconnects with the sea (*The first place I ever felt like there was more out there than myself*, she tells Jack in chapter ten).

That was one of my favorite passages—her talk with Jack about the ocean. I'm tempted to flip ahead, but I can never really read books that way. I always end up going back and picking up what I've missed, even if I've read it a dozen times before. It doesn't seem right, skipping to the best parts and ignoring the in-between.

We're kind of at an in-between right now. I look over at my mom as we ease back onto 30A. I don't know why I said I miss Paula.

I know they would've stayed, if I had asked. They would've stayed in New York so I could finish high school where I started it. But I didn't ask, because I didn't care. Maybe there's something a little bit wrong with me. Or maybe that's just what comes of being the daughter of a fictional puppy killer. Different sensibilities. Different priorities.

"I'm kind of too old for this stuff," Laney says when we present her with the Floopy toy back home.

"Fine then, I'll take it." I go to grab the toy from my mom's hand, but Laney snatches it away.

"No, I want it!"

"That's what I thought," I say, and she makes a face at me but clutches the plastic package to her chest all the same.

three

When I get to AP biology on Monday morning, I find my seat has been taken.

Technically it's not like there are assigned seats, but there is this self-imposed thing where you sit in the same spot every time anyway. It's basically unspoken classroom law.

"Sorry." I hover by the other chair at the bench where Bree and I usually sit. "Are you—did you want to partner with Bree?"

"No," the guy in my seat says. "We switched. I'm Remy."

Remy has close-cut hair and a faint goatee going, like it's something he wants to try out, but his face isn't certain of it yet.

I glance around and clock Bree sliding into a seat in the back, next to a stocky blond kid. She waves at me when I catch her eye and flashes me a smile and a double thumbs-up.

Huh. So either Bree is into that blond kid, or Remy is into me. You don't just up and switch. See unspoken-seat thing. That universally acknowledged tenet of *You sat there on the first day, and if you don't like it, you damn well better get over it.*

I take a seat and glance over at Remy. A shiny class ring gleams on his pointer finger. I can just make out the little sports emblems etched onto it: a baseball and bat flanking the stone on one side, a football on the other.

"I'm Sloane," I say.

"I know," he replies.

It's then that Mason Pierce sidles along the aisle in front of us. He settles into the seat in front of Remy, glances back at us, faces forward, and then does a double take. He looks between us, and his lips curve into a smile that's more like a sneer. Remy, meanwhile, gives him a nod.

"Johnson," Mason says curtly. "Got a new friend?" He manages to make the word *friend* sound like an insult.

"Let's just say I got a new seat and leave it at that," Remy says, with a smile that belies the edge in his voice. Before Mason can answer, the teacher clears her throat, and class begins.

It's a lecture today, no lab stuff, so Remy and I don't interact much. The lead in my mechanical pencil snaps at one point and ricochets off in his direction, to which I say "Sorry" and he says nothing. When class is over, he packs up his stuff, gives me a nod, and then heads out.

So maybe Bree really is into that blond guy. I can't catch up with her after class to ask, but it seems like the most likely scenario.

Until Vera plunks down in the seat across from me at lunch and says, "Remember me?"

I'm at a corner table in the cafeteria, munching on an apple and reading *The Casebook of Sherlock Holmes*.

"From the party," she adds when I look up.

"I remember."

"Good. Because I couldn't forget you. I've never seen Gabe that annoyed with someone who wasn't me."

"Is that a good thing?"

"Annoying Gabe is a great thing," she says with a grin. Then she angles her head, taking in the title of my book. "Sherlock?"

"Yeah." I don't know why I say it, but I do: "My, uh, my dad used to read them to me, when I was a kid." Now he reads them to Laney, and if I happen to stand in the doorway and hear a few, then so be it.

"They're the best," she says. "I just wish there was one where they finally admit that they love each other."

"Sorry?"

"Sherlock and Watson. They never really say that they love each other in the canon, but it's so freaking obvious. Like, Sherlock would straight-up kill for Watson."

I smile.

"Are your friends on their way?" she says, glancing around the room. "I don't want to take someone's spot."

I hold up the book. "Sherlock and Watson are my friends."

She looks at me for a moment, something alight in her eyes. Then she says, "We're going to eat lunch together, okay?" And takes a sandwich and an apple out of her bag.

"Okay."

Vera chats while she neatly works through her lunch. It's clear that the garage light from the weekend's party hadn't really done her justice. My mom would describe her as "va-va-voom." Something tells me that there is no product in science or nature that could make my hair look that shiny, nothing Sephora has to offer that could turn my eyes that bright.

That being said, I get the feeling it's not really her looks that do it, or her hair, or her makeup, because if you took all that away, there would still be something about her, some kind of magnetism. Vera leans in to talk to me—like we are conspiring somehow—and the little smile at the corner of her lips sort of makes me want to smile, too.

It's only when we're making our way through the hall after lunch that Vera slants a look over at me and says, "Did he give you trouble? In class?"

"What?"

"Mason. Was he a dick to you in class?"

"Oh. No. I mean—how'd you know we have class together?"

"Remy said."

"You know Remy?"

"Of course. Who do you think told him to sit next to you?" She grins and then grabs my arm and pulls me into the nearest bathroom, where she fixes her makeup. (It's flawless.) When she's done, she holds up her phone, very carefully angles her body so her waist looks incredibly small and her chest and ass look incredibly . . . prominent . . . flashes a smile, and clicks.

Then, "Sorry. That's so rude. You want to be in it? We can make it a photoset."

"Oh, I don't really—"

"Smile!"

I quickly turn to the side like Vera as she clicks again. Upon viewing the picture, Vera looks like a Victoria's Secret model, whereas I look like someone brought in for violating parole.

"I'll tag you—what's your Instagram?"

"Uh, I don't really . . ." *Document my life for the Internet.*

17

"No worries." She flips through filters, and then her thumbs fly: "'Post-lunch selfie with new friend Sloane.'" There is a pause. "Sweet. A hundred likes."

"Wait . . ." I follow Vera out of the bathroom. "A hundred? You posted it like ten seconds ago."

"I know. They think you're cute."

"They?"

"The Internet. I do stuff on the Internet. It's fun."

I will later learn that "do stuff on the Internet" loosely means that Vera has enough followers on various social-media sites to fill a professional football stadium, several times over. Companies send her stuff to promote. Strangers send her jewelry.

But right now, post–bathroom selfie, all I know is that in under a minute, one hundred people had "liked" a picture of me looking dismal and still thought I was cute. Maybe people just look better next to Vera. Like a planet shining brighter in proximity to the sun.

She walks with me to my next class and says, "We meet by the buses after school. You should definitely come."

This begs some questions—like "Who's we?" and "Why?"—but I don't let them loose. I just nod and say, "Yeah, sure."

"Awesome." She gives me a sunny smile, and then she's gone.

four

When I get home later that afternoon, my dad is sitting in his lounger wearing pajamas, with a towel draped artistically over his head. He looks like a shepherd in a Sunday-school nativity play.

"Where were you?" he asks when I come in.

"Hanging out."

"Ooh, with who?"

"Some local youth."

"You sound eighty."

"And you look like a maniac. What are you doing?"

"I'm relaxing." He rubs the towel. "Terry cloth is good for the brain. I read an article on it."

I raise an eyebrow.

"Okay, I read a blog post. On a somewhat less-than-credible web-site. But it did say it could—how did they put it?—'re-energize your photons'?" He fishes for his tablet.

"Really."

"There may have been mention of a lizard overlord. But that shouldn't automatically discredit what they say, right?" He swipes the screen a couple of times. "It's supposed to 'clear the path to rationalization.'"

"Did you write anything today?"

"I wrote a slogan for that website. 'Come 'cause you're stressed, stay 'cause you're blessed . . . by the reptilian messiah.'" He does finger guns.

"Dad."

"Elder child." He tosses the tablet aside and slaps his knee. "Come. Tell me about your day. Tell me about these youth."

I sink down onto the couch. "They're from school."

"I figured as much. Gimme some names and faces."

Well, first, there was Aubrey, who sidled up to me in front of the buses and said, "Hey, it's new friend Sloane." Upon my look of confusion, she held up her phone. "I follow Vera," she explained. "Like half the continent."

"Oh, cool," I said, still a little confused. "So you're like . . . a fan?" Was Vera so Internet famous that I could be recognized by proxy?

"I'm a friend," she replied. "She said to meet here after school?"

"Oh. Yeah. Sorry."

She gave me a tight smile and then promptly turned to her phone as Remy approached us with a wave; apparently he was part of Vera's *we*, as well. Finally, Vera arrived and declared that we'd be going to Opal for snow cones.

There are a handful of towns along the coast collectively termed the Beaches of Grove County. The vacation towns, like Opal, have very few permanent residents, so the majority of the kids at Grove County come from a town a little farther down 30A called Grayson. But Opal is good for snacks, the last vestiges of summer still operating.

Come the end of the month, summer hours would end, and snow cones would be harder to come by.

So we went, and sat, and ate. They chatted. Aubrey texted. I listened politely. Not a bad afternoon. All in all, it was . . . an afternoon.

I relate this, for the most part, to my dad, who listens with his eyes shut. When I'm done, he looks over at me.

"Sounds like a productive day."

"I guess?"

"You made three friends. People only make three friends in one day on sitcoms."

"We're not . . . friends. We ate snow cones. They talked about the Avengers."

"How do you think friendships are forged? Mutual interests. Food. Repetition. If you see them two more times, they're your friends."

I don't quite believe him. It's not like there's some kind of formula to it. And even if there was, I certainly wouldn't be the one to pull it off.

"Hey, you want to go pick up Laney from her thing?" Dad says. "After School Cultural Whatever It's Called?"

"Culture Camp?"

"Ugh. Yeah. Culture Camp. Have you ever heard anything more ridiculous?"

"Yes. Re-energizing your photons."

He grins. "Touché."

"Don't you want to go?" I ask. "You could, you know . . . put real clothes on."

"And lose sight of the path to rationalization? Hell no." He waves me away. "Go get your sister."

21

Laney is not so easily obtained. At nine, she's already a natural social butterfly. I can see her on the lawn in front of her school from across the circle. They have long plastic folding tables set up, piled high with art stuff. They all appear to be painting geometric designs; Laney later informs me that it's "tile art," and my mom hangs hers in the kitchen.

Right now I watch as Laney leans in to whisper something to the girl next to her. They both giggle and consult a third.

It was easier back then, wasn't it? A few good packs of press-on earrings or some credits on Club Penguin and you were in. Or maybe Laney's just better at that stuff than me. I didn't do my best this afternoon. Mostly I stared into the depths of my snow cone and wondered how on earth someone could know so much about the Marvel universe (Remy), smile so frequently (Vera), or text with such vigor (Aubrey).

I greet the adultish-looking person at one of the front tables, who calls Laney over.

"Time to go," I say.

"Ten more minutes."

"Mom's making spaghetti."

"Yummmm, okay." Laney abandons her friends in the way of a nine-year-old, meaning she goes back to the table and hugs each of them good-bye as if she'll never see them again. It takes at least ten minutes.

We walk home together and she tells me about her day, and then it's Mom's dinner as promised. My dad takes Laney for a walk on the beach afterward, as the sun is going down. It's too early to see the stars, but Laney brings her constellation guide anyway—*A*

Comprehensive Guide to the Stars by Dr. Angela Fellows is one of her latest obsessions. Once she learned that different constellations were visible at different times—*Like the sky is changing, all year long! We're seeing different parts of the galaxy, Sloane!*—it was a done deal.

I don't join them tonight, instead opting to stay in for the usual. Homework. Practice. And when all is said and done—Laney is tucked away, my mom is watching the news, my dad is re-energizing his whatevers—I get online and search the screen name I saw on Vera's phone at lunch: @vera_marie.

The accounts come up instantly: vera_marie is on all the networks, including ones I've never even heard before. What is Flipit? ("Kind of like Snapchat, but videos only," Vera will say later when I ask.) What is Heartmark? ("Kind of like Flipit, but with emojis.")

The numbers are staggering. Followers, likes, views, winkydinks (courtesy of Heartmark). I click over to the image tab, and dozens of Veras stare back at me: Vera posing in front of a mirror in a crop top, Vera at the beach, Vera with her head pillowed on her arms in class.

Her Twitter is a study in affirmations and exclamation points. She at-replies more than she tweets, and there are so many words of encouragement and "<333333"s and "XOXO"s, to rival the number of "please answer it would make my life" and "omg ily"s in her mentions.

Her profile is the same across all platforms: *Vera Marie Fuller. 17. Loving life, my friends, my girl.*

I click on *my girl* and it brings me to another profile—@natashah19. A girl who looks, if possible, even more glamorous than Vera. The most recent picture shows the two of them together, lying across a beach blanket in the sand. Natashah19's arm is extended, holding the camera, but they're looking at each other instead of into the lens. Vera's hand is wrapped in Natashah19's dark hair, pulling her in, and Natashah19 is grinning widely.

Gorgeous, the top comment reads, followed by one of those heart-eyes emojis.

I click over to one of my own neglected profiles and follow Vera. Then I shut down the laptop and go to bed.

five

"So how'd you start?" I ask, peeling the lid off my pudding cup. Vera sits across from me with one of those prepackaged salads, the kind they throw all kinds of fancy stuff into to disguise the salad taste. As far as I'm concerned, no amount of cranberries or pine nuts is going to transform it into curly fries, so it's not even worth it.

I was surprised to see Vera in my third-period calculus class. She plopped down in the seat next to me and said, "We had this one together the whole time! Who knew? I usually sit up front. Funny what you miss when you're not looking, huh?"

After calculus came lunch, and now here we are, meal two of *If you see them two more times, they're your friends.*

"The Internet stuff, I mean. How'd you start it?"

She shrugs. "I don't know, it kind of just happened."

"So what, you tripped and took a selfie, and it went viral?"

A smile. "Not exactly. I don't know, I started doing it more seriously sophomore year, and it just kind of took off. It's a good distraction."

"From what?"

Her eyes shine. "Everything." She spears a piece of cucumber. "Everyone needs a distraction every now and then, don't you think? It can't all be school and homework and ugh, God, calc is terrible, isn't it? We should study after school. Except I have to work. Put a pin in studying."

"Where do you work?"

"At a boutique in Opal. But since school started, it's only twice a week. Hey, do you need a job? Most places have scaled back because summer season's ending, but I actually know a place that's hiring. I could probably get you an interview."

I have actually never had a job. I don't want to admit that in this moment, so I just shrug. "I mean, sure. I guess. If you know a place."

I had always thought a job would detract from my work. School. Practice. But I could handle twice a week, right?

"I will hook you up, girl," she says with a grin.

"Tell me more," my dad says that evening, tenting his fingers together and resting them under his nose, like some kind of knockoff BBC detective. "What's she look like?"

"I don't know, google her. She'll pop up. She has a social-media presence."

"My publicist keeps telling me to get one of those."

"Everett Finch tragedies, a hundred and forty characters or less?"

My dad clears his throat: " 'Love me,' Jake said. 'I do,' Annie replied. And then she died.' " He grins. "That's it. That's every book I ever wrote."

"Not every book. They don't always die."

"*They don't always die.* There's my Twitter bio. What's your friend's handle?"

"Her *handle?* Geez, Dad, come on."

"Okay, what would you call it?"

"I don't know. It's Vera underscore Marie."

"Sloane?" My mom pokes her head in. "You want to tell Laney it's bedtime?"

"Jill, what should my Twitter bio be?" Dad asks.

She just smiles. "I'll defer to your judgment."

"Something about love," I say when she leaves. "Everett Finch will punch you in the stomach with love and then hit you over the head with tragedy."

"I like that. Get me set up and we'll go with that. But first it's lights-out for Laney."

"That sounded really sinister."

He grins. "I try."

When I head upstairs, the hall is bathed in light spilling from Laney's room.

For her ninth birthday, Laney wanted nothing so badly as a scrapbook. My parents got her one with a red fake-leather cover and binding, gold writing etched into the front: *My Memories.* It was the one she had specifically shown them in a craft store circular as being *totally perfect, this one, Mom, this is the one.*

Laney adds to *My Memories* frequently—so often that she has gone through four additional packs of filler paper already. Photos, pictures from magazines, newspaper clippings, papers from school, God forbid we see a movie—there is a whole page for movie ticket stubs—everything goes into the book.

She's working on it when I look in on her. She doesn't squawk when I appear, so I move into the room and sink down across the bottom of the bed while she clips pictures out of a magazine. It's a brightly colored, glossy outfit I used to love when I was younger called *J-14*. As in "Just for Teens." I really thought that was some next-level shit.

Laney does, too, despite not being a teen at all. I watch as she carefully cuts out the head of a boy-band member. She then glue-sticks the back and presses it lovingly into the book.

"Who's that?" I ask, pointing to the guy. "Is that One Direction?"

"That's Kai, from This Is Our Now, which you already know."

I do, just like my dad knows that it's not called "the MTV." That stuff's just funny, I guess—acting ironically crotchety.

"Mom says it's time for bed."

"What does Papa say?"

"He says 'Don't pit your parents against each other.'"

She makes a face, but after one last pat of the Kai clipping to make sure it's firmly secured, she closes *My Memories*.

I help her pack her supplies back into a plastic bin and stow it under her bed. Then she slides under the covers and I pull them up around her.

"Which stuffie do you want?"

"Mmm, Phoebe."

Phoebe is a soft brown rabbit with a lilac bow around its neck. I pull it down from the shelf above Laney's bed and tuck it in beside her.

I'm about to switch off the light when she says, "Can I ask you something?" And then, "Don't say I just did. Just say yes."

There's nothing she could ask me that I wouldn't at least try to answer. But the sudden seriousness in her eyes worries me. I've been doing my best to keep Laney as oblivious as possible these past few months. If that meant plying her with *J-14*s or watching the TION documentary for the umpteenth time, so be it.

But Kai and the boys are safely shut away in *My Memories*, and there's little to draw Laney's gaze from me.

"Sloane, say yes," she prompts.

"Yes."

"Is Papa depressed?"

That's not what I was expecting. "Sorry?"

"It's like we're not supposed to notice he just sits around the house all day."

"He works from home. People do that."

Even though she doesn't yet have the agency to tell me that she isn't buying my shit, Laney gives me a look that clearly states she isn't buying my shit. "He sits around the house all day, in his pajamas, doing stuff online. He's like one of those commercials for sad drugs."

"Well . . . I think he's just . . . in a slump."

"A slump sounds depressing."

"He's working through some career stuff," I say, because that's what Mom said to me. There's a good chance Laney thinks I'm wiser than I really am, because a lot of the time when my own explanation doesn't cut it, I just end up telling her stuff that our mom has told me first.

"Like what to write next?"

"Yeah."

"But he loves writing. How is that depressing?"

"I don't know . . . I guess it can be hard when it's your job." I shrug. "Every job has good and bad parts to it, right?"

"Skittles taste tester."

"Cavities."

She screws up her face. "Okay, what if you're Kai's manager? And you get to ride on the bus with him and go backstage?"

"Yeah, but then you have to be around boys all the time. And they smell."

She smiles. "Okay, what about singer? Serious singer. Fancy. Like you."

I pause. "You're right. That one's perfect."

"Do you really think so?" she says.

"I don't know," I say, because I don't. I drop a kiss to the top of her head and then lean over and switch off the light. "Go to sleep."

six

Dodge's Market is the fancy grocery store in Opal. *The vacation grocery*, my dad likes to distinguish. *They know you are on vacation, and so they know they can capitalize on either your bliss or your desperation and charge you eight dollars for milk and seventeen dollars for toilet paper and thirty-four dollars for a sandwich with baby kale on it.*

Thus begins the baby-kale rant: *What is its life cycle? When does it progress to mature kale? Will this kale be educated? Who is responsible for the matriculation of this kale?* It happened at least once every vacation.

We shop at the Publix a few miles inland now, because we're not on vacation anymore. But my dad still swings by Dodge's occasionally for a nice bottle of wine or a particular cheese that he read about online. *(This cheese will fix what ails you, Sloane!)*

I swing by Dodge's today at Vera's encouragement. Because she's "hooking me up."

It's pretty small for a grocery store, but it makes up for it in ceiling height, with tall shelves lining the store and one of those library-style ladders wrapping around. It's light and bright and airy, with hand-drawn signs in the large front windows declaring two Coronas for eight dollars or Belgian waffles for twelve. An L-shaped deli counter stands in the center of the store, the case on the shorter side filled with baked goods, the one on the long side piled with salads and entrées and the offending kale sandwiches.

I've been in Dodge's dozens of times over the course of my life—I started coming here before I can even remember—but I don't know where to go when I step in today. There's no one at the cash register in the front.

I hear rustling behind the deli counter, so I head that way. And then someone pops up.

I blink. "Hey."

Gabe Fuller blinks back. "Hey yourself."

He's wearing a baseball cap that has SHOP DODGE'S! embroidered across it.

"Fight anybody recently?" I say, because I haven't seen him since the night of the party, and it's the first thing that pops into my head. "Any face mashings?"

"That's funny," he says, in the kind of way that implies it isn't.

"Vera got me a job interview here. She knew they were hiring." I gesture to him. "I guess this is how she knew they were hiring?"

"Guess so."

"Are you going to do the interview? Because it's going great so far. I really feel like I'm making an awesome impression. I could keep going? Share an embarrassing childhood memory, tell you about my bad habits . . ."

His lips twitch, an almost-smile. "Leigh will interview you—she's in the back."

We both stand there for a moment.

"Maybe you should go get her," I say.

"What, and end all this?"

It's my turn to smile. He heads to the back and ducks through the doorway.

Leigh must be around my grandma's age, with thick glasses and a wide, friendly smile. "Tell me about yourself, Sloane. That's a beautiful name, by the way."

"Thank you." I don't tell her that I was named after Ferris Bueller's girlfriend in *Ferris Bueller's Day Off*. That movie was really formative for my dad. *Why didn't you name me Ferris, then?* I asked, after I had seen it. *Ferris is the one with his shit together. Ferris is the one who has everything go his way.*

Sloane is the heart, he replied. *They need her. Also, frankly, Ferris would be a pretty crap girl's name. I'm sorry.*

"I, um, my family moved to Opal a couple months ago. We vacationed here when I was a kid, and then my parents decided to move for—for my dad's work."

"Ah." She asks me about school (fine), my prior job experience (none, but I spin out a short-lived volunteer job in early high school and some tutoring in junior high), my interests (there's no way to say "classical voice" without sounding supremely full of yourself, so I just say reading, spending time with my family, the typical boring answers). It's when she asks me my availability that I'm pretty sure I've got the job, and it's when she gives me an embroidered SHOP DODGE'S! hat that I'm certain of it.

Gabe is finishing up with a customer, handing a white paper-wrapped packet across the counter when I leave the back office. He raises an eyebrow at me in a way that says *How'd it go?*

I hold up the hat. "Consolation prize. She was thoroughly unimpressed."

"Ha-ha. When are you starting?"

"Sunday."

He nods. And then, "You want some cake? I had to price it out."

"Why?"

" 'Cause I sneezed on it."

I make a face.

"It's sell by today. They'll just pitch it anyway." He puts a slice in a plastic container and pushes it across the counter at me. "I didn't really sneeze on it," he says. "That was—I was being—"

"Yeah, no. I got it." I take the container. "Thanks."

We both stand for a moment.

"Great talk," I say, at the same time he says, "Enjoy the cake."

I smile—I can't help it—but Gabe just grimaces.

"I should probably—"

"Help the growing throng of people?" The place is nearly empty. "Yeah, this place is packed. You should really get to it."

"See you at school," Gabe says with a sense of finality, but I catch the beginnings of a smile as he turns away.

"Why cake?" my dad asks later.

"I don't know . . . because I got a job? Celebration cake?"

"So like, 'Congratulations, you're a functioning member of society' cake? 'You will now be paying into Social Security until your untimely demise' cake?"

"Why will my demise be untimely?"

"Whenever you go, Sloane, it will be untimely, even if it's three hundred years from now."

"Do you really think science could advance so much that I could live to be three hundred?"

"I wish it with all my heart." A pause. "So why'd you want a job anyway?"

"What do you mean?"

"You're in the mighty fortunate position of not *needing* one. So why do you want one? Aren't you worried it might take away from your singing?"

"No." It's not an unfair question. That was my excuse for a lot of things back home. *I need to practice. I need to focus.* "I think it'll be okay." I shrug. "And the kids have jobs here."

"Since when did you care what the kids did?"

"I don't *care*, I'm just observing. They have jobs here."

"And now you have one."

"Can we stop talking about this?"

"Yes. As long as we start talking about that cake. What kind is it?"

"Coconut."

"Ah, I like this boy. He gave you a really divisive dessert right off the bat."

"I love coconut."

"As do I, but some people operate under the impression that it tastes like sunscreen. This kid gets points for a discerning taste in cake flavors. Is he cute?"

"Ew, Dad."

"No, really. Not that it matters. Even a little bit. But do we think he's cute?"

I consider it for a moment, objectively. "Society would think he's cute."

"And what does Sloane think?"

"Sloane thinks her dad is a creeper."

"I creep because I care," he says, and then reaches for the cake.

seven

When AP bio swings around the next morning, Remy is entrenched in the seat next to mine. Vera must have paid him.

We start working on the day's exercises—worksheets about last class's lecture. This version of AP bio is more paperwork than cat dissections. The partners around us are all chatting while they work (or don't work, as the case may be), so I feel compelled to make conversation.

When I glance over at Remy, though, he's not looking at today's worksheet. He's got a spiral notebook in front of him, open to a page with a name printed at the top—*Aubrey*—followed by a dash.

And nothing else. He's gone over the letters in *Aubrey* two or three times with his pen. A couple more rounds and it'll probably tear through the page, but he does it again anyway as I watch, carefully tracing the swoop of the *u* and the line of the *b*.

"Aubrey, like—the girl with the curly hair?" I say. He starts, and then covers the page with his forearm. "From snow-cone time?"

"No," he says, and then makes a face. "I mean, yes. But . . . I was just . . ."

"Lovingly doodling her name? Aubrey, light of your life? Mrs. Aubrey Your-Last-Name?"

"Johnson," he says automatically. "And stop saying her name."

"Or what, I'll summon her like Beetlejuice?"

"I don't—" He looks around, like maybe someone's listening, but everyone around us appears otherwise engaged. "I was just . . . going to write her a note. That's all. I was just thinking. About what to write."

"Do you like her?" I ask.

The responding look on Remy's face is pained.

"So Dan has brought up a point about part C," the teacher says at the front of the room, forcing back the next question on my lips. By the time we've hashed out the issue with part C, it seems like our previous conversation has expired, and I'm forced to start over.

"So . . ." I say, and then pause. An auspicious beginning. "So," I try again. "Did you, uh, make it to the party last weekend?" Mutual ground, at least. We could comment on the drinks selection, or the alarming collection of corn-husk dolls in the bathroom.

But then Remy says, "No."

I think that's going to be it, until he glances my way and says, "I don't go to non-Frank-sanctioned events."

That was the same thing Vera had said that night. *I told you we shouldn't have gone to a non-Frank-sanctioned party.*

"What does that even mean? Who's Frank?"

Remy just stares.

"Who's Frank?" Vera cries at lunch. "Frank Sanger. As in Frank Sanger Presents." This was the same thing Remy had said: *You know, from Frank Sanger Presents.* I didn't know. But then another class discussion erupted about one of the worksheet sections, and we never returned to the topic of Frank Sanger.

"Which is . . ."

"You don't know about Frank Sanger Presents?"

"I don't even know who Frank Sanger is."

Vera looks at me, aghast. "Oh God, don't let him hear you say that."

I glance around. "Is he here?"

"Frank has eyes and ears everywhere. He's the most powerful person in the senior class. And also the most fabulous. He has"—she pauses, her eyes shining, and then finishes with emphasis—"a *universal appeal.*"

I don't know what to make of that. "So he's known for . . . presenting?"

"He's known for hosting parties. The location changes—like they're never at Frank's house; they're always at other people's houses—but Frank is always the host."

"Why?"

"Because he's the best. There are people who just know how to have fun, right? But then there are people like Frank, who know how to get other people to have fun, too. His parties are just . . . better."

"Sounds cool," I say.

"Oh, it is. And this week you're going."

So come Friday, I go.

I expect something spectacular. Maybe not fire-eaters or belly dancers, but at the very least raucous party games or kids doing mad skateboarding moves in an empty pool. Something. But a Frank-sanctioned event looks remarkably like the party Bree dragged me to last week—the kids, the cups, the noise.

Vera leaves me in search of drinks, and I'm hovering in a corner of the living room when just like that, Frank Sanger sweeps into the room. I know it because three or four people yell his name. Also, because if I were going to point out the most powerful and fabulous person in the senior class, he would be the lead candidate running.

Physically, he's kind of unremarkable: He is a little on the hairy side, tall, a little broad. But he has a presence. Like, a *Presence*. So much so that when he moves across the room toward me, I feel that weird, irrational flutter you get when you see someone famous in real life. Like yeah, the stars are just like us, but they're not, in a way. They might buy toilet paper at Target, too, but I know I sure as hell don't go around inspiring that kind of feeling in people. That sort of awe.

"You must be Sloane," Frank says, extending a hand. I reach for it. He shakes once, firmly. "I'd like to formally welcome you to Frank Sanger Presents: Friday Night."

"Thanks," I say, as he relinquishes my hand. "It's, uh, nice to meet you."

"Isn't it?" He smiles winningly. "Have you met everyone yet? Do you know everyone?"

I have met very few people, and I know even fewer. I say as much, and Frank looks at me appraisingly for a moment.

"I see your beverage needs haven't been tended to," he says. "Can I get you something? I have a signature cocktail, you know. It's called Frankly My Dear, I Don't Give a Drambuie." He pauses for effect, but my response must be underwhelming. "Drambuie is a kind of liqueur," he says.

"Ah."

"And I'm drawing on a popular quote from *Gone With the Wind*."

"That part I got."

"Do you want me to say the whole thing again so you can fully appreciate it?"

"I think I'm good."

"Good on the drink, or good on giving it full appreciation?"

"Both," I say with a smile. "But thank you. Solid wordplay."

Another moment of appraisal. And then, "Sloane, are you familiar with a band called This Is Our Now?"

"I am."

"I know we've just met, but if you had to liken me to a member of TION, who would it be?"

"Um . . . I don't know." Except I do know. I have watched the TION documentary with Laney approximately seventeen times. "The spirit of Kai, with . . . Josh's swagger and . . . Kenji's hair?"

Frank Sanger blinks at me for a moment. Then he takes both my hands.

"This is an important moment, Sloane," he says solemnly.

"Yeah?"

"Yes. This is the moment upon which our pure and beautiful friendship will be founded, based on your keen understanding of me as a person. We will look back on this moment from a very old age with both affection and reverence."

I don't know whether to laugh or to nod solemnly back.

"Look into my eyes," he says, and I do. "Sloane, will you mingle with me at this party tonight, and every party night that we are both mutually available and not occupied by fantastic hookups or thrilling misadventures, for the rest of our lives?"

"The rest of our lives? I don't know, that's kind of a big commitment."

His eyes shine. "My girl plays hard to get. I respect that. Think it over. Consider tonight a trial run."

He then slips his arm through mine and leads me into the next room.

"What are we doing?"

"We're mingling. It's going to be fun."

Frank takes me around, introducing me to a number of people who all blend together a bit, and keeps up a commentary of gossip in my ear the whole time. "Hey, Jeff, how's it going?" *Had to be held back in kindergarten. Apparently his fine motor skills weren't up to par.* "Lauren, that top, good God, woman!" *She dated Jeff until the end of last year. Maybe they could've made it work if he was a little better with those motor skills, know what I mean?*—Frank raises and lowers his eyebrows several times—*Know? What I mean? About the skills?*

Yes, I'm catching a subtle innuendo here, Frank, thank you.

My pleasure, darling.

We only pause when he needs to re-up on drinks, and it's then that I see them, clustered in the dining room—Remy and Gabe, with Vera and Aubrey standing just beside them.

Frank appears at my elbow. "Oh they're a gossip gold mine," he says, following my line of sight.

"Really?"

He sputters a "P-*yeah*" and then grabs a couple of drinks off the nearby counter. "Those two," he says, pushing the cup into my hand and then gesturing toward Aubrey and Remy with his own. "Do you know their sad history?"

I don't recall anyone mentioning anything sad the other day. She had a blue snow cone; he had purple.

"They dated," Frank says, with just a little too much relish. "For two years. They were the shiniest golden couple of our class. What a match, you know? Both gorgeous. She's super smart—does student government, debate, choir, all that business. He does the sports and volunteers with his dad's church, has those puppy eyes that make you want to buy him a boat—"

"Do they?"

"Yes, gaze deeply into his eyes next time—you'll feel it." He takes a long draw from his drink and then continues. "Anyway, they were the kind of couple where it's like, separate—they're great. But together, it's . . . star magic."

"Star magic?"

"From the universe. Celestial bodies aligning and shit. That kind of magic." I suspect that Frank is drunk, but if I hadn't seen him drinking, I probably wouldn't be able to tell.

"But then at the start of the summer, out of nowhere—splitsville. No explanation. Just, kaput. One day they were RemyandAubrey and the next they were over."

"What happened?"

"There are several theories, all of which are bullshit, if you ask me. Her family hates him. She's secretly dating a college guy. Nonsense like that. But the universally agreed-upon point is that she ended it. He was just as shocked as everyone else. Came out of nowhere, straight-up blindside."

Across the room, Remy is talking to Gabe, Aubrey to Vera. If Frank hadn't mentioned anything, you'd think it was all perfectly normal, but the scene plays a bit differently with this information. Remy shifting from foot to foot. Aubrey focusing only on Vera. Two people studiously ignoring each other.

43

"He was devastated. Poor little buddy. It's good he's got Gabe—Gabe's a solid dude. They've been best friends for years. Thing is, Vera is equally tight with Aubrey, so . . . the group had to get over it."

"The group?"

"Their little group. BFFs til the grand fucking end."

"Are you in the group?"

"Please. Frank Sanger cannot be tied down to one social group. Frank Sanger is for all people."

"Got it."

He throws back the rest of his cup and says, "Round two."

We finally take a break at the end of the evening, sitting out on the front porch.

"So tell me, was it fun?"

"I learned a lot," I say. "You're like walking exposition."

"Why, thank you . . . Frank said, smiling through the haunted look in his eyes as he relived the devastating moment in eighth grade when he realized he couldn't marry Angelina Jolie or Brad Pitt because they were both too sickeningly into each other."

"That's good."

"I know," he says. "Frank was always good. It was a burden at times, but he wanted so badly to honor his dear father's memory . . ." He breaks off, grinning down into his plastic cup. My face must be doing something, because when he looks up at me, his eyes twinkle. "What, did shit get too real?"

I don't speak.

"If you have tragedy hang-ups, best not roll with that group in there. Vera and Gabe . . ."

"What?"

He shakes his head and downs the rest of his drink. Then he

holds one hand high up in the air. "No, you have to be *this* invested to ride that tragic backstory."

"Tell me."

"Let Vera tell you." He stands. "Want to go dance?"

It's pretty late, and I say so. "Should probably get home."

"You've been drinking."

"I haven't." The cup I'm holding is the same one he gave me earlier.

"You're a wily one, Sloane Finch." Frank offers me a hand up. "Let's see you off."

eight

"Frank basically spent the whole party with you," Vera says with no small amount of awe at lunch on Monday.

"Yeah. I mean . . . yeah." Something in my stomach swoops at that. Vera invited me to the party, after all, and I hung out with Frank the whole time. In the moment I didn't think she'd care, but now I wonder if she's annoyed at me.

But her eyes just shine, and there's that little smile. "I couldn't keep track of you guys. It's silly I don't have your number." She hands me her phone. "Text yourself, then you'll have mine, too."

Her home screen is another picture of her and the girl from her profiles—Natashah19. This one is selfie-style, with Vera's arm extended. Natashah19 has both her arms wrapped around Vera's waist and is pressing a kiss to her cheek.

When I glance up at Vera, she's looking at me. "That's my girlfriend, Tash," she says after a moment. "Isn't she gorgeous?"

"Yeah." I fumble to enter my number. "How long have you guys been together?"

Vera smiles. "Since sophomore year. She was a senior, though. She goes to Florida State now."

"Cool," I say, because it is. My longest relationship has been with Netflix.

She takes her phone back and fiddles with it for a moment. "Now Gabe has it, too."

"Huh?"

"Your number."

"Why does Gabe need it?"

"You never know," she says airily. And then, "You want to study after school?"

That's how we end up at Vera's house that afternoon. We take the bus to Grayson and walk to a little bungalow off the main drag. It has trees growing up on either side of it and a screened-in porch running across the front. The screen door snaps shut behind us, and Vera fumbles with the keys.

"I don't know if anyone's home," she says, pushing through the front door. "Mandy?"

"In the kitchen!" a voice calls back.

Vera shoots me a look. "Brace yourself."

She leads me through the living room and into the adjoining kitchen.

A girl is standing at the counter by the sink. She is wearing a Victoria's Secret tracksuit and puffy slipper boots. Her hair is piled in a messy bun on the top of her head.

"Hey, lady," she says, smiling at us over her shoulder as she finishes pressing a sandwich together. "Who's this?"

She doesn't resemble Vera in the slightest. So I go Sherlock on this situation and do one quick sweep of the room behind us. There is a picture frame on the mantel that has SORORITY SISTERS! emblazoned across it in swirly silver script. Three *Cosmo* magazines are stacked up on the table next to the couch, which features several fluffy throw pillows. The vibe of the place is decidedly . . . youthful.

You have to be this invested to ride that tragic backstory, Frank had said.

Maybe this is a guardianship situation. A tragic car accident, a college student forced to take on her older sibling's teenage kids. Quitting school, working two jobs, caring for them the best she can . . .

But then she turns and extends a hand out to me, and there's the bright gold band, the wink of a diamond on her finger. And it's incredibly clear.

This is no guardianship situation.

I clasp her hand as Vera says, "Mandy, this is Sloane. Sloane, this is Amanda." Her eyes shine when I glance at her, and she draws it out: "My stepmom."

"Nice to meet you," I say, and then my eyes drop down to her midsection, and I really am an idiot. Sherlock would be ashamed.

"Yeah, no, I'm not just fat," Amanda says with a grin.

"I wasn't—I mean—"

"No, it's cool, Kyle tells people wherever we go."

"Kyle?" I glance at Vera.

"My dad. Amanda's husband. The father of her baby." Vera looks as if this is a piece of gossip she would love so fucking much if it didn't pertain to her.

"Congratulations," I say.

"It's still early. Five months. I've barely even popped. Which is why I just look fat."

The rest of Amanda is unfairly toned.

"No, you, uh, look great," I say, and Vera grabs my hand.

"We're going to go study."

She pulls me into her room, and I can't help it: "Are we going to talk about that?"

She drops her bag on the floor and then falls across the bed on her stomach, phone in her hands. "How my stepmom looks spring-break ready?" she says, swiping across the screen.

"No. But. Like, how old is she? Really?"

She looks up at me, eyes shining. "Twenty-two."

"Holy fuckballs."

"Thank you. God, thank you, that's the best reaction I've gotten so far."

"Is . . . I mean . . . what's that like?"

Vera shrugs. "She's not my mom. Obviously. But it's fine, I guess. Overall. She lets us borrow her car, so . . . could be worse." Her mouth twists, a wry smile. "Could be better."

There's so much to ask, but I'm not comfortable with any of it. So I just sink down into Vera's desk chair. "I guess you guys can, like, share clothes? I bet her prom dress is still pretty current."

"Oh my God, Sloane, you're my favorite."

We start on calculus, but I space out about half an hour in. Vera is murmuring about differentials when I start looking around her room. A bulletin board hangs above the desk. Next to it, some movie posters. Farther down, almost in the corner, is a small canvas painted blue with stripes of white and seafoam green across it, little hints of yellow along the upper edge.

"Do you paint?" I ask.

"Huh?" She follows my gaze. "Oh. Yeah, no. My mom was an artist."

"It's nice," I say.

Vera doesn't answer, because there's a sharp knock at her door. It swings open a second later.

"What's the point of knocking if you're just going to barge in?" Vera asks.

Gabe stands in the doorway.

"What are you doing here?" he says.

"Vera brought me to see your super young stepmom," I say, because I can't help it.

Vera laughs, loud and gratifying. "Don't you love her, Gabe?"

Gabe's expression implies that he does not, in fact, love me. But he just says, "Mandy wants to know what you want for dinner."

"Don't care," Vera says. "Sloane? Thoughts for dinner?"

"Oh, I should probably . . . I mean, I'll just head home after we do homework."

"Come on, at least stay for dinner. We can ask Mandy all about UF versus FSU. You're doing college apps now, too, right?"

"Yeah." I have zero percent interest in UF versus FSU, but I don't feel like I can tell Vera that. So I just nod. "Yeah, sure. Cool."

"Yeah, super cool," Gabe says, and it's with a hint of sarcasm, but he's ducking out of the doorway before I can respond.

nine

Tuesday brings the first concert-choir meeting of the semester. Mrs. Simmons, the choir director, smiles at me as I enter. Not a month ago, she stood me up in front of the class and asked me to "sing a few bars."

"We've got to figure out where to put you!" she had said.

"I'm a mezzo," I replied.

She gave me an odd look. "Well, let's have a listen. Do you know 'Amazing Grace'?"

Did I know one of the most basic songs in the English language? "Sure." And I couldn't help but add, "Could I have it in E?"

If Laney were there, she would have made a very specific face at me, brows drawn down, eyes skyward, tongue sticking out, like Mr. Yuck. She did it more when she was younger, whenever I was showing off, but it still happens occasionally, mostly when I get to do something she can't. Getting to stay up later—Mr. Yuck face. Learning to drive—Mr. Yuck face.

I don't know, Jill, my dad had said at the time, eyes shining, *Lane's seven now—I think that's a right fine age for a learner's permit.* Laney had giggled. Dad's always pretty good at banishing Mr. Yuck.

In my inaugural eighth-period music class, Mrs. Simmons made no such face. She quirked an eyebrow but nodded all the same. *Why did I say that?* coursed through me. This was a chance. An opportunity to not be That Kid, that Mr. Yuck show-off. Was it so deeply engrained in me?

She played. I sang.

Everyone looked up.

It didn't come from nowhere. You don't get to be That Kid for nothing. I know that I'm good. Now Mrs. Simmons and the rest of the class knew it, too.

"Have you had formal training?" she asked me after class, as the rest of the kids gathered up their things and left.

"Yeah," I said, because it was too late to downplay it. "Since eighth grade."

It was then that she recommended the concert choir, which would be starting rehearsal in a few weeks. "We could really use someone like you," she said, smiling.

And now, here I am.

I see Aubrey's mass of curls, sitting front and center in the soprano section. There is an empty seat next to her, so I claim it.

"I heard you were some kind of singer," she says, with something that's not exactly a smile.

"I mean, everyone who can talk is some kind of singer," I say. "Whether or not they're a good one or a crappy one is the question."

"I heard you were a good singer," she amends, and whatever kind of smile there was before is now gone.

"Yeah, I don't know. It's a hobby."

Just a hobby. That I spend a great deal of time and effort on.

Aubrey doesn't seem to buy this. She just turns to face the front as Mrs. Simmons begins the warm-up.

"Aubrey said you were like an opera singer," Vera says the next afternoon. We're lying across her bed, and I'm tapping my fingers idly against a notebook while she pores over history notes. "Like so talented. I had no idea."

"She said that?" Aubrey doesn't seem particularly forthcoming. I can't imagine her saying something about me in general, let alone something nice.

"Yeah, and she'd know—she's been doing choir for ages. That's so cool." Vera swats my arm. "You'll have to sing for me. Tomorrow I'll come over to your place. You can give me a performance."

That's the thing about Vera, one of the many things about Vera. So many people generalize—*We should do something sometime.* But Vera is ever specific, enthusiastic, excited. She grins at me now. "You can wow me with your killer pipes."

"I'll do my best."

So the next day we head to my house after school. My mom is still at work, but my dad nods at us from the kitchen, one hand on a glass of juice, the other holding his tablet.

"Ladies," he says.

It's only when we're headed upstairs to my room that Vera says, voice lowered, "Your dad looks kind of familiar."

"Yeah, he writes books." He's been on TV to talk about the movie adaptations—slinging one arm around Dex Finnegan on the *Today* show—but I don't mention that.

"What kind of books?"

"They call it 'literary romance.'"

Vera stops short. "Oh my God." Her eyes widen. "Oh my God."

Then she spins around and heads back downstairs.

I follow, just in time to see her burst into the kitchen.

"You're Everett Finch," she says, and looks at me accusingly. "Sloane Finch! You're Sloane Finch and your dad is Everett Finch!"

"All of these statements are correct," I say, and she spins back to my dad.

"You wrote *Summer Burn*. And *All Is Hope*. And *Sand on Our Beach*. And *Love Knot*."

Dad nods. "I did. Guilty as charged."

"I read *Summer Burn* on a flight to Denver last year, and I cried the whole way. That scene in the gas station? When he flushes the drugs? And she punches the mirror? Oh my God." Vera clutches her chest.

"Hey, thanks. You know, ironically enough, I wrote that scene on a flight to Denver."

"You didn't."

"I didn't. It was to San Diego. But that's not as pat."

"Oh my God." Vera spins around and looks at me. "Why didn't you tell me your dad is Everett Finch?"

"No one really goes around leading with their dad's job, do they?"

"No one's dad is Everett Finch. Except you."

"And Laney."

"Who's Laney?"

"My sister."

My dad grins. "You two do know each other, right? You've met on at least one other occasion?"

"We're fast friends," Vera says, grinning back. "So what should I call you? Mr. Finch? Everett? Is that your real name?"

"It's not. How about Mike?"

"Weird," I say, because I should get a vote here. My dad. My friend. "How about Mr. Finch?"

"Done." She approaches Dad and sticks out her hand. "It's nice to meet you, Mr. Finch. I mean, I met you before, just now, but I didn't know that you were more than Sloane's dad, you know what I mean? I'm a big fan of your books. Obviously."

"That's always great to hear, thanks."

"Maybe—like if it's not too much trouble—maybe you could sign some books for me, like if I brought them over sometime? And then I could give them away online. I do stuff online."

"She does," I add, even though I know my dad knows about Vera's stuff. "She's very prolific."

"You looked me up?" Vera is positively glowing. "Aw, I'm flattered."

"I'd be happy to sign whatever you put in front of me," my dad says. "I'm not much for that social-media stuff, though. My publicist's always trying to get me to make a Twitter or a Heartmark or whatever."

How did my dad know about Heartmark? I barely knew about Heartmark.

"I could get you set up on whatever site you wanted," Vera says. "Anytime. Just let me know! Or let Sloane know, and she'll let me know. Got to warn you, though, it's kind of addictive. But it's a great way to make connections!" She loops her arm through mine. "We should study, huh? And then you're gonna sing for me! Thanks for the chat, Mr. Finch. We'll leave you to it."

And she pulls me upstairs, leaving my dad to it.

"She's a whirlwind," Dad says that night. "A force of nature." He is not wrong.

ten

"It's a great way to make connections," my dad says when I get home from school the next day.

I find him in his office, in front of his desktop computer. His laptop sits open beside it, and his tablet beside that—all systems go.

"Sorry?"

"That's what Vera said, about the social media, the Internet thing. *It's a great way to make connections.*"

"Yeah, I mean. I'm sure it is."

"I have made a connection, Sloane," he says, and when he finally turns away from the screens, he doesn't look tired or stressed. Rather, there is some kind of bright, manic energy in his eyes. His hair is sticking out in all directions, like Doc Brown, and his eyes are red-rimmed.

"How long have you been online?" I ask.

"I looked up Vera" is his reply. "She has almost as many followers as that lizard church. Can you believe that? I suppose I can—she has an effervescence."

"Where are we going with this?"

"Last night, after we met, I looked her up, and it's changed every-thing. I've had a breakthrough."

"What kind of breakthrough?"

"She is subscribed—following? Liking? She is looking after a number of different people, so I wondered, who are these people that this charming young woman chooses to associate with on the Internet? What are their occupations, their pursuits? And one of them—one of them is this guy, do you know this guy?" He has about two dozen tabs open, but he manages to locate the correct one on the fly.

"No." The guy looks vaguely familiar, though.

"Turns out, he's on this show. This show, Sloane. It's a game changer."

He clicks another tab, and a promo for a TV show begins.

A group of attractive people are slow-motion walking across an empty field while an aggressive guitar riff plays underneath. Flashes of scenes from the show cut in, with lines like "The stone . . . it's the key to all his power!" and "Get out of there! Now!"

"*Were School*?" I say, at the promo's pounding conclusion. "Kind of shitty grammar."

"Not were school. *Were* School. Like *were*wolf. Have you heard of this show? It's on one of those young-people networks. It's about a bunch of supernatural kids at a suburban high school. *Harry Potter* meets . . . *GQ,* I don't know, they're all stupidly attractive."

"Ew."

"Don't worry, in true Hollywood fashion, they're twenty-seven-year-olds playing sophomores. This guy James? He's a dish. Your mom would leave me for him." He scrolls down to a stark black-and-white picture of he who must be James, wearing a tight black T-shirt and brooding at the camera. Dad considers the picture for a moment. "There's like a thirty percent chance I would leave your mom for him."

"*Dad.*"

"Yes, sweetness?"

"What does *Were School* have to do with anything?"

"Are you familiar with fandom, Sloane?"

He makes it sound like a person, like Fandom is someone you could meet at the grocery store.

"Kind of." I'm familiar with the concept of being a fan of something, at least.

"The way I understand it—and I'm no expert, so forgive me if my explanation is insufficient, I've only been in the *Were School* fandom for approximately sixteen hours, and eight of those hours were spent watching season one—"

"Did you even sleep last night?"

"Fandom," he continues, like I hadn't spoken, "is something you can join, like a club or a team, but also something that you *are*. People make up a fandom. But the fandom is also the various arts that people create in the name of the thing they are enthused about, and the consumption of those arts, and the feelings that they produce that feed back into their love of the original thing. . . . God, it's dynamic and it's wonderful. And you know what my favorite part is?"

"I honestly have no idea."

His eyes are alight. "I have been reading *Were School* fan fiction. No, let me rephrase that: I can't stop reading *Were School* fan fiction."

"Okay." This is not what I was expecting. But to be fair, I'm not sure how you would come to expect any of this from your dad. "And . . ."

"And it's brilliant. It is brilliant. Do you realize people just write the stuff and post it up there for free? Anonymously? Because they want to? Because they love *Were School* so much?"

"Yeah, I mean, that's how fan fiction works, right?"

"It's miraculous. It's creativity in its purest form."

"Yeah, okay. So . . . how is this helping with . . ." *Your current situation* is what my mom would say. "How is this helpful?"

"I've been struggling with the basics, wanting to strip this all down to its most essential parts—why do we read, why do we write, why do we choose to write what we write—and this is it right here, it's all there." He points at the screen, which is now playing a laundry detergent commercial while another *Were School* promo loads. "This is the key to everything."

I don't see it. But that doesn't really matter when it comes to my dad. He just has to see it, and that's enough.

eleven

I find myself at Vera's again after school on Monday. She texts me during last period: Study buddy study time! After class! and it appears I have little choice in the matter.

We've been crushing calculus for an hour or so when I break for the bathroom. Vera waves vaguely in the direction of it when I ask, so I head down the hallway and pick the first door to my right.

I push it open. But it's not a bathroom.

It's bedroom-size, but it's no bedroom, either. Big windows line the wall across from the door, looking out over the backyard. An easel, a drafting table, and a half-dozen boxes have been pushed into the middle of the room, and the floor has been covered with some drop cloths. Someone has clearly been at work with paint swatches on the walls: Four different colors—varying shades of green—cut wide swaths through the blue on one side of the room.

"What are you doing?"

I jump. "Geez."

Gabe.

"I thought this was the bathroom," I say.

"It's not."

"Really?" I'm about to say something stupid, but then I catch sight of his face.

He cuts by me and steps into the room, taking in the walls, the pile of art stuff. Then he wheels around abruptly and pushes back through, motoring down the hall and turning into the living room.

A muffled conversation follows.

"Gabe, I get it, I really do, but honestly, we need to be practical here—"

"Were you even going to tell me? Give me some fucking warning?"

Gabe reappears in the hallway, with a man who must be his father close on his heels.

"Language, Gabe."

"Language. Yeah. That's the most important thing here."

I press against the wall behind me and try to look inconspicuous as Gabe passes and goes back into the room that's definitely not a bathroom.

"It couldn't stay that way forever," Mr. Fuller says, following him in. "It's not . . . healthy. And what's more, we need the space. Like it or not, the baby needs a room, and this is the one we've got."

Gabe turns in a slow circle, surveying the room silently.

"Where are the paintings?"

"Which?"

"Mom's paintings."

"I've got a few in my room. Mandy took the rest to Meira."

Gabe tears out again and bursts into the room to my left. I can hear Amanda, faintly, "Gabe, what are you—"

"Where is it?" he says, exploding back into the hall.

"Sorry?"

61

"*The Dream.* Where is it?"

"I don't know what you're—"

"Blue frame. The three figures. It was in Mom's room. It was off to the side, I set it apart, special—"

Mr. Fuller shakes his head. "I don't know, I . . ."

"It's blue? With the people in the center?" Amanda appears in the doorway.

"Yeah."

"I . . . I think I brought it with the last batch to Meira."

Gabe squeezes his eyes shut. "Are you serious?"

"I thought it was supposed to go with the others. Wasn't it . . . ?" She looks at Mr. Fuller, eyes wide. "I wouldn't have—if I had known it was important, I definitely wouldn't have—"

Gabe glares. He seethes. And all the while, I stand pressed up against the hall cabinet, trying to be invisible.

"I put it aside," he says through clenched teeth. "On purpose. So you wouldn't fucking sell it."

"*Gabriel,*" his dad says. Amanda, meanwhile, just looks a bit like I imagine I must look. Confused, trying to become one with her surroundings so as to avoid this confrontation. "Look." Mr. Fuller takes a step toward Gabe. "You haven't been in there in—in *months.* You haven't looked at those paintings in a long time. Now, I saved the ones that are special to us—"

"Yeah, right," Gabe mutters.

"I *asked* you if you wanted to go through them, if you'd pull out the ones you wanted to keep."

"And I did. I set it aside."

"How was I supposed to know that? How was I supposed to know you did that if you don't fucking talk to me, Gabe?"

"Kyle," Amanda says, now the admonisher.

"No. Seriously. If you want to have this conversation, let's do it. Let's not hold back, right?"

"I don't want to." Gabe's expression is a lot like the one he wore in the kitchen that night, right before Mason grabbed his face.

"Of course you don't. You want to sulk and hate me, because that's way more productive, right?"

"Right," he says, and then leaves.

Mr. Fuller runs a hand over his eyes and looks at Amanda.

"I'm sorry," he says. "I didn't mean to upset you." Then it's as if he notices I'm there for the first time. "I . . . Sorry, who are you?"

"Vera's friend," I say, and the word sits strangely in my mouth. "I didn't mean to—I'm just heading out." I start to back down the hall. "Sorry for . . . that was . . . personal . . . didn't mean to—"

I don't have to finish, because thankfully I pass around the corner at that moment and leave the Fullers to themselves.

Well, not all of them. First I go to Vera's room, grab my stuff, and say my good-byes.

"But we still have the practice quiz," she says.

"Yeah, sorry. Gotta get home. I just . . ." *Feel too awkward.* "I'll see you tomorrow."

She nods. "Okay. Text me later."

I pause. "About what?"

"Whatever you want," she says with a smile.

I push outside. The screen door bangs shut behind me, and I'm all ready to head off when I hear a sound coming from the side of the house.

I peer around the corner.

Gabe is standing there, his back up against the wall, his face toward the sky. His eyes are shut and his fists are clenched at his sides. He's breathing fast and ragged, like he just finished a sprint.

"Hey," I say, and he startles.

"What?"

"You okay?"

"Yeah."

"Are you sure?"

"Why would I say yeah if I wasn't sure?"

"Because sometimes people lie when they think it's easier."

"Do you do that?" he asks.

"No."

"Did you do it just now?"

I smile a little. "Are you okay?"

He shakes his head.

"Come on," I say.

I take Gabe to the ice cream shop on Opal's main circle drive.

He is remarkably compliant in his anger. I make him sit at one of the tables outside, with a big yellow umbrella running through its center. When I emerge from the shop, I see him there, and it strikes me at once that he isn't on his phone. If you leave someone alone in public for nearly any length of time, they're almost always on their phone when you come back. But I guess Gabe is consumed by an angst that not even the embarrassment of being alone can penetrate. Or maybe he just doesn't get embarrassed like that.

He only looks up when I scrape an aluminum chair back from the table and set a spoon and a large plastic dish in front of him.

He looks from the ice cream to me and back again.

"What is this?"

"Vanilla ice cream with gummy bears and chocolate sprinkles."

"I know that, I just mean . . . why did you get me this?"

"It always cheers my sister up," I say, digging into my own. "I mean, she's nine, but . . . guaranteed results."

"I don't need ice cream," Gabe says.

"No, you need an attitude adjustment. Maybe the sugar will help."

Gabe's eyebrows slant downward into an impressive glare. "Seriously? I'm the only one here reacting normally. I'm the only one willing to say how fucked up this whole situation is."

"Okay, number one, I was joking. Number two, I don't know what the whole situation is. So tell me what it is, and I'll tell you if it's fucked up."

Gabe looks at me for a moment, and I just look right back. I get the feeling that he isn't used to being challenged.

"How long has your mom been gone?" I say when he doesn't speak.

"You make it sound like she left, like she did it on purpose."

"I was trying not to say *dead*, but if you want me to say it, I'll say it. How long has your mom been dead?"

"Two years," he says tightly.

"So your dad met Amanda, they got married, and she's pregnant— all that—in two years."

Gabe nods.

I nod, too. "Okay. It's a little fucked up." It's quiet. "So who's Meira?" I ask as he pokes suspiciously at a gummy bear. "They're not poisoned, in case you were wondering."

Gabe takes a bite, chews, and then says, "She has a gallery here. I don't know her, but my dad—" He doesn't finish.

"So he's selling the paintings off."

"First it was to pay for medical bills, and then it was to help with the house . . . but now it's not even for the money. Really it's that he wants to get rid of everything that reminds him of her because he doesn't want to be, like—fucking—inconvenienced by having to remember her. And now they're almost all gone, and he gave away the one—he sold the one that was for *us*, it was special, she said it was about us being together, but of course he doesn't—of course that's the one that—"

He doesn't continue, just shakes his head and stabs at an unsuspecting gummy.

"How do you know it was sold?" I say.

He raises an eyebrow in question.

"How do you know she sold it? Amanda brought the painting to Meira—it doesn't mean Meira sold it. Maybe it's still there."

"They sell fast," he mumbles. "She was popular before, but now that she's . . ."

"Dead?" I say, and he gives me a look. "You said not to say *gone*. You said."

"I did," he says after a moment. "Thanks for the consistency."

My lips twitch. "We should go look, don't you think?"

He doesn't speak.

"This painting was important to you?" I prompt.

"She wanted us to have it." He doesn't meet my gaze. "It was just for us."

"So let's look. Where's the gallery?"

"Here. In Opal."

"Kismet," I say, and scoop up another gummy.

The Newforth Gallery is two streets over. "She used to show at a place in Grayson," Gabe says as we walk. "But my dad thinks they sell better in Opal, so he moved them here, after—after."

"People here are willing to pay ridiculous prices for baby-kale sandwiches," I say. "So maybe he's not wrong." Then I give Gabe the baby-kale rant, because it fills the silence, and even if his laughter is a little obligatory, at least it's something.

A bell sounds as we open the gallery door and step into a space with high ceilings, parquet floors, and white walls. A TV sort of art gallery, with an eclectic array of paintings lining the walls. A truly hideous portrait of a French bulldog. A woman dancing in a red dress. Several renderings of an outdoor café. But there—in the back—

On the far wall of the gallery, six paintings of varying sizes hang. They're water scenes, mainly; the style is delicate, almost fragile, but there is some kind of movement to them, some sort of energy. Those little gallery lamps throw pools of light down on the paintings, but they hardly need it—they glow with some kind of inner light. The frames look handmade, painted as well in some cases, bits of string and shells and detritus along the borders, so that the paintings seem to be bursting off the canvas.

I gravitate toward this back wall. A little table stands nearby, hosting a pile of postcards and a stack of books titled *Laura Fuller: A Retrospective*. Someone has placed a handwritten sign next to them: COMMEMORATING THE LIFE AND WORK OF LAURA FULLER.

I look up at the paintings for a long moment. "They're really pretty,"

I say finally. But *pretty* isn't the right word. *Pretty* is too innocuous—it undersells them. They're . . . dynamic.

When I glance back at Gabe, he's still standing near the door.

I'm about to say something more, though I'm not sure what—the look on his face is hard to describe. But then a woman emerges from a door off to the side. She matches the surroundings—a TV sort of gallery owner, in a long patterned skirt and tight tank top. Lots of turquoise jewelry. She's maybe a little younger than my mom. Presumably, it's Meira.

"Can I help you?" she asks, looking from me to Gabe.

He just shakes his head, his eyes on the wall of paintings opposite us. "It's not here."

"Are you looking for something in particular?" Meira says.

"Yeah," I say. "Is this all there is? Of his mom's stuff?"

"I'm sorry?"

"Laura Fuller's paintings."

Something clicks for Meira; I can see it on her face. "You must be Gabe," she says, looking his way. "Gosh, you're all grown up. There's a picture of you and your sister in the book; have you seen? I'm guessing you've got one of these already—" She starts to move toward the table, piled high with copies of *Laura Fuller: A Retrospective*.

"We were wondering about a particular painting," I say, as Meira picks up one of the books. I get the feeling that Gabe isn't in the mood to stroll down memory lane. "Called *The Dream*? It's, uh, it's in a blue frame?" I glance at Gabe. He nods once, curtly.

"Yeah," Meira says. "I remember. That one sold quick, a few months ago."

"Do you remember to who?"

"I'd have to look back."

"Could you?"

Meira looks between the two of us, and then says, "I can't really give out their information. I'm sorry."

"Yeah, but it's not like . . ." I want to be diplomatic; I don't want to overstep. But I can't help it: "It's not like there are gallery rules, right? It's not like being a doctor, or a priest taking confession."

"No, it's not. But this is a business, and there's a certain etiquette. Not only to protect our clients but to protect ourselves. I'm sorry. I really am." She looks at Gabe. "What I can do is pass a message along to the client who purchased the painting. But because your dad is the seller, I'd need him to contact me first to request this."

Gabe just shakes his head.

"Why not?" I say. It's not ideal, but at least it's something.

"It's fine. Thanks, though."

He turns to go, but Meira steps forward, still holding the book.

"I, uh, I met your mother, once. It was at a festival, a few years ago. She was . . . just such a lovely woman."

I don't know how I would respond to this, but Gabe's face softens a bit. "Yeah, she was. Thanks."

"Why don't you just ask your dad to call her? And then Meira will call the client, and we can get the painting back."

Gabe is moving swiftly down the street, back toward the center of town. "I don't want to get him involved."

"Why not?"

"Because." He shakes his head. "This was a stupid idea."

"You're only saying that because it wasn't your idea."

"It's gone. There's no point."

"We'll get it back," I say.

"Not everything can be gotten back. Right? So. Let's forget about it."

"Is that what you want?"

"Yes," he says, and he looks like maybe he means it. Or at least that he wants to mean it.

But I know different. He didn't see his own face, standing there in the baby's room. His expression when Amanda said she had taken the painting here. Like something had been broken. *The one that was for us,* he had said. *It was about us being together.*

Maybe there's a way to fix it. To unbreak it. Because I don't necessarily agree with him. Not everything is absolute. Not everything is irreparable.

"Okay," I say, but I know there's no way that I'm letting this go.

twelve

I'm working on homework later that evening when my phone lights up with a text from Vera.

> I heard what happened. Sorry if Gabe freaked you out

It then quickly buzzes a half-dozen more times:

> He said you bought him ice cream
> With gummy bears
> You bought my brother, the most humorless person on the face of the earth, ice cream with gummy bears
> You are a queen among mere mortals
> Queen Sloane
> lol

I type back, You know you could just send all that in one message
Not as fun, she replies.

> Anyway I think in chunks

Got to type them as they come
Is it annoying though?

A little, I say, because I can't lie.

You know, annoying you might be as fun as annoying Gabe

Why? I type, before she can continue with another barrage.

You're both so serious.

I'm not serious, I say. Anyone who knew me knew that, right? I made a dozen stupid comments a minute. Almost as fast as Vera texted.

Have you ever met you? she replies.

I don't answer back, and it doesn't buzz again for some time. When I look back, expecting Vera, it's from a new number.

Thanks for the ice cream.

I blink and recall Vera and me exchanging numbers at lunch after the Frank party, how she passed mine along to Gabe.

Sure no problem, I reply.

The little bubble pops up, indicating that Gabe is typing a reply. I watch as it disappears and reappears. And then disappears again for good.

I go to pick Laney up from Culture Camp a few days later with a detour in mind.

But first I have to wait the requisite amount of time for Laney to say heartfelt good-byes to everyone around the craft table. I watch her throw her arms around a small blond girl and am reminded suddenly of an after-school ritual of my own, when I was about her age.

Culture Camp wasn't a thing at my elementary school, but there was a program called Banana Splits. I didn't fully understand it at the time, but Banana Splits was for children of divorce. All I knew was that they got the newest games with all the pieces still intact, and that they had ice cream on Thursdays, and that my friend Ella was in it, whereas I was not.

Ella and I would stop outside the cafeteria, where Banana Splits was held. We would link pinkies and each kiss our thumbs before pressing them together. This was not unique to us—lots of girls in our class did it. It was a way to seal a secret or a promise. I guess Ella and I used it in the same way, but the promise was more benign—*See you tomorrow.*

It was a ritual we grew out of. I haven't thought of it in a long time.

When Laney finally finishes up, we head off and detour down Hadley Street on the way back home. I come to a stop in front of the Newforth Gallery. Laney keeps going a few feet but then stops, too, turns, and squints up at the sign on the building.

"Unauthorized stop," she says.

"We're just going to check on something," I say as I lead her into the gallery.

"Hi," Meira says from behind the desk. "How can I—oh, you were here the other day, right? Gabe's friend?"

"You have a friend?" Laney eyes me suspiciously.

"Go look at the art," I say, pointing at the Laura Fuller wall.

She heads that way and then stops, stock-still, in front of the paintings.

"Look at them," she breathes. "Look how they move."

"Was there something I could help you with?" Meira asks.

I look next to Laney, at the little table with copies of *Laura Fuller: A Retrospective* sitting on it.

"Yeah," I say. "How much are those books?"

Meira gives Laney a gallery postcard with a Laura Fuller painting on the front of it. It's of a little blue boat, floating in an inlet of water. It goes straight into *My Memories* that night. She even flips the page, leaving one blank between her latest clippings of Kai and This Is Our Now and the postcard. All by itself, in a place of honor.

I tuck her in and say good night to my parents, and then I cozy up in bed and crack the cover on *Laura Fuller: A Retrospective*.

A picture of her is centered on the first page. A beautiful dark-haired woman with Vera's laughing eyes.

Laura Fuller (née Morales) was born in the Dominican Republic and moved to the U.S. at the age of ten with her mother, a teacher; and her father, a chef. They settled in Panama City, Florida, where Fuller's father opened a restaurant. Fuller's love of art was apparent from a young age . . .

The book is divided into sections. First is a brief selection of her works from college—landscapes, mainly, but also some still lifes. It transitions into her work following that—water scenes, the beach, the ocean. Then the final section:

Fuller completed five paintings in the last month of her life. They are arguably her most compelling pieces, wrought with emotion and charged with energy. While her early

works capture an elegance and refinement, there is a raw
power to these, which would be her last paintings. Among
these are High Tide, *a continuation of the water motif with*
a dark twist; Sleeper, *which is one of Fuller's few docu-*
mented forays into figure painting; Omnibus, *an impres-*
sionistic take of a town at dusk—likely the town of
Grayson, where Fuller resided; The Dream, *an affecting,*
abstract look at life after death; and Probability, *which is a*
return to the beach, and to Fuller's more traditional style.

I quickly turn the page. *High Tide, Sleeper,* and *Omnibus* follow.
But *The Dream* isn't included.

Of the three shown, *Sleeper* is my favorite. It's the only one in the
whole book that depicts a person. But it's not realism. It's more of an
indication of a person, a dark silhouette standing in a doorway. There's
an impression of space beyond the figure, a depth that's somehow
both scary and comforting at the same time. The person's head is
turned slightly, as if caught between looking forward and looking
back.

I look at the picture for a while before I fall asleep.

thirteen

When I get up to my room after school the next day, there's a neatly stacked pile of papers sitting on my bed. My dad is an avid believer in the inherent magic properties of paper. *You have to* feel *the pages, Sloane.*

I pick up the first sheet and start to read. It doesn't take me long.

I find my dad in his office when I'm finished. "So someone printed out a *Were School* fanfic and left it on my bed," I say.

"Huh. Gee. That's odd."

"Seriously?"

My dad swivels around in his chair. "Did you like it? It's one of my favorites. I'm compiling a rec list."

It contained phrases like "pain so potent it tore through him" and described James's love for Mickey as being "like a dying star—too bright, too hot, destined for collapse."

"I didn't dislike it," I say.

"A resounding endorsement."

"It was nice."

"But . . ."

"But . . . I don't know. That's not . . . It's not even a little bit realistic."

"Well, look at the source material. They're were-teens at a were school in a version of Massachusetts that looks an awful lot like a soundstage in Los Angeles. Of course it's not realistic. But does that in any way diminish your enjoyment of it?"

I shake my head. "I don't mean like that. Obviously the supernatural stuff is its own thing. I just mean . . ." I shrug. "All the love stuff. The gushy stuff. Nobody talks like that—nobody feels stuff that way."

"What do you mean?"

I hold up the pages. "*The love of a dying star?* Really? No one would ever think that, let alone say it out loud."

"Then I have to assume you think of my books the same way."

"Kind of. But this is like your books on crack."

"It's like my books without the pretension. It's . . . unguarded and sincere. It comes from a complete and total love of the characters, and a love of their love—of the *idea* of their love—and that's what I'm here for, Sloane. Characters you care about. Feelings that are authentic. It doesn't shy away for one second. I wish I could write something like that."

"But come on." I shake my head. "I mean, no one loves anyone that much. Right? No one . . . *feels* it like that."

"People absolutely feel it like that. People one thousand percent feel it like that. Maybe they don't think of it in those terms necessarily, but . . . Jesus, Sloane, of course they do."

I look down at the pages. "It's a little heavy-handed, is all," I say finally.

"Agree to disagree," my dad says, then fiddles with his computer for a moment. "I'm printing you another one."

"*Dad.*"

"Fine, I'll send you some links."

It's quiet as he presumably searches for said links.

"How was school?" he asks eventually.

"Okay."

"Anything interesting happen?"

"I, uh . . ." I don't know how much to tell him about the painting. At this point, getting it back is mainly just an idea. But it's an idea that I can't let go of. "I'm starting this new project. I'm not sure how it's going to go."

"Is it a group thing?"

"Not as of now."

"Well, maybe it'd help to have a partner. What class?"

"How about that rec list?" I say.

"On its way," he replies, successfully diverted.

I glance over at Remy in biology on Monday. *Maybe it'd help to have a partner.*

I clear my throat. "Hey, so, did Gabe . . . did Gabe tell you about the painting? Their mom's, that got sold accidentally?"

"Yeah."

"Really?"

"He's my best friend—he tells me everything."

He says this entirely unironically.

"Oh," I say. "Well. I sort of want to get it back."

I tell him about going to Meira's, about how she couldn't give out the client's info. "So . . . ," he says when I'm done.

"So I need your help. Gabe doesn't . . . He said to forget about it."

"But you're not going to do that."

"Of course not."

He cracks a smile. "Yeah, okay."

I don't know Remy super well, but it strikes me as very Remylike. Most people would follow that up with some questions: *Where are we going, what are we doing?* But Remy just accepts it, nods, and then is quiet.

Until he says, "I . . . sort of need help, too. Getting something back."

"What is it?"

"Aubrey."

I glance over at him. "Aubrey's not a thing. You can't just *obtain* her."

"But you know what I mean. I want . . . I want her back."

"That's sort of a two-person decision, isn't it? Doesn't matter what you want if she doesn't want the same thing."

"But maybe there's something I could do," he says, and he sounds so earnest. "Maybe there's something I could change, or do better, and then maybe she'd want to date me again. And even if she doesn't, that's really—if I can't get her back, that's all I want, to know why. When she ended things, she didn't . . . I don't even know why." He looks at me. "It's the worst. Have you ever—" He stops himself, and I'm not sure if it's because he's overcome with emotion or because I don't look like anyone who has *ever.* "Just . . . maybe you could find out why it didn't work out."

"Why do you want me to do it?"

"You're the outsider."

My face must've done something I wasn't aware of at that, because Remy's eyes widen. "I don't mean—not the outsider like . . . You're just new, is all. We're all used to each other, and we've all gotten set into how we are together. You're different. I think . . . I think she'd talk to you."

"Why?"

He shrugs. "You just . . . I just think she would."

"Okay. Well, I'll talk to Aubrey if you help me with my painting scheme."

"It's a scheme now?"

"Hell yeah it's a scheme. And by the way, if Gabe truly is your best friend, don't you think you should want to help him out of the goodness of your own heart, and not because I'll help you with your lady problems?"

"He doesn't like people helping him. I'm actually going against him by doing this."

"That's stupid and you know it."

He shrugs. "That's Gabe."

I meet Remy in the appointed place for strategizing after school that day—room 324, tucked in the back corner across the hall from a janitor's closet. I'm surprised to find that, of all things, it's a radio station.

A small one, yes, but it's got the trappings all the same, with the big microphones and the soundboard and the unnecessary shelves of now irrelevant CDs. Music is blaring when I enter, which Remy turns down, sliding the headphones off his ears.

"You're a deejay," I say.

"DJ Smooth, to be precise."

"DJ Smooth?" I repeat.

"I told him it was a terrible name," a muffled voice says.

"It's better than DJ Gabe," Remy replies, and there is Gabe, emerging from a door tucked in the corner.

"Hey, Gabe's here," I say.

"I am."

"He is."

I look at Remy. Remy looks back at me. I raise my eyebrows emphatically, but he just scrunches his lower in confusion.

Don't say anything about the painting, my eyes are trying to say.

I have no idea what you mean, his eyes are saying back.

So we have yet to achieve nonverbal communication. Maybe it doesn't come to lab partners until the second semester or so.

"That thing we're supposed to work on," I say finally. "Maybe we should wait to talk about it until after the show? After you guys are done . . . and everyone's . . . gone their separate ways?"

Gabe is looking at me strangely, but Remy seems to understand. He nods. "Sure. Yeah. We just have one more break if you want to hang out."

I sink down into the ratty couch in the corner. Dangerous, having a couch in a high school. The radio room must be make-out central during off-hours.

Remy clicks a button and the ON AIR sign lights up, just like on TV.

"Hey, this is DJ Smooth in the studio here with my pal—"

Gabe leans into the mic. "DJ Gabe," he says solemnly.

"Got a news item here fresh off the press," Remy says, in a Radio Voice: peppy and big and very unlike anything I've heard come out of him thus far. "Looks like a Destin man has been found safe and reunited with his family after twenty-four hours missing. He was last seen leaving work at approximately four p.m. in a forest-green SUV with license-plate number—you know, I don't know why I'm telling you that part. It's not that helpful, seeing as he's actually been found—"

"I don't know, it'd be helpful if you were trying to kidnap him again," Gabe says.

I laugh, and he looks up immediately. Something flickers quickly across his face—something like amusement—but then he's back to flipping through a CD booklet.

"Anyway, just trying to end our day here on a high note. Reunited families, that's always good news. And to round off our show, here's 'Take On Me' by A-ha. Have a great day out there, Grove County. This is DJ Smooth—"

"And DJ Gabe."

"Signing off," they both say together, like huge nerds. And then "Take On Me" pipes through the speakers, and the ON AIR light switches off.

"Nice song choice," I say.

"I know how to throw it back," Remy replies with a grin.

"Are you going to ride the bus?" Gabe asks Remy as they gather their things.

"Nah, Sloane and I are going to work on that thing."

"We have a class together," I say, which is the absolute truth.

Gabe nods. "Okay. Well . . . see you guys."

"I don't think we should tell him," I say, as soon as the door closes behind him. "About the scheme. Just in case . . . you know, like in case we don't get the painting back. No use in getting his hopes up, right?"

"Got it. No telling. Vera, too?"

"Right. She'd just tell him. Or they'd, you know, twin-telepathy it out of each other."

"So what's the plan?"

This is the hard part. "I don't exactly have a concrete plan, per se . . ."

"What does that mean?"

"It means that coming up with the plan is part of the plan."

Remy grins.

We come up with a plan.

Really, we come up with an advertisement and a list of places to post it. Remy and I craft the copy ourselves, to much debate.

"Just put a bunch of dollar signs at the end," he says, once we've parsed the wording.

"But then people will think we're going to give them money if they have information."

"We said no such thing. We just put a bunch of bomb-ass dollar signs in our ad. That could mean anything. Maybe we'll give them money, maybe they give us money . . . It's just eye-catching. Trust me."

I add them, and we stare at our handiwork:

SEEKING: Laura Fuller painting called "The Dream."
Sold in blue frame from Newforth Gallery,
Hadley St., Opal Beach, Grove County.
With info, please call 646-555-2910.
$$$$$$$$$$$$$$$$$

"Are you sure you want to put your phone number?" Remy asks.

"Why not?"

"I don't know, what if people . . . send you pictures of dicks or something?"

"I will show you any and all dick pics I receive. Then we'll both suffer."

"That doesn't make me feel better."

I look at the screen. "I think this is good."

"I don't know—maybe there are too many dollar signs."

"Disagree. Not enough. Add ten more."

"If you're not taking this seriously—"

"You're the one who said to put dollar signs!"

"Send it," Remy says with a smile.

fourteen

My dad is busy that evening when I come home. He doesn't even
have dinner with us.

"What's Papa doing?" Laney asks. My mom just shrugs.

"His own thing."

I knock on the door to his office before I go to bed.

"Uh-huh?"

I crack it open.

"Are you writing?"

He doesn't look up. "Yup."

"A new book?"

"Not . . . quite."

I step into the room and eye him. "Are you writing *Were School*
fan fiction?"

"I said I wanted to write something *like Were School* fan fiction."

"And?"

"And yes, I am writing *Were School* fan fiction."

"For real?"

"Yeah, I'm doing a coffeeshop AU to start—you know, a

classic—but I turned it on its head. Usually Mickey is the barista and James is the harried businessman, but I swapped roles—no one sees James as the coffeehouse type, you know, this carefree, laid-back kind of guy, but I really think he has that in him. In another 'verse, without the tragic backstory, he really could've—"

"Dad."

"Okay, yeah, well, that one's whatever. But I have a couple other ideas going, too."

"What's AU?"

"Alternate universe," he says, like it's the most obvious thing in the world. "Look at this."

He brings up a picture of the cast of *Were School* on his computer, using the cursor to draw a circle around a guy in the middle.

"Everyone's really keen on Luke, the hot, young, newly turned werewolf. Luke and his girl problems. Luke and his doting mother. Luke's fine, but the chemistry between James and Mickey totally overshadows him, if you ask me." He points them out accordingly. "But the most underutilized character, without a doubt, is Kiko." He points to a pale girl to the far right, whose dark, flowing hair billows out behind her, no doubt a result of the requisite photo-shoot wind machine.

"Let me guess," I say. "Kiko is a mermaid."

"Mermaids aren't real in the *Were School* canon."

"Okay, Kiko is an automaton."

"Kiko is a *ghost*," he says witheringly. "And if you ask me, it's the most underplayed device of the whole show. She's capable of taking corporeal form by briefly inhabiting someone else's body. When she leaves them, they have no recollection that she'd been there at all. And they are *wasting* this on having her take over Emily's body so that she can get closer to Luke and manipulate him into using the Kisney stone to bring her back to life."

"That sounds pretty legit to me."

"Yes, but there's so much potential to use this to develop Jickey's relationship and the writers are completely ignoring it."

"Jickey?"

"James and Mickey. See, you could take it to a comedic place. Kiko plays matchmaker—wants James and Mickey to be together—so she alternately takes each of them over, trying to get them to end up in the same places at the same time, throwing them together in all these romantic situations. Or, or, okay. This is the big one I'm working on. An AU in which Kiko is desperately in love with James. Maybe they knew each other as kids? Maybe she gave up her life trying to save him! But she sees that James is in love with Mickey, so she inhabits Mickey's body, knowing it's the only way she'll be able to spend time with James. At first, James is thrilled, but he quickly realizes what's happening, and he's devastated, obviously, so he starts ignoring Mickey. Meanwhile, Mickey has been pining for James for years—okay, well, he's seventeen, so, he's been pining for at least a semester—and he doesn't understand what's changed between them, thought there was a tentative truce, maybe even some interest, but now James is acting like he's poison, and it's all because of Kiko—" He shakes his head. "Okay, I don't know, it's pretty dub-conish—I'd have to work that out—but . . ."

He trails off and then starts typing furiously.

"Dad?"

"Oh my God, Sloane, that's genius."

"I . . . didn't say anything."

"I know. I mean the idea I just had. It's genius."

"Should I be worried?" I ask after a pause.

"No. But you should start on season one."

"That's hilarious," Vera says at lunch the next day.

"It's not hilarious if he's having a breakdown."

"I'm sure it's not a breakdown," Vera says. "I mean, I'm sure it's probably not a breakdown."

I poke at the top layer of pineapple in my fruit cup. "Thanks. Super reassuring."

"It reminds me of Remy, though," she says after a pause. "His radio thing."

"What do you mean?"

She raises her eyebrows. "Have you listened?"

"I caught the end, the other day."

"DJ Smooth." Vera rolls her eyes, but there's an affectionate exasperation to it. "He used to play football, you know. But he quit the team this year. And I'm sure when baseball starts up, he'll quit that, too. He's changed a lot since he and Aubrey broke up."

"Like how?"

She bites her lip. "So his dad's a preacher, right?" I remember Frank saying something about that at the party—*He volunteers with his dad's church.* "He always wanted to be one, too, always, ever since we were little. He was going to take over the church from his dad, and it was always 'God says this' and 'Jesus thinks that.' He was really insufferable."

I grin.

"But then the whole Aubrey thing happens, the breakup, and suddenly it's all about doing the show with Gabe, and he has this internship at a station in Panama City that he's completely obsessed with, and he's just . . . I don't know. Maybe it's like your dad and *Were School*. Maybe sometimes people get super focused on one thing when they don't want to have to think about something else. But sometimes it's like, to the detriment of everything else, you know? I worry about him. I just . . . I just want to make sure he's happy."

I don't point out that there is literally no way to make sure that someone is happy. Happiness is not a certainty. Instead I just nod. "Same with my dad, I guess," I say, because I feel it, too, even if it doesn't make sense.

fifteen

I have a voice mail message when I get out of class on Wednesday.

It's a woman with a bright voice.

"Hi, so I saw your ad online, and I have a Laura Fuller painting, but I don't know exactly what it's—Jackson, Jackson, get down from there, for God's sake—sorry, sorry, uh, yeah, so I have a Laura Fuller, I got it from my mother-in-law and I'm pretty sure she bought it at the place on your ad. I don't know what it's called, but I'd be willing to sell if you're—Jackson, I swear to God—yeah, just let me know, my name is Tisha, just give me a call back and that'd be—"

The voice mail cuts out then. Ran too long, I guess, or maybe Jackson got hold of the phone.

I call Tisha back. She picks up on the eighth ring.

She has a Laura Fuller painting, purchased at Newforth, in a handmade blue frame, and she's enthusiastic about us coming by.

"I would love for someone to take it off my hands."

"Can you send me a picture?"

"Yeah, for sure," she says, and then starts rattling off her address. I make arrangements to go visit on Saturday afternoon.

Got a lead, I text Remy when we get off the phone.

He sends a half-dozen high-five emojis back.

I work that evening, and on my fifteen-minute break, I take a seat on the deck out back and crack open a book. The back of Dodge's faces the Opal Motor Court, which is a series of small, squat little buildings, a motel that's masquerading as down-home and rustic but really—just across the street from the beach—charges more for a week than a month's rent at an average apartment.

It's not long before someone drops down next to me.

"What are you reading?" Gabe asks.

I hold up the book so he can see the cover of *Sand on Our Beach.* "One of my dad's."

He has a bag of chips, which he opens loudly and holds in my direction. I shake my head.

"Kinda weird, isn't it?"

"Not liking cool ranch?" I gesture to the bag.

He makes a face. "Reading your dad's book."

"Why, because he writes about sex and stuff?"

"Ugh, no, I didn't even think about that. I just meant, isn't it like . . ."

"Like a musician sitting at home listening to their own album?"

"Kind of."

"I don't know. I'm not the artist here, so I guess I can still appreciate it. It must be like you and Vera—" I almost say *looking at your mom's paintings*, but I cut myself short. I get the impression Gabe knows where I was going, anyway. He bobs his head and looks out at the Motor Court.

"What's it about?"

"It's kind of . . . It's pretty depressing, actually. And it didn't . . . I mean, it sold a lot of copies. But it wasn't exactly, like, critically acclaimed. The *New York Times* called it 'the worst thing to happen to Huntington's disease since Huntington's disease.' "

"Rough," he says, lips quirking. "So what's it about?"

"A woman with Huntington's disease," I say. "Surprise, surprise. Well, really, her grandfather had it. But it's hereditary, and she doesn't know if her mom had it or not because her mom died when she was—" I did it again. But Gabe's face doesn't change; he just looks thoughtful. I cough. "So she doesn't know if she has it or not. It's a neurodegenerative disorder; it's really devastating, so . . . she moves to this small town to be alone and get her shit in order in case she does have it. And then she meets someone."

Of course. That part is inevitable.

"And they fall in love?" Gabe says.

"She resists it."

"Because she thinks she's dying?"

"She thinks it's not worth burdening him if she really is sick."

"So why doesn't she just find out if she has it or not?"

"That's kind of the crux of the book. Is it better to know or not know?"

"Does she find out?"

"I don't want to spoil it."

"Oh, come on."

"No, this is a strict no-spoiler zone."

He looks at me for a moment and then says, "Maybe I'll just watch the movie."

"Those are fighting words," I say.

And then it's quiet, save for the crunch of Gabe's chips.

"Got plans for the weekend?" he says after a while.

"Not really."

"I was thinking of seeing a movie on Friday," he says. *Crunch, crunch.*

"Thrilling."

His mouth twists, a suppressed smile. "You could join. If you want."

"Could I?"

"If you want," he says again.

"Sure. I'll ask Vera. Or, you know, you could ask Vera, since you live with her and stuff."

Gabe nods, staring into his chip bag. "Can do."

"Think my break's up," I say. "See you inside?"

"Yeah, sure."

I head in, but I can't help but peer out the glass door to the back as I slip my apron on. Gabe's leaning back on his hands, shoulders hunched, the empty chip bag crumpled by his side.

sixteen

We don't end up at the movies on Friday. Gabe doesn't mention it again, and when I ask Vera, she says, "It's Friday night! We can't miss FSP!"

But I don't go to Frank Sanger Presents, either. Instead I stay in and watch the Disney Channel's latest endeavors with Laney. Vera texts me, presumably from the party.

Where are you?

At home. With my family, I say.

Boooooooooooo, she replies, and then a moment later: No but that's sweet though.

When morning comes, it's time for my voice lesson. Mom and I make the trek to Tallahassee, and Eileen and I spend our session hammering out an art song I've been working on.

When we pull back into the driveway that afternoon, Remy is sitting on our front porch.

"Hmm" is all my mom says, her eyebrows raised.

"We have a project to do."

She's wearing a big cheesy grin, wiggling her eyebrows suggestively. "Which someone seems eager to start on."

I look at her. Right in the eyes. "I don't like Remy like that, Mom. There are no romantic feelings. Do you understand?"

She nods.

"You're nodding, but like, I really need to know that you understand. I need verbal confirmation."

"I understand," she says, and her smile softens a little.

"So you'll let me and Remy be friends without any kind of insinuation or shipping or anything."

"Shipping?"

"Ask Dad." I get out of the car.

Remy stands. "Ready?"

We go to DeFuniak Springs to see Tisha. Tisha and Jackson—*Jackson! Get down from there*—and their dog, Maximus.

Their front lawn is littered with toys. Predominantly human-child toys, but there are some dog toys mixed in as well, among the Tonka trucks and plastic pails and one of those motorized cars that I always wanted as a kid but *It's practically a death trap, Michael—we're not getting our child a car*. There's a turtle-shaped sandbox and a plastic Fisher-Price jungle gym and an assortment of beach/foot-/soccer/basketballs trailing from the front around to the side of the house. I'd bet money that the backyard looks much the same.

HAPPY SMILES DAY CARE reads a hand-painted sign on the side door.

"It's a side business," Tisha explains as she leads us into the house. "At least, it started that way, but now it's kind of my full-time gig. Just easier—we were paying so much for day care for Jackson while I worked that it was basically losing us money, can you imagine? Jackson? Jackson!" she calls into the depths of the house. I can hear

95

the slap of a child's feet against the floor. A kid, probably four or so, turns the corner and barrels down the hall at us, a big black Labrador retriever on his heels. He nearly crashes right into Remy.

"Sorry, sorry," Tisha says as boy and dog dart into the living room/ dining room. "It's just through here." She leads us after them to where a large rectangle wrapped in brown paper sits atop a table. "Had to keep it covered. Jackson gets into everything, as you can probably imagine." She begins to peel the paper back.

I had asked Tisha to send me a picture of the painting, and she hadn't. I even texted her last night, asking again. She had replied this morning, with a sorry, just saw ur msg! See you in a bit!

When the painting is revealed, it is indeed in a blue frame, though if I had to classify it, it's a bit more green than blue. Mottled a little, like turquoise. Maybe we should've been more specific in our ad. Then again, it's not like we had many specifics to go from. Just Gabe's halting description in the hallway, midargument with his dad.

"What do you think?" she says. "It's cute, huh?"

Cute doesn't do it. The painting shows a red dock jutting into an expanse of water, bright midday sun shining down on it. The beams of the dock seem to glow with it; it somehow looks like the perfect summer day—the heat of the sun tempered by the coolness of the water.

"My ex's mom got it for us. I got it in the divorce. Lucky me." It's said with more than a hint of bitterness. "Not that it's not beautiful— it is—it's just, I kind of would've rather had the TV, you know?" She huffs a laugh. "Is that bad? That's probably bad. I'm more than happy to get rid of it, though. So is it the one you were looking for?"

Remy glances at me.

I shake my head.

Tisha bites her lip. "I was worried about that. See, I was looking over it last night, and I actually saw something on the back." She flips the painting over. The canvas looks handmade, with excess fabric hanging over the sides where it's stretched across the wooden frame. She pulls the flap back on the bottom corner, and it reveals a word written across the bottom: *Sunday.*

"What do you think, though? Are you interested?"

"I . . . sorry, no. We're looking for a specific one. But thanks for showing us. We really appreciate it."

"I could give you a real deal on it. Cheaper than a gallery, for sure. Believe me, every little bit helps."

I can't really afford to buy a painting that's not *the* painting. But I feel an odd pull anyway, looking at the red dock. I think Remy can sense it.

"We'll probably keep looking," he says, glancing at me. "But we'll keep it in mind for sure."

"All right," Tisha says with a sigh and starts wrapping the painting back up. "Thanks for coming out."

We get back in the car. Tisha gives us a wave from the stoop. Jackson and Maximus stand in the front yard and watch us go.

"She could've told us she found that on there. She could've called us last night and saved us a trip," Remy says in the car. The radio is on low, churning out the Top 40 hits of the day, and we're easing back onto the highway.

"She was hoping we'd buy it anyway. We did put a shit-ton of dollar signs in that ad."

He glances over at me. "How did you know, though? Before she showed us the title. I thought all you knew was blue frame, and it sort of had a blue frame."

"*The Dream* is supposed to have people in it." Gabe had said. Three figures in the center. "There were no people on that dock."

Remy makes a face. "You should've said that before—we could've put it in the ad."

It's a good point, but I'll never concede to it. "But then you would be less impressed with my deductive skills."

"What are we going to do now?"

"I don't know. Go home?"

"I mean about the painting."

"We can redo the ad if you want."

"And then?"

"I don't know. Hope that someone else contacts us?"

He sighs. "Send it up to the God Man, then. That's the plan."

Vera's words come back to me, about Remy: *It was always "God says this" and "Jesus thinks that."* "I guess." And then it's quiet until I glance over at him. "Why is he a man?"

"Sorry?"

"The God *Man*. Why is he a man? Why can't he be a woman? Why does he have to fit into a gender binary at all?"

"I don't know." Remy shrugs. "To me, it's a guy. I think you can imagine him—or her, or them—however you want."

"So I could have, like, the God Starfish?"

"Sure, why not? God is in all things, right?"

"Is he in that air freshener?"

Remy gives me a look. "You don't always have to run everything up the flagpole, you know. You can believe in something without making fun of it."

"I believe in stuff."

"Like what?"

I shrug. "I don't know. Stuff." And because I don't like to let a conversation hover on me too long, I turn it around: "What about you, then? You've got the God Man. What else?"

"I believe in lots of things."

"Santa? Radioactive spiders?"

He doesn't reply, just makes a face as he switches lanes.

"You must've believed in you and Aubrey," I say. I'm not even sure why. I don't want to needle. But part of me wants to know—what happens when your faith betrays you? At one point in time, Aubrey must've believed in them, too.

But "Yeah" is all he says.

"How did it end? What did she say?"

"Nothing."

"So she mimed it."

"Jesus, Sloane."

"Don't you mean God Man?"

He doesn't dignify that with a response. "There wasn't much to it," he says instead. "We just broke up. One day she came over and . . ."

"What?"

"Okay . . . so we sort of have this thing, among us. As friends. Where if there's something that you need but you can't say why—like a favor, you know, like you need someone to cover for you about sleeping over or something—then you can just say this phrase, and everyone has to go with it, no questions asked, and never speak of it again unless spoken about by the invoker of the phrase."

"Sounds . . . handy, I guess. What's the phrase?"

Remy mumbles something. It sounds like *penguin party.*

"Sorry?"

He clears his throat. "Penguin party."

Huh. "And this is because . . ."

"Because we all liked that movie *Happy Feet* when we were kids. And it's a nonsense, random made-up phrase anyway—the phrase itself doesn't matter—but when you say it, that's it. It's unbreakable."

"So when Aubrey broke up with you . . ."

"She said, 'We need to break up.' And then she said . . ."

"Penguin party."

"You got it."

"So that's why you can't ask her. Why you need me to do it. Because I'm not in on this sacred covenant of the penguin party."

"Yeah."

"You guys are so much weirder than I thought."

He smiles a little.

"I'll try," I say. "But then . . . I mean, you don't want to get creepy about this, right?"

"Of course not. I just . . . When someone breaks your heart, you kind of want to know why."

I nod, even though it doesn't make sense to me. If someone broke my heart, I don't think I'd want to know why. Then I could make up something to suit my own vanity. Maybe they were incapable of loving. Maybe it had nothing to do with me. But knowing—

Well. That was the crux of *Sand on Our Beach*. Knowing or not knowing. My dad had already written 374 pages on the subject. And the *New York Times* had already excoriated it.

Remy turns up the dial on the radio and says, "This is our competition. The guys at the station say their morning team is the worst." And I accept the change of subject, say something stupid about the dee-jay on now, and we talk of nothing of importance for the rest of the ride back.

seventeen

Remy ends up staying for dinner that evening. I text Vera and she comes over, too, and after dinner we watch the *Were School* pilot. Half because by this point I'm intrigued, and half to get my dad off my back about *appreciating the canon*.

It's very much like you'd expect. Gratuitous shirtlessness. Dim lighting. There's an extended fight scene in the school at night that's so dark, Remy gets about six inches from the TV, cupping his hands around his eyes to see better. Vera laughs her head off.

The episode ends abruptly.

"What the hell?" Vera squawks.

I can't help but agree: "That's it? It's over?"

"I literally don't know what I just watched," Remy says.

"Wait until season four," my dad says gleefully from the kitchen. "There are cliff-hangers out the wazoo."

"You're on season four already?" Vera asks.

"Dad's been through all the seasons already."

"Twice," he adds, without a hint of shame.

We watch two more episodes, and then Vera and Remy get ready to leave. They're slipping on their shoes at the front door when Vera looks up at me.

"Hey, so what were you guys doing this afternoon? Your mom said you were out."

I glance at Remy. I don't want to lie. We just saw firsthand what happens when Luke lied to Mickey about being a werewolf—Mickey ends up tied to a chair in the secret warehouse lair of a gang of wendigos.

Remy doesn't seem to have the same qualms. "AP bio stuff," he says.

"Ugh. Should've opted out like me. Regular biology is more than enough." She throws her arms around me. "Good night, lady."

I put one hand on her back. This is the first time she's hugged me. "Night."

"Do I get a hug?" Remy asks.

"From me, or from Sloane?"

"Ew, I don't want a Sloane hug."

"That means he likes you," Vera says, her eyes shining. I meet Remy's gaze over her head in a way that says *Yeah. Right.*

They head out, and I watch them go from the porch.

The door swings open after a moment, cutting a swath of light across the front yard.

"It's nice, huh?" my mom says. "Having friends over. Doing friend stuff."

"Say *friends* again, Mom."

"Friends, friends, friends," she says, and grins at me.

"So what was the secret trip about?" my dad calls from his office that night as I pass from the bathroom to my bedroom.

"Sorry?"

"This afternoon. The secret errand. With the secrecy."

"There was no secret errand."

"Is it drugs? Guns? I can't help you if you don't let me," he says, straight-faced.

"It's a painting," I say, and with that, I have to tell him the whole story.

"Perfect," Dad says when I'm finished. "Perfect. It's just like Luke and the Kisney stone."

"I thought you said the Kisney stone was to undo curses."

"Obviously it's not *exactly* like Luke and the Kisney stone. But you know what I mean. Lost gem. Epic quest."

"It's not much of an epic quest right now. More like a needle in a haystack."

He smiles. "All epic quests start somewhere, right?"

eighteen

Remy and I start shotgunning *Were School* episodes after that. Sometimes my dad joins in, giving commentary on his favorite episodes and occasionally rewinding scenes and making us watch them again to fully appreciate what he calls "the sizzle."

"The writing is pretty terrible," he says. "The plot holes have plot holes. But the chemistry! God, I just want to bottle it up. And the fics . . . the fics make up for anything lacking in the show itself."

"Dad, you're like weirdly passionate about this."

"We should all find something to be weirdly passionate about, don't you think?"

It isn't until the next Frank Sanger Presents that I find out that Frank is weirdly passionate about my dad.

"Your dad is Everett Finch," Frank says for the third time since it came up. We're sitting out on the front porch of Ava Carmichael's house. There's a hint of coolness to the air—perfect hoodie weather.

"Well, technically, my dad is Michael Finch. It's a pen name."

But Frank doesn't hear that. "Holy effing shit, have you met Dex Finnegan?"

Dex Finnegan has starred in three of my dad's movie adaptations. The first, *Summer Burn*, was Dex's debut film role. My dad became friends with him when he went to visit the set. Dex came to our house for Thanksgiving that year, after my dad found out he didn't have anywhere else to go. I was eight at the time.

"What did he smell like?" Frank grabs me by the shoulders and shakes. "For the love of God, woman, what did he smell like?"

"Like the air after a rain," I say, because I have no earthly recollection of what Dex Finnegan smelled like. "Mixed with that smell like when you blow out a candle. Mixed with the smell of baby sweat. Like a baby who's just done a lot of cardio."

Remy snorts. "Baby sweat?"

"It's really rare that a baby sweats. So, you know, it probably smells magical. It probably has healing properties."

"It's probably really terrible for the baby," Aubrey says. "Their internal thermostats are very sensitive, and if a baby is sweating, he's—"

"He smells like a baby who just taught four spin classes back-to-back," I continue, because I can't help it. "He smells like a baby who just kickboxed another baby."

"He smells like a baby who's climbing Mount Everest," Gabe says quietly. "With ten other babies, and things get rough, and they have to cannibalize and eat three of the babies, so that baby is literally sweating the blood and tears of his friends."

The porch is silent.

And then Vera and Frank explode into laughter, and Aubrey rolls her eyes, suppressing a smile. Gabe catches my eye for a second and then looks away, and it's almost like he's trying not to look pleased.

"There's something seriously wrong with you guys," Remy says, but he's smiling in that quiet Remy way, like a teacher in the back of the class after a good presentation.

Frank stands, dabbing imaginary tears from his eyes. "You slay me, kids. Truly." Then he lets out a belch. "I'm hungry, and I know where Ava's mom hides the good cheese. Who's in?"

Vera and Remy stand. But I'm perfectly good without any of Ava's mom's secret cheese. So they go in, and Aubrey, Gabe, and I stay out.

Gabe stretches out across the plush wicker couch, occupying the spots where Vera and Frank had sat. Aubrey is nearer, sitting on a cushion on the ground with her phone in her hands. I scoot my chair closer to her. Not because I am naturally friendly like Vera, but because I know an opportunity when I see one. Gabe has his arm thrown over his eyes, by all accounts taking a rest, and I know this is my in for Remy.

"So," I say.

"So," she says, glancing up from her phone.

"How's it going?"

"Good."

"Haven't gotten to chat much."

"No."

"How, uh . . ." I already asked how it was going. God, I'm bad at this.

"What's up?" Aubrey's tone brooks no prevarication.

"I just, uh, I was wondering . . . about you and Remy."

"Me and Remy," she repeats.

"Would be the people I'm wondering about, yeah."

106

"We're not together anymore, if that's what you mean."

"No, I know. Everyone knows."

She raises an eyebrow.

"Not like it's super obvious—it's just Frank mentioned it when I first met him, and I was just wondering—"

"Wonder whatever you want. We're not together, so I don't care."

I blink.

"I didn't—"

"I think I'm hungry," she says, and stands abruptly. Then she's gone.

I glance over at Gabe but he's quiet, one arm flung over his face, chest rising and falling steadily. I let out a sigh, but if he hears it, he doesn't acknowledge it.

I sleep over at Vera's that night.

A night-light sits on the table next to Vera's bed, a little plastic base with three stars sticking out of it: yellow, orange, and pink. It casts a golden glow, competing with the wash of white light from Vera's phone.

"Me and Aubrey usually just share," Vera had said after we changed into our jammies, pulling down the covers and climbing into bed. So I followed, but I couldn't help but think of Aubrey, her tone when she said *Wonder whatever you want. . . . I don't care.* And I think about Frank, describing "the group"—*BFFs til the grand fucking end.*

I glance over at Vera now, tapping away on her phone. "Maybe we should invite Aubrey next time," I say. "So she doesn't . . ." Feel left out? Resent me for moving in on the group?

"We wouldn't fit" is Vera's simple reply.

"One of us could sleep on the floor. Or we could have it at my house . . . camp out in the living room or whatever."

She doesn't speak for a moment, and then: "Things between me and Aubrey have been kind of weird."

"Weird how?"

"I don't know. Just kind of"—she shakes her head—"different."

"Why?"

Vera shrugs, fiddles with her phone a bit, then places it faceup on the nightstand.

"It's just kind of hard to talk to her sometimes. But she's my best friend," she says finally. She then amends, "She's one of my best friends," and I'm not sure if that's for my benefit. How long do you have to know someone before you can declare yourselves best friends? And what if it's one-sided—to one person they're best friends and to the other they're not? I hadn't really thought about it before, but it's complicated—along the same lines as dating and romance and love, almost as murky and potentially heartbreaking.

"I never really had a best friend," I say after a moment of thoughtful silence. And it's true. I had friendships growing up. I think of Ella, playing on the playground together, our parting ritual every afternoon. By junior high, we weren't nearly as close. We'd wave at each other in the hallway, or sometimes I'd eat lunch with her and her friends. But she had sort of just drifted away.

"Or if I have, I guess it's my dad," I continue, because it's the truth. "We talk about everything."

"He's a cool dad," Vera murmurs. "Not like mine."

"Society would think your dad is cool. He has a twenty-two-year-old wife and seventeen-year-old kids."

"That's not cool—it's douchey."

"It's not douchey if he really loves her, is it?"

"You can say that because it's not you. It's different if it's your dad."

"Gabe says it's fucked up."

"It is." She turns on her side to face me. "My mom was so great, Sloane. Like A-plus mom, good person, funny and kind and she knew everything, and he loved her so much. And she loved him back the same way, and you don't just . . . piss in the face of that love by marrying the fucking Hydrox of second wives, you don't just . . . cheapen that, like he did. How can you go from the kind of love he had with my mom to her and think it's okay? Unless—" Her voice breaks, just a little.

"Unless the love wasn't as strong as you thought," I say. Even though I don't want to. It just comes out. She nods at me, vigorously, and her eyes are shiny in the light from the shooting stars as she rolls onto her back again.

It's quiet for a while. I think maybe she's asleep, but I see her out of the corner of my eye, one hand darting out to her phone on the nightstand. Maybe one more text to Tash. One more reply to someone out there in the universe who needs her.

nineteen

"I hope to see you all at auditions for the spring musical next week,"
Mrs. Simmons says at the end of choir on Tuesday. Aubrey glances at
me as we gather our things. We've been sitting next to each other at
every practice, but I wonder if Aubrey does it more out of obligation
than anything. Or maybe just the tenet of that unspoken seat thing.
You sat there once and now you're stuck.

"Are you going to audition?" she asks.

"Theater's not really my thing," I say. "Are you?"

She shrugs.

"What do you mean, you're not going to audition?" Vera says that
evening on the phone. "I'm auditioning, and I don't even sing!"

"It's not really my thing," I say again.

She lets out an exasperated huff. "But it's *Anything Goes*! You
have to be Reno Sweeney. You *have* to be."

"Why?" I've seen the show before. Reno Sweeney sings a lot of
songs—she's this charming, attractive, madcap force of nature. I don't
really think I'm qualified.

"Because the best singer is Reno Sweeney, and that's you!"

I'm warmed by her confidence in me. But I just shake my head, and because Vera can't see me through the phone, I say, "Yeah, no. I'd rather not."

Something in my voice must sound final, because Vera just sighs. "Okay. Well, I expect you at the auditions for moral support."

That I can agree to. "I'll be there."

Friday comes, and instead of a party, Frank suggests a movie night.

"Frank Sanger Presents: Your Cinematic Faves," he says, brandishing a Red Vine like an old-fashioned cigarette holder. We're all sprawled in the living room at Vera and Gabe's house. Vera is sitting next to me on the couch, hugging one of the fluffy throw pillows.

As soon as the opening credits finish and the movie begins, Gabe rises up. "Well, this has been great."

"Where are you going?" I ask.

"Gotta change" is all he says, heading out of the room.

I look to Vera, but her eyes are glued to the screen.

Gabe returns five or so minutes later, in dress pants and a button-down shirt, with a tie. Vera finally tears her eyes away from the movie. "Isn't it sickening how guys can just do that?" she says. "From sweats to formal wear in the time it would take me to line one eye. Pause it, Frank."

"What, why?" Gabe says, grabbing keys off a hook by the door.

"We're taking pictures."

"No, we're not."

"At least one," she says, handing me her phone and jumping up. She reaches behind Gabe and flicks the lights on, then throws

111

one arm around him, resting her other hand on her waist and jutting out one hip like a starlet on a red carpet. She then looks at me expectantly.

I forgot I was the designated cameraperson. I stand and snap a few pictures. Gabe looks put-upon for the first one, but when he actually smiles, it does something strange to my stomach.

"So where are you going?" I say, handing the phone back to Vera.

"Gabe's going to homecoming at Jade Coast Christian," Vera says for him. "With *Alice*," she adds, with emphasis.

"Ooh, the famed Alice from Jade Coast Christian?" Remy says. "So tell us, is tonight the night you guys finally hold hands?"

Frank jumps in: "When you dance, will there be *room for Jesus* or are you just going to go for it? Groin to groin? Even though the good sweet Lord could strike you down at any moment?"

"Screw you guys," Gabe says, but he's grinning.

"Our love to Alice," Vera calls, as Gabe leaves.

Vera then hits the lights, and we start the movie again. When I bite down particularly hard on a Red Vine, she glances over at me. "What?"

"Nothing."

She pokes me.

"Nothing," I say. And then, "Who's Alice?"

"Gabe's lady friend. They do date stuff, but he always claims they're not dating."

"How can you do date stuff but not be dating?"

She shrugs. "I think he just likes the routine."

"Shouldn't he like the person?"

"That, too. But also the routine."

"Can we be quiet while Hollywood icon and Broadway star Dex Finnegan is talking?" Frank says from his spot on the floor.

"He's not a Broadway star," I say.

"Is so. He's opening in a show soon—Shakespeare or something, trying to bank that serious acting cred. Don't play like I don't follow my boy on Twitter. Now we definitely need to rewind, I'm not even kidding. I don't want to miss a moment of that man's angelic face and his heavenly voice, it's like a choir of angels singing—"

"That's a lot of angel imagery, Frank," I say.

"I can't help it if I'm not at my best. The blood leaves my brain where Dex Finnegan is involved."

"Ew, Frank, we don't need to know about your . . . blood-flow situation," Vera says.

"Very subtly put, darling, thank you." Frank grins. "Now be kind and rewind."

How was the movie? Gabe texts me later that night.

The movie was horrible. Frank loved it, Remy, Vera, and I hated it, and Aubrey declared no opinion one way or the other. "Didn't you feel anything when she gave up the internship for him?" Frank cried, holding one of the throw pillows to his chest.

"Yes," Remy said. "Revulsion."

Ugh, I reply. Gabe sends me a laughing face back.

How was the dance? I ask, after the part of me that wants to know wins out over the part that really doesn't.

Okay, he replies, and nothing more.

You should've stayed for the movie, I say after a while. Everyone missed you.

This is probably not true, if I stop to really examine it. In fact, the only time anyone mentioned Gabe was when the romantic lead ran through the pouring rain to the protagonist's apartment, clutching a bouquet of sunflowers. Vera rolled her eyes and said, "That's the kind of shit Gabe would pull."

My phone buzzes: Haha.

No really, I say, and I'm not even sure why.

Come on, he says. I'm like the yellow Starburst of this group.

My lips twitch. You're at least the orange Starburst.

> I think that might be worse.
>
> Nothing is worse than the yellow Starburst, Gabe.

He sends me a smiley face. I contemplate saying something back, just to keep it going, but then I feel . . . run-through-the-rain-with-sunflowers cliché, so I shut off my phone and go to bed.

twenty

I get a call from a random number during AP bio that Monday. We're doing worksheets again, so I don't feel bad ducking out quickly to grab it. I've only gotten a few calls from our ad, and I don't want to play phone tag with someone who clearly doesn't have what we're looking for.

"Hello?"

"Hello, yes, this is Ann Smith. I'm calling about an ad I saw online. For the painting?"

I'm no great judge of ages, but Ann Smith has a reediness to her voice that I'd place with an over-seventy crowd, and just a hint of that Southern twang.

I thank her for calling and reiterate the contents of the ad: *The Dream*, Laura Fuller, Newforth Gallery.

"Yes, yes, well, I thought I'd give you a ring, because I did have it, up until recently. Bought it from Meira, I think it was the very same day she first hung it up. One of the last ones Laura Fuller ever did, you know. I read about it in that book."

"It has a blue frame? Figures in the center?"

"That's the one. Lovely piece, goodness gracious. Wasn't in the house but a week or so when Dr. Mark was in from Mobile, saw it, fell in love. Wanted to hang it up in his practice."

"So he bought it?"

"Yes, indeed. Made twice what I spent. And fortunate, too, because Mr. Smith didn't love it. Said it made him sad. I had it in the bathroom—what could be sad about that?—but he said it brought him down. Something about the colors. 'Who wants to feel that kind of melancholy when they're brushing their teeth?' he said. Well, can you imagine such a thing . . ."

"Dr. Mark," I say, before Ann Smith can go on. "Do you have his number?"

"Oh, not off the top of my head, dear, but you can just plug him into the Google and he'll pop right up. Most prominent private practice in Brecken—that's right outside of Mobile—he's a sweetheart, Dr. Harold Mark, we've known him for years—"

Ann Smith talks for another ten minutes, but all I have to supply are *mm-hmm*s and *ah*s in the appropriate pauses in her monologue. Eventually Ann Smith rings off, with a "Thanks for the chat, darling!" and I am left alone.

"So it's gone?"

"To Dr. Mark, in Mobile. She told us to google him."

Remy huffs a laugh—"Figures"—and then it's quiet.

"It's a lead," I say. "Like an actual lead. We have something to go off of now."

"Yeah, it's great." I can tell there's something else he wants to say, but he's not saying it.

"What?"

"What are we going to do if we actually find it?"

It doesn't go unnoticed by me that he uses the word *we*. Remy and I. We are a *we*. For a second I try to pinpoint when that happened. Maybe halfway through *Were School* season two.

"What do you mean, what are we going to do?" I say. "We'll buy it back." He gives me a look, so I clarify: "I'll buy it back."

"You said she sold it for twice what she bought it for. The paintings in Meira's were already pretty steep."

"I've got money. Christmas and birthday money like for the past ten years." I'm a saver, not a spender.

"You'd just buy it for them, just like that?"

"Why not?"

"What if Dr. Mark won't sell it to you?"

"We're retrieving it for the dead artist's kids. If he's a good person, I won't even need to buy it back—he'll just give it to us."

"We need a backup plan, in case he doesn't want to sell."

"A trade? We'll take some pictures of the other ones Meira has, offer one of them up?"

"What if Meira doesn't agree to that?"

"They're not Meira's paintings, in case you didn't notice. They still belong to Vera and Gabe's dad until they're sold, and if he doesn't want to get this back for his kids, there's something wrong with him."

"You're like weirdly passionate about this."

I smile. "We should all find something to be weirdly passionate about, don't you think?"

twenty-one

I sneak in the back of the auditorium and watch Vera's audition for *Anything Goes* on Wednesday.

With my objective singer hat on, I have to say she's not particularly great—a little flat, a little loud. But she manages to catch a nice vibrato at a spot or two. What sells it most is her face—bright and beaming—and the little sweeps of her arms and gestures with her hands during certain passages. She is not great, but she packages the not-greatness with charm, and that somehow makes it work.

She joins me in the back when she's finished.

"Great job," I whisper, as a freshman takes the stage.

She shrugs. "It was fun." For a moment I think she's going to say something about me not auditioning, but she just turns her eyes to the stage and says, "I was talking to this kid backstage. He said he's going to freestyle rap."

The opening bars of his music start up.

"Nothing would make me happier," I say, and she smiles.

★ ★ ★

I read all the fics my dad sends me in the coming weeks, paying closer attention to the ones he prints out and leaves around for me to find. *(The printed page, Sloane!)* And while they vary in Jickey's occupations (Mickey owns a comic-book store, James is a writer; Mickey is a florist, James is a Hollywood stuntman) and AU (coffeeshop, fake-married, college, soul mates, movie star, Civil War—*"Civil War, seriously?" "It's BEAUTIFUL. I CRIED"*), the bones are the same: James loves Mickey. Mickey loves James. Sometimes it's the wrong time for them, and then it becomes the right time. Sometimes one of them realizes before the other and pines, because they think he could never feel the same way. Sometimes they both think they aren't good enough for the other. But it always works out. There may be fics where it doesn't, but my dad isn't sending me those. Even when the situations are dark *(Embrace the angst, Sloane!)*, everything still manages to sort itself out. James is in a coma; presto chango, Mickey's love brings him back. Mickey gets killed; James finds a spell to resurrect him.

"Isn't that weird, though?" I say after dinner one evening. "James literally orchestrating a resurrection to get Mickey back? He straight up *Jesuses* Mickey and we're supposed to be okay with that because we believe so deeply in their love?"

"Yes," my dad says simply.

The thing about Mickey and James is that they both have tragic backstories, and most fics inevitably feature these scenes where they reveal pieces of their past to each other. But the thing that strikes me is a particular take on this scene that comes up a lot: James reveals something tragic, then Mickey reveals something tragic. And vice versa, again and again, back and forth.

I lost the only family I had when I was a kid.

My family cast me out when I became a were.

It's my fault that Luke got bitten.

It's my fault that Kiko died.

Neither of them could just let the other have their grief, their moment. I know it wasn't the intention—they're opening up! Sharing the tragedies that made them who they are! The regrets and fears they can't share with anyone but each other!—but Christ, it seemed like one-upmanship to me. Where is the fic where Mickey says, *I lost the only family I had when I was a kid* and James just says, *I'm so, so sorry.* And they sit in silence, and maybe they hold hands, or maybe they don't, maybe that's all there is. One of them says what they need to say, and the other one just listens, absorbs, acknowledges it. Lets their sadness have a place to land.

I'm reading a fic on my laptop at Vera's one afternoon while she answers messages online. She gives my screen a glance between responses and says, "More Jickey?"

"More Jickey."

"Did your dad pick it?"

He hadn't. "No, I found this one."

She doesn't reply, but when I look over, her eyebrows are raised.

"What?"

"You're looking for them now, too?"

I shrug. "You can find whatever you want."

Literally, you can. There is enough *Were School* fic out there to satisfy almost any whim or desire. A *Were School* culinary-school AU. A *Were School–Lord of the Rings* crossover. An arranged marriage where one or both parties are royalty—there are entire rec lists of

Were School arranged-marriage royalty AUs. Not to mention any kind of sex stuff you could possibly imagine (and some that I could never have imagined, even in my wildest dreams). What interests me most is the idea of tags—themes helpfully supplied by the authors, so you can search for exactly the kind of content you're interested in. Hurt/Comfort. Obliviousness. Pining. Slow burn.

"You can pick any kind of relationship in any kind of setting that you want," I say, when I realize Vera is still eyeing me skeptically.

"I just didn't think you liked the show that much."

"It's not really that much about the show after a while, I guess?"

"So what's the point?"

I can't describe it quite right. So I just shake my head. "I don't know, it's just funny, I guess. Because it's so ridiculous."

I turn back to the screen, but she doesn't turn back to hers.

"You know, the cast list for the musical went up today."

"Yeah?"

"Alexa Petrie's going to be Reno Sweeney. Do you know her?"

"Nope."

"She's in my lit class. She thinks she's the shit because she played Annie when we were in elementary school."

"Good for her."

"Not good for her, Sloane, geez. It should be you. You should be Reno."

"But I'm not."

"But you should have been! I don't get it. I know it's not because you're scared, because one, you've been doing this for ages; and two, you're not scared of anything. I think it's because if you did it, you'd have to actually do it, and not make fun of it, and you're not capable of doing something that you can't make fun of. Or joke about, or tear down in some way. That's what you do, and maybe it's holding you back a little bit."

The sting is unexpected, but sting it does. "I don't . . . do that" is all I say.

"Seriously? You just did it about the *Were School* fic. Literally just now."

"I don't—"

"No, Sloane, listen. It's okay if you like *Were School* fic. There's absolutely nothing wrong with it. You can like it without anybody judging you. And you can do musicals without anybody judging you. You can like sequins and tap dancing and singing and werewolves having sex with each other. All that stuff."

"I know that."

"But do you, though?"

I blink down at my keyboard. The letters blur a bit and then pull back into focus.

"Yeah," I say, and then I look across the room at the painting in the corner. Calm and composed and reassuring. "Um. You know, I should go. I forgot—I'm supposed to—"

"Wait, Sloane—" Vera goes to grab my hand, but I pull away, closing my laptop and shoving it into my backpack.

"I'll see you later." I leave as fast as I can.

I don't go to FSP that night. Gabe texts me.

Are you mad at Vera?

No, I reply. And I'm not. But I don't know what I am instead.

> She's acting weird. Did she fight with Tash?
>
> Why don't you just ask her?
>
> She's with Aubrey.
>
> Then how do you know she's acting weird?
>
> Because I can see her.
>
> Creeper.
>
> What are you doing? Why aren't you here?
>
> Tired.
>
> No one's too tired for FSP.
>
> I didn't feel like it.
>
> You should have come.
>
> Why?
>
> I don't know, you just should have.

I look at that for a moment. Careful, I send back. It might sound like you miss me.

I don't hear from him again for the rest of the night.

twenty-two

Remy and I locate Dr. Harold Mark online. Ann Smith was right—he comes right up when you type him into the Google.

The problem is, we haven't been able to get through to Dr. Mark himself. I've encountered his receptionist, who is more interested in whether or not I would like to make an appointment than she is in putting me through to the doctor for a non-health-related inquiry. And when Remy called and asked if she knew whether Dr. Mark had recently acquired any new artwork, she flat-out hung up on him.

So we decide to go in person. Dr. Mark's office is open on Saturday mornings. With some finagling, I get out of my lesson that week, and I go to pick up Remy at six in the morning.

He looks at me, and his face says something like *Ungodly early*. I hand him my dad's New School travel mug and grunt in agreement.

The drive isn't terrible. We're quiet most of the way, just remarking on random signs we pass (WORLD'S BIGGEST MUSHROOM CAP, 14 MILES!), and making inane comments about whatever's on the radio.

Until Remy glances over and says, "You missed FSP last night. I think Frank was hurt."

"Why?"

"Because you're his favorite. He was afraid you went to Pete Mendez's thing instead."

I blink. I thought *Will you mingle with me at this party tonight, and every party for the rest of our lives?* was a joke. "A non-Frank-sanctioned event?" is all I say. "An event that hasn't been Franktioned? How could I even fathom it?"

"Franktioned?" Remy repeats. "Oh God, wait til he hears that."

"It's way more efficient. I don't know why you guys haven't been saying it all along."

We reach Brecken, a suburb of Mobile, in just a couple of hours and find ourselves outside a squat one-story redbrick building. The sign out front declaring this to be the office of DR. HAROLD MARK is covered in fake cobwebs with a few plastic spiders set in—just in case I could have possibly forgotten that today is Halloween, despite Laney's weeklong countdown.

"What's our cover?" Remy asks. "Should we pose as a married couple?"

"Why would we need a cover?"

"I don't know, it makes it more fun."

"We're not doing fake relationship," I say.

"Are you sure . . . Mrs. Applebaum?" He extends his arm toward me.

I sigh and take it. "Lead the way, Mr. Applebaum."

Once inside, no aliases are necessary. The receptionist is wearing a pointed witch's hat and jack-o'-lantern earrings, but despite this bit of whimsy, she doesn't look like she'd be very receptive to a couple of high schoolers who are clearly not the Applebaums. I'm certain she's the same woman who hung up on Remy.

But she can't very well hang up on us in person, so we explain the situation. She looks confused at best, annoyed at worst, but when we're done, she huffs a sigh and gets to her feet. "Well, Dr. Mark did pick up something on his vacation. It's through here."

She leads us into the back, down a hall, and past a series of closed doors. She stops in front of an alcove housing a scale and a measuring stick attached to the wall.

"There."

Hung on the wall is a large picture of a sailboat in a blue plastic frame. It is not even a little bit a Laura Fuller.

"Um, no," I say after a moment. "We're looking for—it has a different blue frame. But Dr. Mark got it recently, we know he did."

"I don't know what to tell you," she says. "But you've really got to get along here. I've got plenty to do out front—"

"Are there any other paintings around? In any of the rooms?"

"If you'll follow me back—"

"Evelyn, the phone's ringing out there," a man says, emerging from a door to our right. He's wearing a white coat and, underneath it, a black shirt and an orange-and-black plaid tie.

"Hello," he says, smiling genially at us both.

"Hi, Dr. Mark," I say, recognizing an opportunity when I see one. "We're looking for a Laura Fuller painting called *The Dream*. You bought it out of Ann Smith's bathroom?"

Dr. Mark blinks at me.

"I never really thought of myself as an art aficionado," Dr. Mark says, settling down on a low rolling chair. We've ducked into one of the examining rooms for a quick chat, much to Evelyn's chagrin. He gestures to us to sit, but the only seats are a chair in the corner and the examining table. I take the chair, and Remy just hovers by my side.

Dr. Mark is probably in his fifties and has gray-white hair and a mustache. "I like pictures of boats," he says with a smile. "Sailboats, dinghies, sloops. Gimme a little empty rowboat on a nice blue pond. Peaceful. Unassuming. Boats don't try to *tell* you anything, you know? They're just boats. That's the kind of art I like." He gestures to one of the walls, which indeed features a framed painting of a boat. "But this painting—*The Dream*—it just . . . spoke to me. Which sounds like something a fancy art person would say, doesn't it?"

I smile and, when I realize he's waiting for an answer, say, "Yeah, yeah it does."

"Art never made me *feel* something like that before. I bought it right off Ann's wall, right then and there."

"So you have it? It's here?"

He sighs. "Well, that's the thing . . ."

"Of course not," Remy says in the car. "Of course he doesn't have it."

"Worth a try?"

Remy shakes his head. "Why would he give it up if he loved it so much? If it made him *feel* and all that?"

"I guess they made him an offer he couldn't refuse."

"What do we do now?"

"Onwards and upwards! The search continues!"

Remy's quiet as I pull out of the parking lot.

"What?" I say.

"What do you mean, what?"

"What are you thinking that you're not saying?"

When he speaks next, I can tell he's choosing his words carefully, and it irks me for some reason. Like I'm delicate. "Why do you care so much?" he says. "About the painting?"

I shrug. "I just . . . want to do this for Vera and Gabe."

"Is that all?"

"Yeah, that's all. What else would there be?"

"I don't know, that's why I'm asking you. I don't think Captain Ahab had anyone sit down and be like, *Okay, dude, I really think we need to talk this through*."

"I'm not . . . This isn't like that. I'm not going Ahab here. This isn't going to be my undoing."

"You know, anytime someone says that, they're definitely fore-shadowing their own undoing."

"Shut up," I say, but I can't keep back a smile.

"Do you want me to drive a bit?" Remy asks, as I'm pulling onto the freeway.

"No. But text my dad." I pass him my phone. "Tell him Dr. Mark sold it to a patient."

twenty-three

When I get back to my place after dropping Remy off, I find Laney and Vera in the living room. Laney has my mom's makeup bag. She blinks dark, sparkly eyelids at me.

"Vera's doing makeup for my costume!"

"She requested a 'smoky-eye look,'" Vera informs me.

"Sorry, but Vera's way better at this stuff than you are," Laney says.

Vera closes the makeup bag. "Let's take some pictures. Then you can show your mom." She snaps a few pictures and then flips through them. "Gorgeous, girlfriend." Laney smiles broadly.

"Go find Mom," I say. Laney does her Mr. Yuck face but runs off down the hallway all the same.

"Hey." Vera puts her phone aside and stands. "I brought you something."

"You gonna teach me a smoky-eye look, too?"

"If you want," she says with a little smile. She crosses over to her bag and pulls out a clear plastic container and hands it to me.

It's a cookie—chocolate chip, by the look of it—that says I'M SORRY SLOANE across it in frosting. The I'M SORRY is in big block letters, but the letters of SLOANE underneath get increasingly smaller, so that the *E* is barely squeezed on there.

"I had Gabe make it at work. I told him to watch the spacing, he always screws it up."

"You don't—you didn't have to get me a cookie."

"No, I did. I'm sorry. I didn't mean to pressure you about the show, and I didn't mean to, you know, cast judgment or whatever. You're Sloane, and you're perfect in your Sloaneness."

All I can do is stare at the cookie. "That might be overstating it a little."

"It's understating it. A lot."

"Don't overdo it."

She makes a face. "Are we friends again?"

"Were we not friends since yesterday?"

"You know what I mean."

I make a face. "Only if you share the cookie with me."

"Deal."

We sit out on the back porch and eat the apology cookie. I snap a picture before we do and send it to Gabe: Excellent handiwork.

He doesn't reply. Maybe he's with Alice. Maybe they're doing a couples costume.

"Are you going to the party tonight?" Vera asks. "FSP, Halloween edition?"

"Nah, I'm going to go around with Laney and my parents."

"You're going to trick-or-treat?" Vera's eyes shine.

"No," I say, defensive. But then, "I mean, kind of. We always do a family costume, and I stand in the back but they usually just give me candy anyway."

"And you secretly love it."

"Of course I love it. Trick-or-treating is the best."

"Laney said she was going to be Wednesday Addams. So who does that make you?"

"I'm not telling."

"Sloane. You have to."

I shake my head, breaking off a piece of the apology cookie. "It's classified."

"Are your mom and dad going to be Morticia and Gomez? Your dad would make a great Gomez."

I *hmm* noncommittally. It's quiet then for a bit, just our munching and the buzzing of the tree frogs.

"When's his next book coming out?" Vera asks finally, and when I hesitate, she says, "I try not to geek out on you as a fan of your dad's since we're friends, and I don't want you to think it has like zero-point-one percent influence on why we hang out. But like, I'm also very curious."

I smile. "It's fine. It's just, he doesn't have another book coming out."

"But *Sand on Our Beach* was ages ago."

"Yeah, I mean, he's kind of been struggling."

"Writer's block?" Vera says in a hushed voice, in the same way one would say the name of a terminal illness.

"Kind of? I think he's just . . . not sure what he wants to do next. I don't think he ever really planned to be this big romance writer."

"What did he want to write?"

"Serious stuff." Tortured-artist types finding themselves.

"His books are serious, though."

"Different serious. *Literary* serious."

I was gonna be Fitzgerald, Jilly. Fucking Fitzgerald.

Yeah, but you're not. You're you. And maybe this is you. Have you ever considered that? Like really considered that?

"So why doesn't he just write something different?"

I shrug. "*Sand on Our Beach* got kind of crucified. I think he's just . . . more hesitant. Not only to do something different, but like . . . to do anything."

"Crucified how?"

I reach for my phone. I could find any number of articles, but there's one in particular that pops right up. It got a lot of traction at the time.

EVERETT FINCH'S 'SAND ON OUR BEACH':

Hackneyed narratives and tortured prose underscore
everything that's wrong with literary romance.

By Darryl Samberg, *New York Times Book Review*

"Shit," Vera murmurs.

Sarah Watson is dying. Or . . . maybe she's not. Either way, she's packed it in and headed to the small coastal town of Somewhere. But predictably, her story doesn't end there. Perhaps we as readers would have been better served if it had.

Enter Jack, the widowed town handyman. He's haunted by grief but willing to love again. She's dying and afraid to take the risk. They will heal each other's wounds. Slowly. Reverently. Inevitably. Interminably.

It's nothing new—it is, in fact, a palimpsest of pernicious clichés and overdone tropes. But that in itself is not what is so truly repulsive about Everett Finch's latest endeavor.

I watch as she reads. I don't need to see it again. It's seared pretty firmly in my mind. It goes on and on:

> There's the absolute travesty that is Sarah's "career" in "crafting." The cringeworthy dialogue, which oscillates between the overwrought ("Love is for the living," Sarah unabashedly declares) and the almost offensively simplistic ("I like sandwiches," says Jack, a grown man supposedly in possession of his mental faculties).
>
> In the final act is the very nadir of Mr. Finch's attempts at emotional manipulation. The height of tragedy pornography, the morose cherry on the maudlin sundae: the death of Avery the puppy.

It doesn't get better from there.

"Shit," Vera says again, when she's finished.

"I know," I say. "But you have to admit, it's a little funny."

Vera just frowns. "I think it's mean."

"Are critics ever nice?"

"They don't have to be *nice,* but they weren't even fair. They left out everything good about that book, the heart of it, the . . . hope. All your dad's books have hope. That's the best part about them."

I shrug. "I don't know. But that stuff has made him . . ." Afraid? Not really. It's tough to think of my dad as being scared. "You know. Cautious."

★ ★ ★

There's a knock on our front door around nine that evening. We've already been all throughout the neighborhood, and Laney is up in the bathroom with my mom, having her Wednesday Addams smoky-eye look removed.

So it's a little late for trick-or-treaters, but maybe they go later here. I grab the bowl of candy off one of the side tables and go to answer it.

Vera and Gabe are on the front porch.

"Nooo," Vera says when I open the door. "We wanted to see your costume!"

"I thought you guys were at the party."

"We were," Gabe says. "But Vera wanted to see your costume."

"How are you gonna put it all on me?" Vera says as I open the door wider and usher them in. "Gabe wanted to know, too. What were you? Were you Pugsley? Or were you Cousin Itt? Gabe thinks you were Cousin Itt."

I can see them better in the hallway. Vera is wearing a red jacket with a short black dress underneath and has dark, dramatic eye makeup. Gabe has on a tight gray shirt, and his hair is gelled out so that most of it is sticking backward.

"What are you guys supposed to be?"

"We're famous twins," Vera says.

"What's wrong with your hair?" I ask Gabe.

"You're like the twelfth person to say that." He looks at Vera. "I told you no one would get it."

"We're Quicksilver and Scarlet Witch!" Vera says, like it's the most obvious thing in the world. "You know. Famous twins! Famous super-hero twins!"

I see it now, and I tell them as much, but Gabe just rolls his eyes.

"Next year, I pick."

"Next year we'll be in college," Vera says.

"Do you always do a costume together?" I ask.

"Every year except sophomore year, when Tash was here. She and I went as Captain America and Bucky."

"Are they always superhero-themed?"

"Not always but mostly," Gabe says. "Were you the hand? I feel like you were the hand."

"Who do we have here?" My dad comes down the stairs. He's still got his Gomez mustache, but he's changed out of his pin-striped suit into sweats. "Quicksilver and Scarlet Witch?"

Vera beams, but I look at my dad, who gives me a wink, and I'm pretty sure he heard us from upstairs.

"Hi, Mr. Finch," Vera says. "Great mustache."

"I drew it myself, can you believe?" He looks at me. "Are they here to take you to a party? Better hurry up and get your Uncle Fester costume back on."

"Uncle Fester!" Vera crows. Gabe's eyes light up.

"Dad, geez," I say.

"Are you going out?"

"No." I look to Vera and Gabe. "No, I was going to stay in. You guys should go back, though."

Vera just shrugs. "It wasn't that great. Let's watch something Halloweeny."

"I have it on good authority that *Hocus Pocus* is saved on the DVR," Dad says.

"Yes!" Vera grabs my arm and leads me into the living room.

"Nice hair, son," I hear my dad tell Gabe in the foyer.

twenty-four

Frank Sanger Presents the following week is apparently a rare and sacred event—Frank hosts the event at his own house. Which happens to be a beachfront property in Opal, with private stairs leading right down to the water.

"God," I say, walking up the front path with Remy. "I didn't know Frank was so . . ."

"Stupid rich?" Remy supplies. "Yeah. It's something, isn't it?"

Something more for the legend of Frank Sanger. It's fitting.

We make our way inside, into a wide living room giving way to a massive kitchen. It's already packed with people, and I scan the gathered masses for Vera. I see Aubrey, standing with Gabe and a couple of others, but no Vera.

I barely notice when Remy suddenly slips his hand into mine.

It takes me a moment. I look down at our hands, then up at him, and then over at Aubrey, who has clocked us from across the room.

I yank my hand away, grab him by the front of the shirt, and pull him back outside.

"What the *hell*?" I say.

"What?" He looks a little confused, but mostly guilty.

"I'm not a *pawn* in this, okay? I'm not going to let you use me to make Aubrey jealous. That's gross. That's not how you treat someone if you really care about them, and you claim to care about Aubrey, but if this is just some kind of game to you, then I'm out."

"I don't . . . I didn't think—"

"No. You didn't." That was a favorite line of my mom's, and I have to say, it is very effective. Remy looks positively repentant.

"I just got nervous," he says.

"You can hold my hand if you get nervous," I say. "But don't hold it because you want to make her think something that's not true."

He mumbles something.

"Sorry?"

"She was standing with Marshall Peters."

"So?"

"So . . . he's like, big football jock king. And she was standing with him."

"I stood next to freaking Dex Finnegan. It doesn't mean we're doing the do, does it?"

"I panicked."

"Well, try to keep it together. Should we try this again?"

"Yes. Yeah. Sorry," he says, and I lead him back inside.

The porch off the back of Frank's house overlooks the beach. We all end up out there this evening—me and Vera, Gabe, Aubrey, Remy, and Frank.

"Let's tell stories," Frank says, lying back against the pillows of a luxurious chaise and sipping from a mud-colored drink. (Orange and grape sodas, he says later, account for its unique coloring.) He has a blanket—a *cashmere throw*, he informs us loftily—draped over his shoulders. Although it's much warmer than it would be back home at this time of year, there's a nip to the air, a reminder that it's really November.

"What, like ghost stories?"

"No, real-life ones. Let's tell first-kiss stories. Those are always fun. Mine was in seventh grade. Well, my first girl one was in the seventh grade, with Lucy Freedman, at Jen Smith's birthday party. Do you guys remember that? The skating party?"

The group affirms the remembrance of the skating party.

"We couples skated to Panic! At the Disco, and then we went over to the snack stand and ordered nachos. And while we were waiting she said that if we were going to kiss, we should do it before we ate nachos—I have such an affection for Lucy Freedman, she's a deeply practical woman—so I was like, fuck it, let's do this, and I just full-on went at her face like some kind of radioactive super piranha from a bad sci-fi movie."

"How did she react?" Vera asks.

"Panic! At the snack bar?" I murmur.

"No, she came back at me, *Sharknado*-style," Frank says.

"What does that mean?"

"She dug it. It was a success. Ten out of ten, Frank Sanger wins at life. How about you, Gabe? First kissy-kissy?"

"Pass," Gabe says.

"No fun," Frank scoffs. "Aubrey?"

Aubrey is examining her nails, and she looks up like she's surprised to be called on. "Mine . . ." She grimaces a little. "It was, uh, it was with Remy."

We all look at Remy.

"Same," he says. "With Aubrey."

"Well, isn't that precious," Frank says, but even he knows how awkward the moment has turned.

"Mine hasn't happened yet," I say, compelled to replace that awkward with a different kind of awkward, just so Aubrey and Remy can stop staring at the ground like twin searchlights have been fixed on them.

"Are you serious?" Frank says. "On all that is good and holy in this world, are you serious?"

"You know, everything is, like, fifteen times more dramatic when you say it."

"No, but am I crazy? Look at you. You're a stunner."

"Debatable," I say.

"This is a crime," Frank continues, as if I hadn't spoken. "THIS IS A TRAVESTY."

"So . . . kiss me."

He raises one finger dramatically. "Don't say that unless you mean it."

"I mean it. I don't care. Kiss me."

Frank springs to his feet. "Get up. We'll do this right."

I stand.

"Now slap me," he says, a devilish gleam in his eyes.

"Sorry?"

"We'll do it like in one of your dad's books."

"That's weirdly Freudian, Frank."

"No, it'll be hot! I'll pick you up and push you up against the wall. But you have to slap me first. Or, I mean, we could just do it like sixth grade–style, if you really want to. I could come at you sci-fi movie–style." Frank leans forward and opens his mouth wide.

I smile. "Okay, I'll slap you."

So I pretend-swipe at Frank's cheek.

He makes a face. "That was weak. Remy, make the slapping sound. Really aim for it."

I wind back and aim my palm at Frank, and this time Remy claps his hands, and it's probably pretty realistic-looking.

Frank grabs the side of his face dramatically and then looks at me with fire in his eyes. Before I can do anything, he hitches his hands on the backs of my thighs and picks me up off the ground, pushing me back into the wall behind us.

"Geez," I hear Gabe mutter.

My breath catches in my throat, because even though it's a joke, Vera is right—Frank does have a universal appeal. His face is half stubbly and his eyelashes are impossibly long, and I feel a little thrill course through me that I wasn't expecting.

Frank growls, low in his throat.

"I should've left you on that island," he says.

That may have broken the spell. "What?"

"When I found you. On that deserted island. With our mailman. I should've left you there to die. But I couldn't, because of the fire for you that burns deep in my loins."

"I never loved our mailman," I say with as much ardor as I can manage, cupping his face with my hand. "I loved the free first-class shipping."

"I can ship you anywhere in the world, baby." His voice sinks, deep and gravelly. The fics would describe it as *laden with promise*. "I have . . . international flat-rate boxes. So many."

"That's good," I murmur. "My eBay business is really taking off."

He is eyeing my mouth now, his face inching closer.

I let my eyes drift shut. Frank Sanger is going to kiss me.

Except that he doesn't. He holds me for an impossibly long moment. And then he blows a loud raspberry into my neck.

I laugh. He loosens his grip on me and I slide down, back onto solid ground.

"What the hell?"

"I can't," Frank says with a smile. "I can't. Look at you."

"Swamp creature? Deathly unkissable?"

"I can't take your first kiss. It's sacred."

"But you said—" I'm a little put off. That thrill still thrums through me, unfulfilled. My skin feels a bit itchy, some kind of pull deep down.

"I was acting on base impulse. I should know better than to try to steal something that someday, someone will absolutely cherish. You deserve better than ol' snack-stand Frank Sanger here."

"Do I smell bad?"

Frank leans into me, his lips by my ear. "You smell like a baby," he whispers, "who has just had a *grueling* sesh of Bikram yoga."

I smile a little.

He pecks my cheek. "Want more drinks?"

"I'm good."

"I'm getting another round."

And he disappears into the house.

Outside the spell of Frank and his undeniable magnetism, the porch rematerializes, and the rest of the group along with it. Except Remy and Gabe are now absent. I look out onto the beach, and I can see two cell-phone lights down by the water, illuminating the sand.

"What are they doing?" I ask, sinking down next to Aubrey. Vera has drifted toward the other side of the porch, her phone pressed to her ear.

"Hi, baby, what's new?" I hear her say softly.

"They're looking for hermit crabs," Aubrey says, and then it's quiet.

I get the impression that Aubrey doesn't like me. She certainly wouldn't be the first. But with her, for some reason, I feel the irrational desire to win her over. I don't know if it's because she's Vera's friend, or because Remy's so crazy about her, but it nettles that she's shut off to me.

"Hey, I heard you got a part in *Anything Goes*," I say. "That's so cool."

"Yeah. Should be fun."

Silence. I watch the lights bobbing down below.

"So do you want to do musical theater for college?" I'm really reaching into the depths of the small-talk barrel here.

"No. It's just a hobby."

"So what do you want to do?"

"I don't know. Something practical."

"What do you mean?"

Before she can respond to that, Frank returns.

"You can stop missing me now," he says, settling down on Aubrey's other side with a large drink. He offers the cup to her. "Ma chérie?"

She just shakes her head, standing and pulling out her keys. "I'm gonna get going."

"More for me," Frank says, giving me a wink.

twenty-five

Remy and I strategize on Sunday, over AP bio notes. There's a test coming up, but we've been through the stages of mitosis umpteen times, and eventually our conversation drifts to the painting.

Dr. Mark gave us only one bit of information about the painting's whereabouts, because apparently HIPAA forbade more than that. He said we'd do well to check galleries in the Birmingham area.

We've called around where we can. One gallery has a Laura Fuller, but it's not ours. No one has *The Dream*. There are three galleries we haven't been able to reach by phone—two in the city and one farther out. So Remy and I start planning our road trip to Birmingham. It's a four-hour drive.

"Maybe we should get a hotel room," Remy says, as my dad walks in.

"Maybe you should get a what now?" he asks.

"For our gallery tour of Birmingham," I say. "To find the painting, remember?"

"Of course I remember. What's the plan?"

"That's what we're trying to figure out." I glance at him as he takes a seat at the head of the table. "It's kind of a long drive, and we have a few places to see."

"Well, how about this—what if your old man comes with?"

"Really?"

"In addition to, or as a replacement for me?" Remy asks.

"You're welcome along, too, Remy," Dad says. "After all, I don't want to hijack your quest. What do you guys think? It'll be fun!"

I look at him for a moment. I can't tell if this is a genuine-interest-in-our-pursuit thing or a protective-dad thing. Maybe a little bit of both.

So I just look at Remy, who shrugs, and that's that.

Dad books a room that night and forwards me the information with the subject line "ROAD TRIP!!!!"

Vera and I are packing up from lunch on Monday when she says, "Frank's was fun, wasn't it?"

"Yeah. His house is super nice."

"You and Remy showed up together."

"We were hanging out before."

She nods but doesn't speak. It's not until we're heading to class that she takes a deep breath and says, "I feel like . . . Okay, tell me I'm crazy, but I feel like you guys are sort of . . . hiding something."

I blink for a moment. "I . . ." Do you lie to your friends? Is that what friends do? Would Luke lie to Mickey? Well, yeah, Luke lied to Mickey all the time. It was usually to try to keep him safe, although it almost always ended up backfiring. I'm not trying to keep Vera safe, though. I just . . . don't want to tell her about the painting until we have it. Until I can hand it right to her.

But maybe I could tell part of the truth.

"Because you guys are always talking, and you hang out some-times without me or Gabe, and Aubrey said she saw you *holding hands* at FSP. Do you . . . I mean, like do you have a thing for Remy? Because you can just tell me. If you guys are dating."

"We're not dating," I say emphatically. This is what I was afraid of. I silently curse Remy for the hand-holding thing. "We're not. I'm actually . . . He just . . ." I take a deep breath. "He just asked me to find out what happened with Aubrey."

"So that's what you guys are doing? You just sit around and talk about Aubrey?"

"Sometimes we talk about *Were School*."

She smiles a little. "Well, if that's all it is, why can't I come? I like Aubrey. I like *Were School*."

"You said it was incomprehensible."

"I did not."

"Did so. You tweeted about it."

"I said it was full of WTF moments. But I didn't say that was a bad thing." She bumps her shoulder against mine. "Come on. I don't mind sharing you with Remy, but, like, I found you first, right?"

I don't like the sound of that. Like I'm a fad she'll tire of soon enough. Like I'm crop tops or leggings as pants.

"Though I guess technically, you found us," she continues. "Right? I'll never forget it. You popping out of the crowd like that, tearing Mason Pierce a new one. I've never seen Gabe look like that before."

"Like what? Annoyed?"

"Smitten," she says.

"Shut up. I don't think Gabe's ever looked smitten in his life. Smitten is for, like, little kids and cartoon cats."

"Awed, then. Just . . . full of awe."

"I don't think we were witnessing the same event," I say.

"You couldn't tell because you were busy fucking Mason's shit up."

"Beautifully put."

"It was," she says, and links her arm with mine as we head to class.

twenty-six

I find a new fic on my bed the next afternoon, and I know immediately that it's an original. It's not printed in the font of the fanfic site my dad uses but rather in his preferred writing formatting. Single-space Arial, size 11.

You're just going to have to change it later.

I have a deep connection to Arial size 11, Sloane. My love for Arial size 11 knows no bounds.

I settle in with the pages.

It wasn't quite war, it begins, *but it felt like it.*

    Another supernatural onslaught. Another Tuesday night in Crescent Heights.

    Mickey is lost. More lost than usual, that is. It's one thing to be lost in a pack meeting, listening to Jessica argue with Atl about the proper technique to track and kill some creature that's no doubt too horrifying to even possibly imagine. It's another thing to be stuck in this fucking fog.

"Splitting up was a great idea," he mutters, tripping over something and barely catching himself on the nearest tree—which he only sees looming in front of him as he flies through the air. "Grade-A awesome idea, five stars, would recommend again."

He tries to get his bearings, turns—and he can barely see it, but there's a space up ahead, a clearing. And so Mickey forges onward.

He's maybe ten feet out when he sees the dark mass in the middle of the clearing. One step, two steps closer. He can just make out the shape:

It's a body.

A person.

He realizes.

His person.

Jesus Christ, it's James.

I hear movement, and when I glance up, my dad is in the doorway to my room, holding his tablet.

"Keep going," he says, moving to sit in my desk chair.

"I can't read with you watching me."

"I'll keep busy."

I make a face. "Are they gonna . . ." I gesture indeterminately.

"Do the do? No. You're safe."

He's still moving forward, but suddenly the air feels thicker. It clogs his lungs as he breathes in. Exhales, but it's as if he can't expel it all, so the next breath is shallower, sharper, hurts more. Holy hell, it's James, utterly still, facedown, a dark pool of liquid underneath him.

Mickey stops, a foot away, just above. The stillness intensifies.

"James?"

Mickey has heard of out-of-body experiences. Who hasn't? The near car wreck, the operating-table code—the person leaves their body, hovers above, observes. He had wondered if it was actually some kind of supernatural phenomenon (because what wasn't, these days?). It's kind of amazing, really, that your body, in the face of extreme pain or extreme hardship, actually forces you out of it. You're dissociated, you're . . . evicted, spiritually, so that whatever mad shit that has to go down can go down. Maybe so you can witness it, to process it all. Or maybe so you can avoid experiencing that kind of hurt firsthand.

God, if only something could force him out of his body right now, so he wouldn't have to reach out. He wouldn't have to turn James over and see those dark eyes turned glassy and lifeless. No spark. Empty and gone, like Mickey will be if there isn't some breath of life left in James's chest.

His fingers pause—*please don't fucking do this to me, James, please*—and maybe he doesn't have to find out. He could stay frozen here—Schrödinger's cat, the unopened box. James is neither dead nor alive until he turns him over and sees.

Mickey can hear James's voice in his head, wry like

always, half annoyed, half fond: *What am I doing, then, dumbass? Sleeping?*

Maybe. Maybe not. *Maybe I can just refuse to find out.*

But Mickey couldn't survive in a moment like that forever; he knows that. And so his fingers close around James's shoulder, and he turns him over. James slumps, lifelessly, all slick leather and thick blood that has already run cool, and those eyes—so fucking expressive, so often bright when they looked at Mickey, shining and reverent in a way that Mickey never deserved, ever—now fixed blankly on a point in the distance. Mickey lets out a sound that he didn't even know he was capable of, something high and strangled, because all at once, everything is over. Everything is broken and empty, and to say it feels horrible would be grossly insufficient. To say this is the worst he's ever felt in his life—entirely inadequate.

He shifts James into his lap and cradles him in his arms, and he waits for the switch to flip—for the dissociation, the gentle eviction. He waits to leave himself. Because the pain is too much to take, and eventually his body will realize that and shut him out.

She appears beside him, a cold mist.

"How?" Mickey's not sure at what point he started crying, but his voice is wrecked, and tears stream down his face, blurring the image of the form beneath him. "How could this happen, how, fuck, Kiko—"

"I'm sorry," she says. Her voice is equally broken. "I'm so sorry."

"What the fuck?" I look up at my dad. "That's it? James is dead?"

"Don't say *fuck*."

"Mickey just said *fuck* like four times."

"Mickey just lost the love of his life."

"Is he really dead? How did it happen?"

"I don't know. I just wanted to write some angst."

"It can't just end with Kiko saying 'Sorry.' You can't do that to people."

"Should we call it a work in progress?"

"Yes. Progress this work. Please."

He makes a face. "But then I can't post it. No one ever wants to read a WIP. Or at least, I never want to read a WIP."

"Why not?"

"Because you have to wait for it to come out, chapter by chapter, and there's always the chance that the person will just stop writing it. And you'll be left there forever, not knowing how it's going to end."

"You're a writer; can't you just write your own end?"

"It's not the same."

I roll my eyes. "Whatever you say."

twenty-seven

The next day is a perfectly ordinary Wednesday, except that Vera is not in calculus. I text her between classes, but when I check back at lunch, she hasn't answered. So I text Gabe instead.

Is Vera here?

She stayed home, he replies a minute later.

Sick? I just saw her yesterday, and she seemed as sparkly and lively as ever. Maybe it was something swift.

No, Gabe answers. But she's not feeling well.

I don't know what that means.

If I were a good person, or like, a character in a movie or a teen drama, I'd probably ditch my last two classes and go and see Vera. But instead I just send her a video of four pug puppies in a bathtub while I'm in world civ and a picture of a "Hang in There" kitten during English.

And then after school I go and see her.

I knock on the screen door, but no one answers, so I duck my head in after a moment. "Hello?" I call. "Vera?" With less enthusiasm, "Amanda?"

Still no answer. I slip inside and head down the hall toward the bedrooms, torn between whether I should make as much noise as possible to alert anyone of my coming, or if I should be as quiet as possible so that no one suspects a home invasion and comes out swinging.

The door to Vera's room is slightly ajar. I peer through. A blanket-covered lump occupies the bed.

I knock lightly. "Vera?"

The lump moves, and Vera's head appears at the top of the blankets. "What are you doing here?"

"Gabe said . . ." That you weren't sick? I shrug. "I brought you the homework."

"Because you thought calc problems would help?"

"I know complex math always make me feel better."

Her head disappears.

I step into the room and drop my bag, sinking down into the desk chair. "Do you want to talk?"

"No." It's muffled. "I'm sad. I don't want to talk. I want to be sad."

"Can we be sad together?"

She doesn't reply. But after a moment, she shifts over.

I stretch out across her bed in the opposite direction, so my head is where her feet must be. I think maybe it will be less oppressive that way. Less demanding.

"Why are we sad?"

It's quiet for a long time.

"Because we miss my mom," she says finally.

"Can I do anything?"

"No."

Silence. When she speaks again, it's so quiet I can barely hear her. "I get jealous sometimes," she says. "When I see Aubrey with her mom, or you with yours . . . I get jealous and I wonder what it is that I did wrong, like why did it have to happen to me? And then I feel so fucking guilty, but at the same time, how is it fair at all?"

"It's not," I say. "It's supremely unfair. And shitty."

She adjusts the covers after a pause, and her face appears.

"No one will ever love me like that again," she says. "That exact way that she did. It'll never be like that again. And so I miss her—I miss everything about her. But I also miss that."

I don't know what to say. My mind flashes to all those Jickey fics: *It's my fault that Luke got bitten.* According to them, I should follow it up with my own bit of tragedy; try to soothe her hurt by sharing my own.

But that would be unfair, too.

"What can I do?" I say.

She shakes her head. "Nothing."

"You want to see Tash?"

"I can't Skype her; she's in class."

"No, I mean, we could go see her. I'll drive you there."

She looks at me. "You would do that?"

"Of course."

She disappears back under the covers for a little while after that, but her hand darts out and squeezes mine hard.

★ ★ ★

The sun is setting by the time we arrive at campus. Vera's been quiet the whole way, but she tells me that Tash is getting out of a lab class, and directs me to the right building. We wait outside.

After a while, a few people start trickling out of the building. Vera shifts back and forth, her arms folded tightly against her chest, until a dark-haired girl emerges, chatting with a couple of other people.

She glances our way, looks away, and then looks right back. "Sorry," I hear her say to the others, and then she's heading toward us.

Vera rushes the distance between them, throwing her arms around her.

"Hey." Tash's arms encircle her instantly. "Hey there." She tries to pull back to see Vera, but Vera pushes her face into Tash's shoulder. "Baby girl," she says softer, gripping her tighter, "hi, hi, hi." She presses kisses to those parts of Vera that she can reach—ear, temple, shoulder.

Vera says something muffled, and Tash replies with something soft I can't quite make out. I'm not sure if I even should. Suddenly I feel glaringly superfluous.

"I, uh . . ." I start to back away. "I should . . . I'll just go . . ."

"You must be Sloane," Tash says.

"She drove me," Vera says, still muffled in Tash's shoulder.

"I'm Natasha. Nice to meet you."

"Yeah, same." *Though I wish it were under better circumstances* goes unspoken.

"Why don't we go for dinner?" Tash says. "All three of us."

"No, I don't want to intrude. I can just . . . you know, hang out or whatever—"

155

Vera mumbles something I can't hear, and Tash just strokes her hair, murmuring a reply.

"I can take her back in the morning," Tash says to me. "Thank you. For coming down here. Will you be okay driving back?"

"I'll be fine."

"Bye, Sloane," Vera mumbles, but then she turns her face toward me, cheeks red, eyes bloodshot. "Thank you."

"Anytime," I say, and I mean it.

I've just fallen into bed that night when my phone buzzes on the nightstand. I think maybe it's Gabe, but it's from an unknown number.

stole your # from V lol, it says.

Then it buzzes again.

thanks for taking care of my girl

I save the number as "Tash" but then change it to "Natasha." Tash seems more like their thing.

No problem, I reply.

ur a good friend, she sends back a moment later.

I stare at the text on-screen, glowing blue-white in the darkness of the room.

Finally I send back a smiley face, because it's easier than saying *No I'm not. Vera's the good friend,* which is the absolute truth.

twenty-eight

Frank Sanger Presents is in a big house in Opal on Friday night, right off the main circle by Laney's school. It was always one of my favorites growing up—peach-colored with white trim, a wraparound porch on the first and second floors, and a lovely little tower jutting up above the trees. Apparently Luke Nelson's family owns it: "He's a dear old friend," Frank says as he greets us in the foyer. I would be surprised to meet someone at one of these things who isn't a *dear old friend* of Frank Sanger's.

It's the usual routine: dancing and gossip and drinks, Frank sweeping around like a society matron in Regency times, making sure everyone is well taken care of.

Vera is here, much to my surprise. She missed school again on Thursday but showed up today, fresh-faced and smiling like nothing out of the ordinary had happened. It made me think of a description in *Sand on Our Beach*—how maybe grief was like a chronic illness, something that could hide dormant in your system but activate at any time.

We're sitting out on the second-floor balcony, talking about nothing much, when Vera gets a text. She reads it, rolls her eyes, and stands.

"What?"

"Aubrey says Gabe just got punched in the face."

"What? Why?"

"I'm guessing someone was being disrespected. Come on, let's go find him."

We split up: Vera takes the first floor, and I head outside. Gabe isn't in the back (though the Nelsons have a lovely inground pool), so I take the footpath around to the front.

And then I see him, standing a little ways away, under one of the green-domed streetlights that casts a perfect round circle of light onto the ground.

His back is to me when I approach.

"I said I'm fine," he says, not turning around.

"Are you sure?" I reply, and he looks back, surprised, just for a second before facing forward again. A second is all I need. "'Cause you look pretty wrecked."

"I thought you were Aubrey," he says, muffled and a bit nasal, like he has a cold. "She said she was going to get ice. Or . . . a towel, or something."

"Hopefully both," I say, and cross in front of him. The bottom half of his face is hidden behind his hands, one holding his nose shut and the other shielding it. Blood is running pretty freely down both. I wrap my fingers around one of his wrists, trying to guide his hand away, but he doesn't let me—just slips out of my grasp and steps to the side.

"It's fine," he says.

"Was it Mason?"

I think he might not answer, but when I look over at him, his expression—the top half of it, anyway—is wry. "No. I hate to break it to you, but there's more than one douchelord at this school."

"And you're responsible for them all?" I say, but then shake my head. "No, wait—you're just responsible for everybody else, right?"

He shrugs.

"No but really, what's worth getting punched in the face for?"

"I would do anything for my friends," he says. Totally serious.

A fondness wells up in me, unbidden. I look away. "That's . . . ridiculous."

"Why? Wouldn't you?"

Normally I would make a joke. Deflect. But for some reason, I just go with the truth: "I guess it's never really come up. I, uh, didn't have a ton of friends back home." If I had, maybe it would've been harder to leave. Maybe I would've asked my parents to stay. It's funny to think about now, on the street in the middle of Opal, under stars brighter than I had ever seen at home—if I had, maybe I wouldn't be standing here right now. "At least, not punched-in-the-face-for kinds of friends, anyway."

"Everyone should have punched-in-the-face-for kinds of friends. Everyone should have . . . you know. Like the people you call when you need to hide the body."

"Why is there a body?"

"If there was a body. Hypothetically."

"I'd like to avoid all forms of murder, including hypothetical."

He lets out a breath of laughter, and then: "I think everyone has it in them."

"Hypothetical murder?"

"No. That kind of friendship. When they meet the right people.

I think anyone can have that kind of friend or . . . be that kind of friend." He looks off down the street. "Especially you. I think you're a hide-the-body friend."

"Oh yeah?"

"You're at least a drive-round-trip-to-Tallahassee-on-a-weeknight friend."

It shouldn't be a surprise that Vera and Gabe talk to each other. But I guess it's just weird to think of them talking about me when I'm not around. Thinking about me.

When I look back at Gabe, the blood is still horrific. It's like someone let the tap run.

"The fuck is Aubrey with that towel," I murmur, and before I can think too much about it, I'm shrugging out of my jacket and then unbuttoning my sweater. It's a cotton cardigan, a back-to-school buy from a couple of years ago that I have no particular attachment to. I put the jacket back on, ball up the cardigan a bit, and force Gabe's hands down.

"No, come on," he says, as I press it lightly to his face. "You're going to ruin it."

"You're going to ruin your face if you keep picking fights with people."

"I don't pick them—they pick me."

I snort. "How noble."

He doesn't reply, just looks away. I'm still holding on to one of his wrists, even though he's not resisting. I could probably let go. I don't, though. I just give it a gentle squeeze.

"Who was it, though?"

"Doesn't matter."

"It matters to me."

"Why?"

A cough comes from behind us. We both turn. Aubrey is there, holding a dish towel.

"Well, I could've done that," she says.

"Your shirt is nicer," I reply.

Her lips twitch. "Here," she says, handing Gabe the towel. "You're an idiot."

"Joke's on you, because I'm *your* idiot," he says, and I relinquish him, left holding my bloody sweater. "I mean, not yours specifically," he says after a moment, with a glance at me. "I'm just, you know. The group's idiot. Collectively."

He's not Aubrey's, is what he's trying to say. In truth, he's Alice from Jade Coast Christian's, and we all know that.

"I think we should go," Aubrey says, and to me: "Do you know where Vera's at?"

"She was looking for him."

Aubrey pulls out her phone and steps away from us.

"I'll take that," Gabe says from behind the dish towel, pointing to my sweater.

"Why? So you can do some powerful blood magic?"

"To wash it, God." He takes it from my hand before I can protest, much like I had shoved it in his face before he could protest.

"We're out front," I hear Aubrey say. "Yeah . . . he is . . ."

"Gabe?" I say, before Aubrey ends the call.

"Yeah."

"I'm glad you're our idiot."

I can't see his smile behind the dish towel, but the corners of his eyes crinkle a little, and that feels just as nice.

twenty-nine

My phone buzzes a few times on my nightstand that night, lighting up the room. It's one-thirty in the morning. Messages from Remy.

> sloinbee
> lol
> fijnger slippin
> i should use auitocrec
> *auutocoorect
> *autocorrect
> nailed it

He then sends three atomic-bomb emojis, a banana, and a high five. I'm not sure what any of this means, so I call him.

"Sloooooooane." He picks up on the fourth ring. "It's you. You called."

"It is. I did."

"D'you see your name? Sloinbee. Instant nick"—a pause, a belch—"nickname."

"Are you drunk?" I ask, though it's completely unnecessary.

"Define *drunk*."

"Did you drink a bunch of alcohol?"

"Define *a bunch*."

"Why'd you text me, Remy?"

"I'm at Sliders with the guys from the station. You know Sliders? They have chicken wings! They are the best chicken wings I ever put in my mouth."

"What's going on?" I say, trying to get this back on track.

"I need a ride, they're going somewhere else . . . said I can't come . . . too wasted . . . And I'm like, then you should've stopped buying me drinks if you didn't want me to"—another pause, another belch—"Sloinbee, please come pick me up. Please, pretty please."

He could've called Gabe or Vera. But he didn't, and I know I can't say no.

I sigh. "Yeah. Okay."

I leave a note on my pillow, on the off-chance either of my parents comes in to check on me. I guess I'm not really the "stuffed-up pillows to make the shape of a body" kind of person. I'm slipping out, but I pause outside my parents' room when I hear voices: "—not what I'm saying." Dad's voice has an edge to it.

"Then what? What do you need from me?"

"I just need you to be patient."

"Patient," my mom says, and the word is loaded. "Patient, yeah. Because I've been nothing but *impatient* with you, is that right?"

"Jill—"

"No. Look at me. Look. I've given you space. I've been your sounding board. I've told you my thoughts when you asked for them; I've

163

held my tongue when you didn't. I've been so supportive, so receptive, so fucking *there* for you, Mike, and I don't know what else there is for me to do—"

"You can accept that this is what I need right now."

"Just like when I accepted that you needed to quit teaching, or when I accepted that you needed to travel, or when I accepted that you needed to drop everything—to completely put our lives on hold—so we could come here. Because you thought this would fix whatever it is that's broken."

"Yes" is all my dad says.

"What if nothing's broken? What if you're just done writing?"

"How can you say that?"

"Because that's how you're acting!"

"Writing is everything to me."

"Then do it! Write a damn book! You've done it a dozen times before—do it again!"

"It's not that easy—"

"It's not brain surgery, Mike—you write books about dying divorcées and the handymen who love them!"

Silence. My mouth has filled with spit in the interim—nervous spit—but I'm afraid to swallow, to move, lest they hear me.

When my dad speaks, his voice is low: "You'll wake the kids."

My mom's reply is hushed, but with just as much intensity: "And how do you think this is for them, huh? Uprooting them like that. Sloane missing her last year at Bishop Dubourg."

"She hated Bishop Dubourg, just like you did. I don't know why you made her go there—"

"I didn't! *I* didn't make any decisions alone—*we* were the ones who made those decisions, together. I wasn't solely responsible for anything—"

"And I'm not solely responsible for this, am I? Because you agreed to do this with me. Together. We agreed together that we would come here."

"I agreed to it because I thought"—a pause—"I thought it would help."

"And it is helping."

"It's helping you, Mike. I thought it would help us."

"I don't understand the difference. What's helpful to me is helpful to us."

"And isn't that just the fucking problem in a nutshell."

A long moment of silence follows. No rustle of movement. Nothing. Are they looking at each other? Or are they looking away? That seems more likely. My mom with her arms folded, my dad hunched in his chair.

"So what do you want to do?" my dad says finally.

I take a step back from the door. And then another. And then I turn and head down the hall—swiftly, quietly, bare feet soundless on the stairs—and I make my way to the back door, slide on some shoes, grab the keys from the hook, and slip out.

I don't want to hear the answer to that question.

thirty

Sliders is a bar in Panama City. I don't know a ton about bars, but I do know that this one is gross.

It's only as I'm parking that I realize I don't know how I'm going to get in. Then again, they let Remy in, and they let Remy get drunk, so maybe security isn't that tight.

It doesn't matter, though, because Remy is out front when I circle the building. A group of people is congregated to the left of the front door, all guys, save for a blond girl standing under the crook of one guy's arm.

They're all probably in their twenties, but it's hard to tell in the fluorescent light from the bar. They're laughing about something when I arrive. It's only when I get closer that I see Remy off to the side, slumped against the front of the building.

"Sloinbee!" he says. "You came!"

I lean down and try to help him up.

"Meet the guys," he says, gesturing to the group by the door. "Want to meet—gotta—"

The guys are paying Remy no notice.

"We're going," I say, slinging one of his arms around my shoulder and holding on to it, just like the blond girl is, though she doesn't appear to be shouldering the weight of her doucheface boyfriend.

"I knew you'd come," he mumbles.

"Yeah?" I put my other arm around his waist and guide him toward the parking lot. "Why's that?"

"Because you're reliable. You are very reliable. D'you know that?"

I don't respond.

"And I couldn't call anyone else. You're not gonna lecture me like everyone else would. Gabe . . . with his disappointed eyes . . . You've seen Gabe's disappointed eyes, right? Like he'd do anything for you—he'd fucking punch the sun for you—but you've let him down." He looks up, like he's just realized we're in motion. "What are we doing? Where're we going?"

"Home."

I decide to take Remy to the back porch. A little couch sits out there, a wicker frame with a couple of cushions, at least. My dad gets up during the night sometimes, so it seems safer to leave him out here. My parents are cool, but I don't think they're unauthorized sleepover cool.

Remy is mumbling as I collect a blanket and a pillow, about how awesome Sliders was, and how I need to meet the guys, and how it was really cool, really fun, but Aubrey would've hated it: "She doesn't like that kind of stuff, shuts off sometimes in big groups, would've hated it, really—"

"I think she has the right idea," I mutter, fumbling to open the back door.

"She always has the right idea. She always knows what's best. That's why I know—I know—"

167

I push open the door to the porch and lead him through, then slip out from under his arm. He sways for a moment on the spot, so I throw out a hand to steady him.

"I'm fine," he says. "I just miss her, is all."

"You're just wasted, is all."

"I love her so much."

"No, you don't. You're drunk."

"Drunkenness has nothing to do with it."

"It does in high school."

"Bullshit. I love"—he turns sharply and then lists a little to one side—"I *love* her. And she loved me. And I don't get it. I don't get why he would do that."

"Who? Do what?"

His eyes shine. "Break us up. Why would he do that?"

"Who's *he*?"

"Him. *Him*." Remy looks to the sky.

It takes me a moment to realize that the *he* in question is Remy's capital-*H He*. The God Man.

"Why would He do that?" he says again. "What is He trying to teach me?"

"That you can't always get what you want?" I say. "The Rolling Stones could've taught you that."

"God, Sloane."

"That is the guy in question, isn't it?"

"Can you be serious for like one second?"

"I am being serious."

"No, you're being Sloane."

"And what does that mean?" I ask, not because I really want to know, but because . . . well, maybe some part of me does.

"You think you know people," Remy says. "That's the thing about you. You think that 'cause you've seen things, you've seen—everything. But you haven't. You think you know everything but you don't, and it's so obvious, because you don't even know that there's a love that doesn't care if you're drunk or in high school or *drunk*—it just is because it is, it just exists because there's no other way than it existing. It's like putting your feet on the ground when you wake up in the morning. That's how I love her. Do you get that? It's not a thing you think about, it's just a thing that is. And she doesn't—she doesn't—" His voice breaks. "She doesn't love me back anymore, and I'm sad about that. And I get to be sad. That shit is valid. Okay? So just . . . shut up."

"Okay." I nod. "Yeah. Okay."

His face crumples. "I don't get it."

"Lie down," I say.

He dutifully goes over to the couch and slumps down onto it, feet still on the ground. I cross over to him and hoist his legs up onto the cushions, and then I set about untying his shoelaces.

"That's why I can't join the church," he mumbles, his face smushed into the pillow. "Because I'm mad. Because I don't understand why He would do this. Why would He make me love her like that and then make it so we're not together?"

"Maybe God doesn't *make* anyone anything. Maybe we just are the way we are. Maybe we just do what we want to do."

He shakes his head and sounds truly miserable: "If you pull that thread, the whole thing unravels."

"What do you mean?" I slip his sneakers off and set them down.

"If God doesn't make anybody anything . . . then what is He for? What does He do? If everyone just is what they are—if they just do what they do because, fuck it—if there's no plan for everything, then what's the point? And that's why I can't, that's why—what if there really is no one? No plan? What if we're all just . . . marooned here alone, and how fucking sad is that, Sloane? How lost are we?"

He screws his face up and cries now, cries for real, and I have no idea what to do or what to say so I just stand there. Maybe he won't even remember this conversation. Maybe he won't remember me being awkward, me once again doing the wrong thing. I should . . . pat his back, or hug him, or tell him that everything will be okay. But I'm not great at affection. And I'm even worse at lying.

Finally, I speak, and I say the only thing that makes sense to me.

"Have you ever heard of dead reckoning?"

Remy has covered his face with his hands, and his voice is muffled: "S'that a band or something?"

"It's a nautical term." My dad had researched seafaring extensively for *Love Knot*. Hardened mariner. Recovering widow. Inevitable romance and heartache. "It's when you navigate without the use of the stars. Can you imagine that? Out there on the ocean, in the darkest night, not a landmark around. . . . But even then, people could still do it. Even with nothing at all to guide them, they could still get themselves where they needed to go." I pause. "So . . . maybe you lost your stars. And maybe you'll find them, or not, but . . . I mean, we're never really lost, right?"

Remy nods. His eyes are closed, and his face is streaked with tears.

I spread the blanket over him. And then I stand there for a moment and get the inexplicable urge to reach out and smooth his forehead.

It's a feeling I've only ever associated with Laney, seeing her sleeping in her little bed as a toddler, so vulnerable. Even now, sometimes, when she falls asleep with a *Harry Potter* book half open next to her face, all drool and rumpled hair and patterned PJs, I look down at her and I just want to create a dome around her, to protect her, to . . . preserve that, somehow.

I feel a rush of that for Remy. My fingers twitch at my side, but I don't reach out. Instead I just swallow and say, "Good night."

I turn to go, but suddenly his hand darts out and grabs mine, and he looks at me through bloodshot eyes, still drunk, still devastated.

I think he's going to say thank you, but he just says, "I might throw up."

I duck into the kitchen and grab the trash can, placing it by the side of the couch. Then I leave.

thirty-one

Remy is gone the next morning. And he's not at Bree's house that evening when we go to roast marshmallows and as Bree put it, "I don't know, whatever the hell else you guys want to do, but my folks will be there so nothing too crazy."

Bree's house is on the inlet in between Opal and Grayson, bordering a protected area of wildlife, all live oaks and saw palmettos. I've been there a few times before, to work on projects for class. Bree's bedroom is covered wall-to-wall with movie posters and clippings from celebrity magazines. The massive Dex Finnegan collage hanging by her bed was a little distracting the first time I visited; it was hard to focus on homework with fifteen Dex Finnegans in varying degrees of shirtlessness staring back at me.

"He replied to me on Twitter once," Bree said proudly when she noticed me looking.

A big deck stands off the back of her house and, farther down, a little wooden dock projects out into the inlet, with a rusted rowboat tied to it. The dunes rise up in the distance; beyond that is the beach, humming with the sound of waves.

The inlet is calm this evening, just little ripples on the surface. Bree's mom lit a fire for us in the pit off the side of the deck, and I've already eaten enough s'mores to last a lifetime.

"I can't eat another one," Vera groans, but takes it from Gabe's outstretched hand anyway. "Come on," she says to me, licking chocolate off her fingers. "Let's go lie on the dock."

So we do. Everyone else stays above. Frank is telling a story about some guy he met online. "I seriously thought I was being catfished, but then halfway through I stopped and really examined myself and realized, Frank Sanger, what if you yourself"—dramatic pause—"are the catfish."

Frank's audience reacts appropriately, and I smile, sinking down onto the wooden planks. The sun is setting pink and gold, fading into deep purple in the west.

"It's too nice out," I say, stretching out and clasping my hands behind my head. Vera finishes her s'more and then settles next to me. "It's cliché."

"I'm sorry, is it too majestically beautiful for you? Would you like me to turn down the sunset?"

"Yes, please." I look over at her. "You're not going to take a picture?"

She shakes her head. "Not worth it."

"Why?"

"'Cause you could never capture it quite right. Something so beautiful."

"You capture yourself."

Vera cocks a look at me, a smile on her lips. "You have to stop saying shit like that. It sounds like you're flirting."

"I'm not. I'm just being honest."

"That in itself sounds like flirting."

"I'm a face-value kind of person. I just . . . say what I mean."

"That must be nice."

We're quiet for a bit, just looking up at the sky. I can hear Frank's voice ringing out from above. The group laughs, and I can pick each one out—Bree's is a giggle, Aubrey's soft, Gabe's begrudging at first but wholehearted when Frank hits on something that really tickles him.

"Do you like it here?" Vera says after a while.

"Sorry?"

"You say you're honest, so be honest. Do you like it here?"

"Why do you ask?"

"Because I want to know," she says, making a face. "Stop hedging."

"I do," I say. "I like it."

"Do you miss home, though? Were you mad about moving?"

"I didn't really care." But it's more than that. "I actually . . . Part of me wanted to come here."

"Why?"

"Everyone loves those sitcom episodes where they go on vacation, right? I thought it would be like one big sitcom episode where they go on vacation."

Vera just looks at me, drawing out the truth in that wrinkled-brow way of hers.

"Okay." I shrug. "I thought . . . Maybe I thought it would make me different."

"Different how?"

"I don't know. Just different. Don't you ever want to be different?"

"No," she says after a pause. "I would change some things, I guess, about my life. But I would keep me the same." She evaluates me for a moment. "Why would you want to be different? What would you change?"

"I don't know," I say, and it's the truth.

"You know what I would change?"

"About me?"

Vera nods. "I would make you realize how much you matter to people. Sometimes I think you don't get it."

I don't know what to say to that.

"What would you change about me?" She turns her face toward the sky.

I glance over at her.

Vera is the most glamorous person I have ever known in real life. She is also the kindest, the most optimistic, and the most generous. But the main thing—perhaps the rarest thing—that I've come to learn about Vera is that she somehow manages to make you feel like *you* are in fact the most glamorous person she's ever known in real life. Or the smartest person, or the funniest person. Vera is a mirror that reflects the very best version of yourself back at you.

"Nothing," I say. "I would change nothing."

"Stop flirting with me, Sloane."

"Stop being perfect."

"Damn, you have game."

"I know. Secret game. Undercover game."

"You should use it on Gabe."

I raise an eyebrow. "Why?"

"Because he'd like it, that's why. You can't just flirt with me and Remy and Frank forever. The safe people."

"Okay, first off, I have never flirted with Remy 'Aubrey is the very gravity binding me to earth's surface' Johnson in my life. And second, Frank Sanger is not *safe*. Frank Sanger is sexual kryptonite."

"Sexual kryptonite!" Vera squawks and draws out her phone. "Oh my God, I have to tweet that."

"He is," I say, grinning. "Frank Sanger is for everyone." I consider the sky above as she taps away on her phone. "Maybe I'm the opposite. Maybe I'm for no one."

"It doesn't have to be all or nothing, does it?"

I just make a noise of assent, and it's quiet between us after that, as we watch the sun slip down below the horizon.

I sleep over at Vera's that evening. We're full on s'mores and crisp night air, so we both drop off to sleep quickly.

I wake in the night, though, and head to the bathroom. It's on my way back that I notice a door ajar down the hallway. A soft light spills through, cutting into the darkness.

It's the door to the studio. The baby's room. Whatever it is now.

I peer in. The room has changed since I last saw it: The walls are now a pale green, and there are a few pieces of furniture. A crib, a changing table, a dresser. The remainder of the art supplies has been cleared away.

On top of the dresser sits a little night-light, shaped like a moon, the source of the soft glow. And next to the dresser stands Gabe.

He is wearing a faded T-shirt and plaid pajama pants, and his hair is in disarray—not like he's been sleeping, but more like he's been running his fingers through it repeatedly. Some kind of a stress response. Some attempt at self-soothing.

He is looking at the crib, and I don't think he realizes I'm there until I push the door open a little wider and a creak rends the room.

"God." He jumps a little at the sound. "You scared me."

"Sorry."

Silence.

"Couldn't sleep," I say, both as an explanation and a question. He nods.

"Remember when I thought this was the bathroom?" I love a good callback. "Good thing I'm not sleepwalking. Could've peed all over the schmancy rocking chair."

Gabe looks at the chair in question. It's white and streamlined.

"Looks like a fucking rocket ship," he says.

"Do we know if it's capable of launching the baby into space? Could be worth investigating."

The ghost of a smile flits across his face, and then it's quiet.

"How's your nose?" I say, because it doesn't seem like I should turn around and go back to bed. It doesn't seem like I should leave Gabe in . . . whatever this is.

"Still attached to my face." I had seen the bruises under his eyes when we were at Bree's this evening.

"Well, that's something."

He bobs his head and then looks at the night-light, reaches out, and fiddles with the cord.

"Everything seems worse at night," I say after a moment. "Especially late. That's . . . that's something I've noticed. Sometimes you wake up and you just . . . you just start thinking, and it's like you're sinking into the bed, you know? Or seizing up inside yourself . . . Your body is the same, but the *you* part—the soul part—is just folding in on itself, and all you can do is think about every bad thing you ever did, everything you're ashamed of, everything that scares you. It's all . . . magnified. Like the daylight keeps it away somehow, and when it's gone it just . . . amplifies."

"Why are you telling me this?"

I think of Remy last night: *What if we're all just marooned here alone? How sad is that, Sloane? How lost are we?*

"Because. I don't want you to think—to feel—like you're . . . you know. Like you're alone."

He just looks at me, so I go on: "I don't know what it's like, what you're going through, obviously, I can't imagine, but . . . everybody's got something, you know? Everyone has those nighttime feelings. So"—I shrug—"you're not alone."

"I know I'm not alone," he says.

"Oh." A pause. "So . . . good."

"You're here."

I nod. "And you've got Vera. And . . . and your dad." He frowns. "And Remy, and Aubrey and everyone. And me."

"We said you twice."

"I'm larger than life. I deserve twice."

The smile sticks a bit longer this time, maybe a full second. Then he looks back at the crib.

"Tell me again how fucked it is," he says.

"Super fucked."

His voice is somehow soft and rough at the same time: "Tell me again I'm not alone."

"You're not alone."

He nods.

"You want me to tuck you in? I'm really good at it."

"I don't need—I'm seventeen."

"Yeah, so? I'm not trying to tuck cigarettes and porn in next to you." I grab his wrist. "Come on."

I lead him down the hall and into his room, which is cramped and covered with clothes.

"Jesus Christ, did the men's department explode?"

"I hate folding."

"Get in. If you can find the bed."

Gabe crosses through the mess and climbs into bed. The covers are all rucked up, twisted and cast aside.

I straighten the sheet over him and then float the blanket up and down a few times, getting it right.

In the dim light from the window I can see him giving me a look. An *I-think-this-is-really-stupid* look.

"You have to put your arms under the covers," I say.

"Why?"

"Because that's how it works."

Gabe obeys, and I pull the blanket up to his chin and then tuck it under his side. Same way my mom did for me; same way I do for Laney.

"There."

I stand back and admire my work. Gabe looks vaguely like a burrito, and I can't help but sputter a laugh. He glares at me.

"Did you do this just so you could make fun of me?"

"I did it to be comforting," I say. "Don't you feel nice and secure?"

"I feel—" But Gabe doesn't finish. I can see the shine of his eyes through the dimness, his mouth pulled down into a frown.

"Get some sleep," I say, at the same time he says, "What do you—"

"Sorry?"

His mouth twists, and then he says fast: "What do you have night-time feelings about? You said everybody has them. So what do you have them about?" *You said you're honest, so be honest.* The Fullers have a way of trapping me.

I think about my parents. The conversation through the bedroom door.

I sit down on the edge of the bed. "I don't have them," I say.

"You said everyone has them."

"I'm special. Like postapocalyptic, dystopian-heroine special. As soon as everything goes to shit and society crumbles and we all divide into postwar factions based on eye color or favorite This Is Our Now member, I'll be the one who leads the revolution to overthrow the government."

"Because you don't have nighttime feelings."

"I don't have them. I just understand them deeply."

"Right."

He looks at me for a moment, and I realize that I'm sitting on his bed, in the middle of the night, and if this were a fic, I would prob-ably offer to stay. If this were a fic, I would be able to hold him until he fell asleep, and stay up long after, stroking his hair and watching the gentle rise and fall of his chest, and I would bask in the knowl-edge that he felt utterly secure with me, and I with him, and eventu-ally I would drift off, too, to a dreamless but comfortable sleep. Or something like that.

But this is not a fic, and Gabe is covered in blankets up to his neck with his arms effectively trapped underneath, and he's looking at me in a way that's hard to describe. There's nothing lustful about it. There's more of an earnestness to it. Almost as if he's looking for something that's not there, an answer to a question that neither of us has said out loud.

"Go to sleep," I say.

"I'm not tired."

"Then just close your eyes." It's what my mom always says. *She just thinks she isn't tired,* she'd say to me about Laney. Like some kind of shared confidence, some adult secret I was being let in on.

Gabe looks at me for a moment more and then shuts his eyes.

And I don't entirely feel that Laney feeling that I did with Remy, that urge to smooth his hair back, to protect him. I feel it in part. But there's also—suddenly, overwhelmingly—the urge to kiss the spot between his eyebrows, and each eyelid, and the tip of his nose. The need to kiss the corner of his mouth, and draw his bottom lip between mine.

It comes out of nowhere, and I don't know what to do with it. So I do none of these things. I just say, "Keep them closed," and then I get up to leave.

It catches my eye as I turn, even in the dimness. The pastel shade is at odds with the rest of the swirling laundry vortex eating up Gabe's room. It's folded carefully and lies across the back rung of his desk chair—my sweater. The pink nosebleed sweater.

I cross over to it and pick it up. It's clearly been washed since yesterday, but there are still bloodstains. I trace my fingers over one of them, faded. Gabe must've washed it himself. Vera or Mandy would know to use cold water to get blood out.

I should take the sweater—it's mine, after all—but . . . I don't know. Part of me likes the idea of something of mine amid the clutter. So I leave the sweater on the chair and slip out.

thirty-two

"Love is for the living," Sarah said.

Page 316 of *Sand on Our Beach*. I have notes I need to go over for a Spanish quiz tomorrow. At the very least, I should practice my pieces some more. But I can't help but burrow deeper under my comforter and dig in on the Sunday evening after the sleepover at Vera and Gabe's.

"And you're not living?" Jack turned around. A fire burned in his eyes. "You're not breathing? Your heart's not beating?" He reached out and grabbed her wrist, holding it up with his thumb on her pulse. "There's no rhythm here, no life, no movement? Nothing?"

He was close now, closer than they had ever stood after that first evening in the rain, crowded under Ruthie's pink umbrella as they waited for Mr. Crowley's tow truck. His fingers burned where they touched her. He must've been able to feel it—her heartbeat quickening. Because he was right: She still had one.

Crack her chest open and it was still there, pumping away, an engine powering a defective vehicle. Every sixty seconds your blood circulates, delivering oxygen to every bit of you that needs it, and every sixty seconds hers did the same. Every sixty seconds feeding her cells, powering the machinery that transcribed and propagated a faulty code. Slowly breaking her down from the inside out.

"Maybe I am now," she said. Her voice cracked as she spoke. "But I won't be forever."

"Nothing's forever, Sarah."

Jack was kind of a smug bastard, wasn't he? Maybe not on purpose, but I couldn't have handled all that if I was Sarah, his unironic truth bombs that he clearly thought were capital-*G* Groundbreaking. He thought he knew everything. What was best for Sarah. How she felt. How she *should* feel. But Sarah doesn't tell him to go screw himself. She just *meets his gaze for a moment* . . .

It was all she could bear, that light pressure still on her wrist, everything about Jack too close and yet too far away. How was that possible, to want to run toward something and away from it at the same time? She wanted to close the distance between them, seal her lips over his, leave them both gasping. But in the same breath, she wanted to turn and run and never look back. She wanted him—she ached with it—but at the same time, it somehow didn't feel nearly as much like wanting him as it did like missing him. How could that be? How could she miss something

she never had, grieve the loss of something that never
existed?

When I abandon my book that evening, I find my dad on the back porch. His computer is next to him but closed. There's just the little black Moleskine resting open on his lap and a pen with a chewed-up cap in one hand.

"What's Jickey up to tonight?" I say, sinking down into the rocker next to his.

"Jickey is resting," he replies. "They just had a bunch of sex."

"Ew. Ew times a thousand."

"Jickey's gonna do what Jickey's gonna do. And that's each other. All the different ways."

"God, Dad."

"Healthy discourse on sex! This is a sex-positive family!"

"Yeah. Well."

He sticks the pen in the notebook and shuts it. "What's up?"

This is how it works, between my dad and me. "I have a question."

"Hit me."

"What is it about being in a relationship that makes it better than being alone?"

My dad looks out at the yard and blows a breath of air through his nose, an audible little puff.

"It just . . . is," he says finally. "Better." He nudges me. "My life's better because you're in it."

"But I don't mean like that. Like family. We have to be a family."

"Should I feel offended?"

"You know what I mean. I didn't *pick* Laney, but of course I love her. You guys didn't pick us, specifically, but we love each other, and yeah our lives are great because of it. But I mean someone you don't *have* to love. Someone you choose to be around, because . . ." I shrug. "Well, because why? I don't know. That's why I'm asking."

A pause. "Sloane, I've written a lot about love. I have written tomes about love. But . . . in real life . . . I don't know if I can explain it. You just . . . know it, when it happens. Or maybe it happens without your conscious thought and you just . . . realize it, later."

It just is because it is, it exists because there's no other way than it existing. Maybe Drunk Remy was onto something.

thirty-three

We leave for Birmingham early on the following Saturday morning, my dad behind the wheel and Remy in the backseat. I have the map up on my phone, and I'm reviewing our stops: Hartwin Gallery, 401 Artplace, and Wilderness Art and Antiques.

My dad stops at a drive-through Starbucks and picks us up drinks, chatting with me about the plan for the day. All the while Remy is quiet in the back.

"What?" I say finally, when we're on the freeway, driving past rows and rows of loblolly pines. "What is it?"

"Aubrey was there with Marshall Peters again last night," he says.

Dad shoots me a look. I wonder if my exasperation is showing.

"You're an expert on love, right, Mr. Finch?" Remy asks, and my dad lets out a laugh.

"I don't know about that."

"But you've written lots of books about it."

"True, but that hardly makes me an expert."

"I guess you kind of have a story like theirs," I say. "*Sand on Our Beach*. Sarah and Jack do get together at first, but she breaks it off."

"Because she thinks she's dying," Dad says.

I look back at Remy. "Oh shit, is Aubrey dying?"

"*No*," he says, but when I glance back again, his face is pulled into a frown.

"She's not dying—that was a joke."

"I know that. I just . . ." He pauses. "What do they do in the fics? If this were . . . Mickey and James, what would they do?"

"If this were Mickey and James, they wouldn't have broken up in the first place," I say. "Their love is eternal, haven't you heard?"

Remy snorts.

"I don't know, fics are usually about getting together, aren't they?" I glance over at my dad.

"Why?" Remy asks.

"The beginning part's more interesting, I guess."

"Fuck the beginning part—I want the back-together part," Remy says, and then grimaces. "Sorry for saying *fuck*, sir. And . . . sorry for saying it again just now."

"Don't despair," Dad says. "There are plenty of back-together stories. Fics or otherwise."

"You have one," I say.

"Which one?"

"*Hour by Hour.*"

"There you go. But you know, you also have to keep in mind that not every breakup is destined to be a back-together story. I mean, if it's Mickey and James, that's usually the case. But you're not Mickey and James."

"What if we were? Which one would I be?"

"You're Mickey," Dad says. "She's James."

"Then who does that make me?" I ask. "Kiko, the belligerent ectoplasm?"

"No, you're Jessica," Dad says with a grin.

Jessica is the pack leader. She wears Doc Martens and drives a motorcycle and has an on-again, off-again romance with a resurrected Aztec warrior.

"More to the point, who does that make me?" he says after a pause.

"Elvin," Remy and I both reply.

"The *aging history teacher*?" my dad squawks. "That's bullshit. Elvin is like seventy years old."

"Elvin is fifty if he's a day."

"I am *forty-eight years old,* thank you very much."

"Fine, you're like Elvin, but two years younger."

"You don't think I could be Wayland?"

Remy chokes on his drink, which sets me off. "Sorry," Remy says, wiping iced coffee from his chin. "Sorry, sir. It's just—he's really—"

"Really what?" Dad says, with mock severity. I know he thinks it's funny, so he'll draw it out. "What is he, Remy?"

Wayland is young and hot. And also really ripped. Wayland has abs you could join a jug band with.

"He's really, um . . . serious?" Remy finishes. "Like, you're really . . . lively, you know, and he's pretty . . . uh, staid."

Dad suppresses a smile. "I'll give you a pass for using an SAT word. But that's the only reason."

★ ★ ★

Hartwin and 401 Artplace turn up nothing. The owner of Hartwin has never heard of Laura Fuller. And 401 Artplace is even more of a dead end, being that it's just an empty storefront now.

"Someone should update their website," Remy mutters as we peer through the windows into the former gallery. There are some crumpled-up newspapers on the floor and a couple of white plastic folding chairs in one corner. Otherwise it's empty.

"In their defense," I say, "if your business goes under, updating the website to say 'We're defunct' is probably just adding salt to the wound."

"Onwards and upwards," Dad says, and heads back to the car.

Wilderness Art and Antiques is a different story.

It's about thirty minutes north of the city, off an otherwise unassuming highway exit boasting a McDonald's and a gas station.

We pass these and turn down a one-lane road, and then onto a dirt road, winding back through a patch of wilderness.

"Aptly named," my dad says. I can tell he's too caught up in the adventure to complain about his car, but we all bounce as the car hits a particularly deep rut in the road.

Before we see the gallery, we see the cars—rusted-out shells on each side of the road that have been brightly painted. Those that still have hoods have been popped open, and there are flowers growing where the engines should be.

Eventually the gallery emerges from the trees. I don't know what I expected, but it's a run-down old house with dark wood siding. It looks small from the front, but as we approach, I can see it goes back quite a ways, a sort of hodgepodge, like additions keep being added on haphazardly.

The cars thin out, but they are replaced with a variety of things: rusty old bikes, farm equipment, large metal feeding troughs, an array of anchors. My dad parks, and we wind our way through the yard to the house.

It looks like someone's home. There's no sign to indicate that it's actually the gallery. But it's the only building around, so this has to be the place.

We climb the steps to the front porch, and my dad goes to knock on the door but then seems to think better of it, gesturing for Remy and me to go ahead of him. I glance at Remy and then knock on the screen door. We can see through it into the front room; every square inch is covered in paintings. Some are on canvases, yes, but others are on pieces of metal and cardboard and wood. And everywhere there's more *stuff*.

No one answers.

"Maybe we're just supposed to go in," I say. The door swings open when I try it, and we step into the room.

"Hello?"

"Do we just . . . browse?" Remy asks, hushed, which is silly because it's not like we're in a library.

"How would we even find it in all this?" I say.

"We'll just Command-F the whole building," Dad says, and Remy smiles as the creaking of floorboards indicates someone's approach.

An older woman enters and looks thoroughly surprised to see us. She's wearing a multicolored blouse and armfuls of bracelets. She claps a hand to her chest, and the bracelets rattle.

"Goodness me, you came out of nowhere," she says.

"We knocked," I say dumbly.

"Got the mixer going in the back," she says. "But I heard a little something so I thought I'd check. Come in, come in. How are you? What brings you out? I'm Wanda."

"Hi," I say. "I'm Sloane, and this is Remy and my dad. We're looking for a painting by Laura Fuller? We tried to call ahead but the phone just rang out."

"That phone will be the end of me," Wanda says. "My daughter is always saying, 'What's the point in having it if you never answer it?' but I can never find the dang thing is the problem." Then she looks at me, as if she's just caught what I said. "Laura Fuller, you say?" I nod. "Well, come on back. We've got a few."

She leads us through two more rooms chock-full of art, toward the back, where there's a kitchen with what looks like a family room off of it. It's slightly less full of art but no less full of stuff.

"We keep them back here because my father really loves them."

"Your father?" I say. Wanda looks to be in her late sixties, at the very least.

"He's the collector. I'm just the distributor, that's what I always say. Here we go."

Off the kitchen is a little anteroom with a glass-paneled door at one end. On one wall is a washer and dryer and a set of shelves laden with laundry stuff. On the opposite wall are a half-dozen Laura Fuller paintings of various sizes.

I let out a breath.

I recognize several water scenes from *Laura Fuller: A Retrospective.* There's also one of a house—an earlier work, judging by the style.

"Gorgeous," my dad murmurs. "They're so . . . arresting."

They are. But *The Dream* is not among them.

"These are lovely," I say to Wanda. "But we're looking for one in particular. It was purchased from a doctor in Brecken?"

"Oh!" Wanda's eyes widen. "Oh, yes. That was a beautiful piece. My father picked that up with my daughter when he was there to see Dr. Mark. A darn fine doctor, though the ride down is tough on Pa; it's a bit of a ways. Alisha insists, though. Let me get him. He can tell you all about it."

"There's no need to trouble him—" my dad says.

"Not a bother, not at all. Why don't you just settle in the kitchen? There's drinks in the fridge."

We take a seat around the kitchen table. It's an old metal set with a Formica top, patterned with little white outlines that look like boomerangs.

Wanda returns eventually with an elderly man holding on to her arm. He shuffles into the kitchen.

"This is my father, Robert Quarrells," Wanda says, and we introduce ourselves. He gives us a nod, his head shaking with a bit of a tremor as he does.

"You're here about the one from the doctor's office," he says, as Wanda pulls a chair out for him and he sinks down into it. "Gorgeous piece. Beautiful. Once I saw it, had to have it."

"So it's here?" I say.

He lets out a sigh. "I'm afraid not." If he notices me deflate, he doesn't comment. "Offer was too good. Had to take them up on it."

"Who bought it?" Dad asks.

"Some art lady. Slick. Said she was a—a consultant, for some fancy client. Just passing through town, wanted to check out the *local scene*." He doesn't use air quotes, but they're heavily implied.

"Do you know her name?"

He nods. "Crane."

"That's it?" I say.

"She gave me a card, in case any more came through. I think it's here somewhere." He waves to Wanda. "In the tin, with the others."

Wanda picks what looks like an old recipe box off the window-sill. She pulls out a handful of business cards and gives it to Mr. Quarrells. He spreads them out on the table with shaking hands.

"Got six other Laura Fullers," he says as he goes through them. "Talented lady. Awful shame. Ah." He picks up one card, a sleek black rectangle, and extends it toward my dad, who takes it and passes it to me.

It's embossed with white print: GEMMA CRANE, ART CONSULTANT. A 212 number follows, and an address in midtown Manhattan.

thirty-four

Thanksgiving is almost upon us, so there's a brief three-day week at school. Vera is psyched because Tash will be home for the holiday.

"She's coming tomorrow, so I might skip school, I don't know," she says, as we head to my house after school on Tuesday.

"Got to get in as much Tash Time as possible?"

"Exactly."

We head in through the back door. My mom is working at the kitchen counter, but she looks up as soon as we come in.

"Envelope for you from Clark," she says. "*Big* envelope." And then she looks back at her laptop screen, clearly trying to appear at ease but barely suppressing her excitement.

The envelope is sitting on the kitchen table. I pick it up, and Vera reads over my shoulder: "The Clark School of Music. What's that?"

"I'm not certain, but I believe it's a school of music," I say.

"Sloane, don't sass your friends," Mom says.

"That's okay, Mrs. Finch, we love her sass." Vera turns to me. "Aren't you going to open it?"

So I open it.

"I passed the prescreen," I say. "They're inviting me to audition." My mom jumps up, and Vera—who has only known about the Clark School of Music for all of two minutes—claps her hands.

"That's so exciting!" she says. "When's the audition?"

"I don't know; I have to schedule it."

"Yay, yay, yay!" My mom comes over and presses a kiss to the top of my head. "My baby! The musician!"

"It's just an audition."

"But it means they liked your preaudition!"

"They probably like everyone's preaudition. It's in their best interest to get people to pay the full application fee."

"Sloane, this school is so cool," Vera says, and when I look over, she's on her phone, data mining. "It's one of the smallest conservatories in the country, but the faculty are all like crazy accomplished."

"Yeah, should be fun," I say, and stuff the letter back into the envelope along with the promotional info they sent.

"I didn't even know you were applying for music schools," Vera says, as we head upstairs.

"It's really for my mom," I say, pushing open the door to my bedroom. "I'm applying to normal schools, too. She just doesn't want me to, like, give up on my dream because I don't think it's a possibility or something."

"That sounds like good advice, though, don't you think?"

"But it's not really my dream. I mean, it's just something I like doing."

"Don't you want to do something you like doing for a living?"

"Sure. But with voice, it's like, what could I really do with it in the end? Sing commercial jingles?"

"You could do tons of stuff. Operas, or shows. You could teach. You could sing backup for some artist, or join a late-night talk-show band, or—"

"Yeah, late-night talk-show band singer is a totally realistic dream."

"Dreams don't have to be realistic—that's why they're dreams. You have to work to make them happen. Or else they would just be . . . realities."

"That's great—you should put that on a motivational poster."

A silence follows, and I feel a pang, wondering if I've pushed the button that finally makes her realize how annoying I am.

But she just replies, "Maybe I agree with your mom," voice even, expression unchanging. "It's worth at least auditioning, I think. Just to see. Just to, like, not close the door before ever really opening it."

"That makes no sense."

"You make no sense sometimes, Sloane. You drive two hours for your lesson every weekend. You practice every day. You love it. I've seen you, remember? I've heard you. It's . . . You're good at it, and it means something to you, so . . . why not embrace that?"

"I like that I can sing well in the shower," I say after a pause. "And I like doing recitals at nursing homes, and silly shows with Laney. That's what I want. And it's not . . . unreasonable, or selfish, I think, to want to keep something for yourself, is it? Just because? I can go to college and study whatever I want, and keep this thing for me."

When I look up at her, I can tell she doesn't understand. But she just nods. "Yeah. Okay." And then, "Do you want to meet up with me and Tash sometime tomorrow? She really wants to meet you."

"We met before," I say, even though neither Vera nor I have mentioned that evening since it happened.

"Yeah, but for real this time."

"Sure. As long as you're willing to part with some Tash Time."

"Of course. But we should have a signal for when I want you to get lost."

I smile. "It's a deal."

thirty-five

To my surprise, Frank decides to host a party the day after Thanksgiving.

"Frank Sanger Presents: Black Friday," he tells us at school on Wednesday. "The day after Franksgiving, we come together for a classy affair. All-black dress code, absolutely mandatory."

"Are we just going to let *Franksgiving* go?" I say, and Frank grins.

"It's a day for giving Franks."

"Giving Franks what?"

"Wouldn't you like to know," he says with a wink. "See you on Friday, you beautiful bean sprouts."

Now the moment is upon us. We are all standing in the foyer of Chrissy Li's house.

"We look like we're going to a funeral," I say. "Or like we're crewing a play."

"Frank, I don't think you thought this through," Aubrey says.

"We look like hipsters robbing a bank," Gabe murmurs next to me.

"How would hipsters rob a bank?" I ask.

"With bayonets. And balaclavas made of fair-trade wool."

"They only steal obscure money, like two-dollar bills and buffalo-head nickels."

Gabe laughs, and Frank glares at us.

"It would've worked if everyone put the same degree of *effort* into their ensembles." He is wearing black slacks, a shiny black vest, and a black dress shirt with a black tie.

"Frank, face it," Gabe says. "You look like a fancy waiter."

"I will kill you," Frank replies.

"Luckily we're dressed for the occasion," I say, and both Vera and Gabe snort.

The party gets going, regardless of how absurd we might look collectively. The group hunkers down in Chrissy's living room with a deck of cards. Vera and Tash lose a game of Spades rather spectacularly to Aubrey and Frank, and now Gabe and Remy are playing them. I decline to play, happy just to sit and watch.

"Want to do a movie or something tomorrow?" I ask Vera, as we watch Frank deal.

"Sorry, we've got plans." She wraps her arms around Tash. "And I think Gabe's going out with Alice."

I look over at him. I can't help it. He's making a pouty face at Frank.

"Don't think you can distract me with your smolder, Gabe Fuller," Frank says.

Gabe grins and then glances up, catching my eye.

I look away fast.

"I said we should double," Tash is saying, "but somebody refuses to eat at Southern Grill."

"Grits are gross, I'm sorry," Vera says, but her eyes are on me.

"What?" I say.

"Nothing," she replies, but it's a little too knowingly.

It's not why. It's absolutely not the reason why when my dad says, "I don't think I can take any more Turkey Day leftovers," the next evening, I say, "We should order Southern Grill."

"Really?"

"Yeah. I can ride my bike over and pick it up."

He looks at me for a moment—I guess it's not often that I enthusiastically volunteer to do stuff like pick up dinner for everyone—but then nods. "Sounds good. That coleslaw"—he clutches his chest—"my word. It's a work of art."

Southern Grill has two big rooms, one for family dining and one with a bar. I'm waiting by the front for our takeout when a familiar shape cutting through the family side catches my eye.

It's not like I was *looking*. I'm not remotely interested in seeing Gabe, or the elusive Alice from Jade Coast Christian.

How come she never hangs out with us? I managed to ask Vera last night, ignoring the annoyingly perceptive look in her eyes.

Vera had just shrugged. *She's got her own friends. They do their own thing.*

"It'll just be another five minutes or so," the hostess assures me. I nod wordlessly, and because I definitely don't care that Gabe's here, I wait a solid thirty seconds before moving into the room, lurking behind the drinks stand for a better look.

Gabe has settled at a table about halfway in. The place is packed, but it's definitely him, wearing an orange button-down with the sleeves pushed up. *Ghastly*, I can just hear Vera saying. *Orange is not our color.*

But it's not ghastly. Frustratingly, it's not ghastly at all.

The chair across from Gabe is empty. I watch him fumbling with his silverware. The waitress stops by his table, and they have a brief exchange. It looks like he's ordering something.

But why would he order without his date?

I blink, and it strikes me all at once. It crystallizes before my eyes, that maybe all along this has been Gabe's secret—there are no dates. Maybe sometimes he just needs to get away, to be alone, to think and reflect, and this is how he's done it, under the guise of dates that aren't really dates. That's why he refuses to say that he and Alice are together. That's why we've never met her.

Alice from Jade Coast Christian *doesn't exist.*

This is it—this is the reality of it—and I'm just about to step out from behind the drinks stand, to declare myself, to sit down and say, *We could just sit like this together, you know. We don't even have to talk, we could just sit, you and I, but . . .* together *being the operative word. You don't have to pretend anymore,* I'm going to say, and maybe I'll cover his hand with my hand, and he'll look up at me from under those dark lashes and say, *I never pretend with you. . . .*

I leave the safety of the drinks stand. I'm halfway toward him . . .

And then a tall, willowy girl approaches the table, and Gabe looks up from the menu and smiles.

"Sorry," she says. "I was waiting on Mackenzie for the car."

"I could've picked you up."

"No, no, I said I'd meet you."

I blink. The vision of what I was about to do vanishes before my eyes, replaced by Alice, slinging her purse over the back of her chair and flipping her long straight hair over one shoulder.

What the hell.

When the hell is a more apt question. When did I start thinking life was like one of my dad's books? When did I start *wanting* it to be that way?

Then Gabe looks up.

And locks eyes with me.

It's too late. It's all over. I'm too far into the room to be doing anything but approaching him, and there's no other explanation but the truth, which is that I was lurking around like a full-time professional creeper.

So I give what I'm sure is a very awkward wave and a very winning grimace and then slink off to the front of the restaurant.

With any luck, they will immediately present me with my food and I will disappear from this place forever, but no such thing occurs. The girl just smiles at me—"Two more minutes, hon"—and then takes down the name of a group that's come in behind me.

"Sloane?"

I take a deep breath and then turn.

"Hey."

"What are you doing here?"

"Picking up food."

"But what were you doing . . . back there?"

I blink. Gabe looks at me. I look at him.

"Penguin party," I say.

I wasn't in on it. I wasn't part of the sacred covenant of *penguin party,* and that's why Remy needed me in the first place, but maybe it's different now. Maybe I've earned it.

Gabe just looks at me for another long moment. Then he nods. "Yeah, okay. You want to join us?"

I can think of nothing I would like less.

"Yeah, no. I mean, no, like just no. Ignore the *yeah* part, that was more like modifying the no. I'm getting food for my family, so I should probably—I should just—"

The hostess arrives at that moment and presents me with my food, and I make to get the hell out of there.

I'm stowing the food in my bike basket when footsteps approach behind me.

"Hot Pockets—what were you really doing in there?"

I turn to Gabe, that orange shirt glowing in the setting sun. "Sorry?"

"Hot Pockets," he says.

"Cinnamon Toast Crunch," I reply. "Are we saying things we like?"

"It's a thing. You have to tell the truth. It trumps penguin party."

"Nothing trumps penguin party."

"Hot Pockets does."

I squeeze my eyes shut for a moment. "I thought you were by yourself," I say finally. "I just . . . I thought I'd keep you company. If you were by yourself. If you were . . . lonely. But you're not. So." I point to the food. "I should get home. Nobody wants cold grits." I climb onto the bike. "Is that a thing, too? Someone says *cold grits* and you have to tell them your Social Security Number, or like your top five celebrity crushes?"

"We could make it a thing," Gabe says.

"Okay. It's a thing you say to end a conversation." I give him a salute. "Cold grits."

I don't wait for a reply. I just push off from the curb and pedal away.

thirty-six

We eat dinner, though I'm not really hungry, and afterward my mom and Laney start a movie. I go out onto the front porch and take out my phone to text Vera. But I end up just slinging my sweatshirt over my head and staring at the screen. I'm not even sure what I would say. *Awkward convo with your brother tonight*, maybe, but that just seems like compounding the awkward with even more awkwardness.

After a while the front door opens and closes, and someone sinks down into the chair beside me. "What are you doing?"

"Re-energizing my photons."

"Well, that's never gonna work," my dad says. "The secret is in the terry cloth."

It's quiet.

"Want to talk about it?"

"Nope."

He pulls out his Moleskine. I hear the scratch of pen on paper.

"Can I ask you something? And don't say I just did," he says after a while.

"Sure."

"How should Mickey tell James he likes him in this one I'm work-ing on? It's an AU."

An AU sounds good right about now.

I think I get it, I really do. The appeal of the fic. At least for me. It's the chance to remake something you love so that every little bit of it suits your vision for it. How it should have been in the past or how it should go in the future. How it would happen in an entirely different place, in an entirely different world.

I'd take an AU in this moment. One where I didn't go to Southern Grill. One where Alice from Jade Coast Christian is a convenient fabrication.

But how selfish would that be? The thought of Gabe sitting there alone at the table, Gabe ignoring his phone, playing with packets of Splenda, rolling the mason jar with the fake candle in it back and forth between his hands, waiting for his burger, drinking two sweet teas, smiling at the waitress as she hands him the check, sticking his hands in his pockets, and heading home alone. Is that what I wanted for Gabe? For date nights alone like some weird hermit loner? No. I didn't want that for him. We couldn't both be weird hermit loners.

"What kind of AU?" I murmur.

"Next-door neighbors."

"That's it? Doesn't there have to be more to an AU than proximity?"

"Sometimes proximity is all it takes." He clicks his pen. "So you know how awkward Mickey is. What should he say?"

"I don't know."

"Come on."

"I don't know, Dad." I pull my sweatshirt off my head and stand. "I don't feel like playing."

He looks at me for a moment. "I'll ask your mother, then" is all he says. I head into the house.

Remy texts me later that night: Have you heard back from the art lady?

Gemma Crane has yet to respond to my calls. No, I text back. But I didn't think I would, because of the holidays and stuff. Will just wait it out.

Sounds like a plan, Stan.

Who's Stan? I say.

Har har har, you're hilarious.

I go to send a tongue-sticking-out emoji back, but then I delete it and type what's been at the back of my mind all evening: Hey. Why didn't you just say Hot Pockets to Aubrey?

He replies right away.

What's Hot Pockets?

thirty-seven

Winter formal is a thing that happens the first weekend in December. Barely of my own volition, I find myself packaged into a midnight-blue dress and shoved in front of a camera, my mom on the other side of it, grinning.

"Can you do a twirl?"

"Yes," Laney says, smiling wide. "Do a twirl, Sloinbee."

"Who told you about Sloinbee?"

"What's Sloinbee?" Mom asks.

"Nothing," I say, and begrudgingly twirl.

It slipped out, Vera texts as I'm getting into the car, in response to my WTF, WHO TOLD ABOUT SLOINBEE?

When I was over last, she continues, and in Vera fashion, more texts rapidly follow:

> She asked me where you were
> I said sloinbee's in the kitchen
> Bahahahahahaha no but like it's so good
> Must thank Remy again for sharing that tidbit

I'll thank him when I see him, I reply. And by thank him I mean hit him.

I don't, though. It's hard to, when his mom is brandishing her own camera.

"This isn't a date," Remy says. "She's not my date. She's my ride."

"Squeeze in!" Mrs. Johnson says.

So we just share a look, and that's what Mrs. Johnson captures with her phone. And then two more, because we weren't "smiling properly," and "Why don't you two stand just a little closer, just a smidge, so we know you're together!"

"She's gonna scrapbook that," Remy says. "You'll probably get your own page."

"She did ask me how I spell my name."

Remy throws his eyes toward the sky, his *Lord-give-me-strength* face. It's one of my favorites.

When we arrive, the gym is already hopping. We find Vera quickly. She's wearing an aqua minidress, resplendent with tulle and sequins, and a giant corsage.

"Goodness gracious!" she says when we reach her. "You look so cute!" She holds up my hand and makes me twirl. This is a night for twirling, apparently.

"Was I supposed to tell you that you looked nice?" Remy asks me.

"No because you're not my—" I catch sight of them, probably fifteen yards away but approaching fast. Gabe and Alice from Jade Coast Christian. Who is very corporeal, very much an actual person.

Gabe and I haven't really talked much since that night at Southern Grill. Since he got me with a fake-ultimatum code word. I don't understand why he did it, but I'm too mortified by the whole thing to revisit it.

"Hey," he says, when he and Alice reach us, and he looks happy.

He's got on a white dress shirt with the sleeves rolled up. It looks good to a point that is thoroughly annoying. "This is Alice. Alice, you know Remy and Vera—" Alice smiles prettily. Her lipstick is a perfect matte, and there is not even a trace of it on her teeth, which hardly seems possible. "And this is Sloane, who I was telling you about?"

Her eyes light up. "Your dad's the famous author. Who writes the werewolf stories!"

"Yeah. I mean, the werewolf stories are kind of a more recent development."

"He has so many good books," Vera says, grabbing my arm and leaning in toward Alice as the sound system really kicks in. "*Sand on Our Beach*? Did you see that one, with Dex Finnegan?" She squeezes my arm. "She knows him!"

Alice looks properly impressed. Next to me, Remy is shifting back and forth, and I realize he's scanning the room for Aubrey. Meanwhile, Gabe is looking at me in a way that is both sort of pleased and sort of appraising. Like he knows I should be properly impressed by Alice, so he is waiting for me to show that I am properly impressed by Alice.

"Let's dance," I say to Vera.

"Yes, yes, yes!" she says, because she's a good friend. And then she grabs Alice's hand. "Come with us, Alice!" Because she's also a good person. Better than me.

We dance. A lot. We take long draws from the water fountain by the locker rooms. Vera and Alice take long draws from a flask that Vera has magically acquired from somewhere—"Don't ask, you don't want to know, and whatever you do, don't tell Gabe."

Alice giggles. "He can be kind of a stick-in-the-mud, can't he?"

"A regular fuddy-duddy," I say, and I'm half making fun of her, but she just giggles again. Her face is flushed, and it's very becoming.

I press the tap of the water fountain a little too zealously and get splashed.

Luckily Frank Sanger arrives—a good three-quarters of the way through the dance—and takes me away. He is wearing an all-white suit—"Like Jay Z at his vow renewal," he says—and twirls. He fucking twirls.

We dance for a few songs, and then Frank decides he needs to mingle. "You understand, don't you, darling?" Of course I do. He kisses my hand and then closes it in Vera's as she sidles up to us. I take the opportunity to look at her corsage more closely. It's a cluster of white roses, framed by a liberal amount of baby's breath. A little overdone, maybe, but Vera beams at me.

"I know they're usually a prom thing, but Tash got it for me since she couldn't come tonight. You wanna dance?"

Another slow jam is striking up, the opening upward-lilting chimes sounding through the gym.

"Come on." She pulls me back onto the floor and circles her arms around my neck. "You have to lead."

I put my hands on her waist. "I don't think anybody leads in this kind of dancing."

"You can keep us on beat at least," she says. We sway back and forth, and maybe we're getting a few looks, but I don't notice. Vera commands attention wherever she goes, and if that means she has other people's, it also means she has mine.

Her eyes are bright and her cheeks are a little flushed.

"I think you're drunk," I say.

"You're my best friend," she replies.

"Are you saying that because you're drunk?"

"I'm saying it because it's true."

I look at her for a moment. I'm taller—she has to tilt her nose up a bit to look me in the eyes, and for a second I'm struck by the fact that this must be what she looks like before Tash kisses her. That little upturn of the nose, the little smile teasing the corners of her lips.

"I've never been a best friend," I say.

"Well, I hate to break it to you, but you're mine." She pulls me close now, and her hair crowds me in, all fruity sweet shampoo. "We're keeping you," she says in my ear, and then pulls back and grins at me.

"Can I cut in?" a voice says, and we both turn to see Gabe. In that stupid white shirt. With his stupid eyebrows.

"She's all yours," I say, dropping my hands from Vera's waist.

"Boo," Vera calls as I take off through the crowd.

I don't look back. I see Remy, standing alone under one of the basketball hoops, so I head his way.

"Having fun?" I ask, though it's clear he's not. Unless "forlorn phone browsing" is some new version of fun that hasn't gotten big yet.

He shrugs, and his gaze flicks somewhere to my left. I don't even have to turn around to know.

"Let me guess. Aubrey is here. She looks beautiful. She's dancing with some hulking jock king. You feel a fresh wave of devastation."

"No," he says defensively. "These pants are itchy. I forgot they were itchy." He glances away. "And also Aubrey is here with some hulking jock king."

"Remy."

"I know."

"Do you?"

He looks away, but I step up and put my hands on his shoulders, lean in close, and speak clearly, crisply, so he can hear me without a doubt.

"You need to get over it."

He looks at me. And then he looks beyond me. I glance over my shoulder.

Aubrey is nearby, standing with her hulk, as predicted. The hulk is gyrating behind her, but if she was dancing before, she's not now. She's standing stock-still, looking straight at us.

"God," Remy says, stepping away from me. "She's gonna think— why do you have to do that? Why are you always ruining it?"

"Ruining what? There's nothing to ruin! You took a turn from sweet in a sad sort of way to deluded in a creepy sort of way a while back there. She broke up with you. It's done. Get over it."

It's like scolding a puppy. His eyes are too wide, too brown, and it's more hurt than anger, I know that, but it comes out more angry than hurt all the same. "You're supposed to be on my side," he hisses, stepping close again. "You're supposed to—all this stuff I've helped you with, you're supposed to be helping me, too, and what have you ever done but drive her further away?"

"There's nowhere to drive her! She left the vehicle a long freaking time ago!"

"Everything's just a joke to you, isn't it?"

"I'm not joking. It's not a joke. I hate seeing you waste all this energy on someone who doesn't want you anymore. It's . . . pathetic, and it bums me out."

Harsh, my mom would say, and scratch a line through that dialogue. *Too harsh.*

They need harsh, my dad would reply, and erase her mark.

Remy just looks at the ceiling, his second *Lord give me strength* of the evening.

"Well, I'm sorry to hear that," he says after a moment. "Everyone should take their problems and filter them through you, shouldn't they? Just to make sure they aren't making you sad or *bumming you out,* because your feelings are definitely more important than anyone else's."

"That's not—"

Remy walks away before I can finish.

I shut my eyes, briefly.

I didn't say that right. I didn't do that well.

I care about you. That's the core of it, right? I care about Remy. I could've folded that in there somehow.

But I didn't, and he's disappeared by the time I open my eyes. So I just look out into the crowd. Even in the relative darkness of the gym, I can see Frank in his all-white suit. He's dancing with Vera and Gabe now. There is Bree, over on the fringe of the crowd, with a couple of girls from biology and Alice from Jade Coast Christian, who throws one arm around Bree's shoulder and sways toward her. Someone will probably need to keep an eye on her. I wish I knew where the flask had ended up.

To my right is Aubrey, who is still standing with her date. He's forsaken dancing for goofing around with a group of football players. Aubrey looks . . . well, she looks a little like Remy did, just a moment ago. Hurt and angry. I can't get a balance on her, though, the proportion of each. She also looks like she's about to book it out of here.

And when she does, I congratulate myself on my premonition. Then I follow.

thirty-eight

I find Aubrey outside the front entrance of the school. She's staring into the depths of the fountain, which has been shut off for the winter.

I can't say it right to Remy, but maybe I can still do something for him. I can still try to help him understand what happened.

"Are you okay?" I ask.

"I'm great," she says, but she doesn't turn around. "Everything's great."

"Don't sound great."

She lets out a breath, then turns and looks at me and shakes her head. She smiles, but in a chagrined kind of way, with no joy to it. "No. Figures."

"What?"

"That you'd come out here. Of all people. You gonna sort everything out for me? Blow me away with something really perceptive?"

"I don't know what you're talking about," I say, because I don't.

"I can't even be mean to you. I can't even blame you, because it's not your fault that my best friend likes you better, and my boyfriend likes you better, the whole damn group just—it's like what did I do to deserve you, but at the same time I know exactly what I did. I know exactly why the universe sent you here to fucking—*thwart* me in everything."

"Last time I checked, I had free will. Wasn't under the control of the universe or anyone."

She just snorts.

"I'm not—trying to get in the middle of anything."

"But you are. Popping up, asking me about Remy at every turn. And I don't even know why, because you already have him."

"I don't *have* him. I never—God, is that what you think?"

She doesn't speak.

"If I was into Remy, why would I try to kiss Frank?" is the first thing I land on.

"I don't know, to make him jealous? You saw how fast he cleared out of there."

I didn't, in fact, because all I saw were Frank Sanger's eyes, lips, stubble, inner radiance, etc.

"I don't like Remy," I say. "I mean, I like him, because he's fun and a good person and appreciates *Were School* and stuff, but I don't want to be with him like that. Really."

Aubrey is staring at me like I've grown three heads. So I take this opportunity to go on. I step forward, cautiously, like I'm trying not to spook a wild stallion. "He just . . . wanted me to find out why you broke up with him. That's it."

"This isn't seventh grade," she says. "Why doesn't he just ask me?"

"That's not fair. You said *penguin party*. He is legally obligated by the bounds of you guys' weird friendship not to ask anything."

"I didn't think . . . I didn't really think he would just stay away."

"Yes you did."

"How do you—"

"Because you did."

She looks at me again. "Figures," she says again finally, looking away. "Geez."

"So what is it? What's the big secret?"

"There is no big secret."

"If you stopped liking him, you could've just told him."

"You can't just tell someone you stopped liking them."

"Sure you can. Was that it, then?"

"No," she says forcefully, and then winces. "No," a little bit quieter.

I think maybe she won't explain, but then she speaks.

"We've been friends since we were little kids. Almost our whole lives. Me and Remy and Vera and Gabe. I don't really even remember *becoming* friends with them, I just always was, it was just always something that was true. And I knew—I knew if he and I dated maybe this would happen but"—her mouth twists—"I couldn't help it; you've seen how he is. I always cared about him. I always had fun with him, but then I realized one day that I wanted . . . I wanted to kiss him, and so I did, and when something like that happens to you, when you feel something like that and the other person feels it back, you're like, why weren't we always doing this? How did I . . . function . . . before this, you know? But then. Then . . ." She pauses, shakes her head, seems to remember who she's talking to, and makes a wry face. "I don't even know why I'm . . ."

"Go on," I say. And to my surprise, she does.

"He wanted us to go to college together. He started talking about it, and it's like it wormed its way in and I couldn't stop thinking about it. Because what comes after that? We go to college together, we move in together, get married, have kids, and suddenly I'm a wife and mom and I'm only seventeen! Suddenly everything was . . . set. Everything was specified. And it freaked me out. It . . . scared me." She blinks, her eyes shining. "If you only understood how much I liked him, though. I *loved* him. For real. But I couldn't . . . agree to all that now."

I don't want to see her cry. But she looks down and fumbles with her dress for a moment, and I get the feeling that we're a little bit the same, me and Aubrey. She doesn't want me to see her cry, either.

"Maybe he wasn't asking you for all that," I say. "Maybe he was just asking you if you wanted to go to school together."

"They're tied together, though. They're the same thing."

She sinks down on the edge of the fountain, and when she speaks, it's soft, and it cuts at something right at my core: "It was too much." She shakes her head. "Haven't you ever just . . . needed to get out?"

It's a feeling I'm familiar with.

I remember being little and riding the subway with my parents. I don't know why we were in the city—maybe to see my aunt or go to a show. My mom was sitting, and I was standing with my dad. He held the handrail, and I held on to his legs.

I can see it so clearly—the doors opened at the station, I saw the platform beyond, and I let go. Darted out just as the doors were closing. I don't know what I was after, but for a second, I was triumphant. Then when I glanced back, the train was already in motion. I could see my parents' faces in the window. My mom's hands were plastered against the glass, my dad standing right behind her. Dual looks of horror.

And I was alone.

A woman had seen me. "That was not good," she said. "Naughty thing to do." She shook her head and clicked her tongue. "Take my hand."

I took her hand, and we sat on a bench. "Mama and Daddy will be back," she said. "Let's just wait."

Her name was Cecily. To me she was just a lady—tall to my four-year-old eyes—who had a soft voice and brown eyes. My mom always described her as "the woman who kept you from getting kidnapped when you gave us the biggest scare of our lives." It was usually followed up by my dad saying, "No, you can't ride the subway alone to Jane Bukowski's party; how are we to know that you won't just duck out at Fifth and Fifty-third and we'll never see you again?" They joked about it now, but I knew that was it—the biggest scare of their lives up until that point.

I don't even know why I did it; I just saw the area beyond, and maybe that was all I wanted—to be somewhere else. Something different. I only wanted it for a moment, but it was a moment too long. What would have happened without Cecily?

Sometimes I think of her and her serious eyes and her soft disapproval: "That was not good." And sometimes I think of her saying it to me now, when I've done or said something particularly boneheaded. *Not good.*

Aubrey looks down at her hands and says, "Better just to get out now, I think. 'Cause it would end anyway."

"Everything ends."

"Thanks. You're so wise."

I smile a little. "I'm just saying."

It's quiet. I want to ask, though I'm not sure if I should. But because I'm me, I do anyway: "Why didn't you just tell him? That you felt that way?"

"I didn't want to hurt him."

"But you did anyway."

She doesn't speak. Her mouth just twists, and she continues looking at her hands.

"I'm not trying to be a jerk," I say. "I'm just trying to understand."

She looks up at me. "I get it," she replies after a moment. "Why everyone's so in love with you."

"Nobody's—I don't know what you mean."

"You know exactly what I mean." *My best friend likes you better, and my boyfriend likes you better.*

I think about that for a moment, and I think about Vera throwing her arms around my neck not half an hour earlier, pulling me close: *You're my best friend.* That was Aubrey, once. Maybe it still is. Maybe you can have two best friends, or three, or four. But not with the way Aubrey looked at me before. The thought of it makes something prickle deep within my stomach, some strange mix of fear and . . . envy, maybe, but I'm not sure who I'm envious of. Whoever comes along next, I guess. Whoever enchants Vera. Whoever is enchanted by her. But that could be anyone at all—all you had to do was know her.

I don't have to ask Aubrey this time. I sink down on the edge of the fountain next to her and she just speaks. "You know, when Vera and Tash got together, they were completely obsessed with each other. They spent every waking minute together. And by the time Tash left for school, me and Remy were already—maybe I was annoyed getting left behind by her and Tash, and maybe then she was annoyed getting left behind by me and Remy, so by the time Remy and I broke up, there was already . . . this *space*, I don't know. The only person I felt like I could talk to about the Remy thing was Gabe, so—"

"Wait, Gabe knew?"

She nods. "He's . . . Sometimes it's easier to talk to him than it is to talk to Vera. Vera tries to help, but Gabe'll just . . . listen, and he won't judge, or try to make it better. He'll just . . ."

Absorb it. Let it have a place to land.

"I think you're good for them," she says after a moment. "That's what I'm getting at. I think . . . I don't know, maybe you're good for all of us."

It's a compliment. But I don't know how to respond. "Thank you" seems inadequate.

Aubrey doesn't give me a chance to answer. She just stands. "I'm going back in."

"Your date seems nice," I say, turning as she walks past.

"Shut up," she says, but there's no heat behind it, and when she looks back at me, it's with the hint of a smile.

thirty-nine

We all sleep over that night at Frank's house. There are rooms enough to share, but we end up in the family room: Vera and Aubrey on the massive sectional, me on the big padded chaise (because of course the Sangers have a big padded chaise). Remy takes the floor. Only Alice from Jade Coast Christian accepts the offer of a bedroom. I eye Gabe as we sort these arrangements out to see if he'll follow Alice, but he just sinks down onto the floor with Remy, arranging a nest of pillows and blankets.

When I wake in the morning, everyone appears to be asleep. Only the stretch of blankets next to Remy is deserted.

I find Gabe in the sunroom (because of course the Sangers have a sunroom), eating a bowl of cereal.

I sink down next to him on the love seat and say what I haven't yet had a chance to: "So you knew about Remy and Aubrey."

He looks at me, chews placidly, swallows. "Good morning to you, too."

"No, but seriously. You knew, and he's your best friend and you didn't tell him."

"She told me not to."

"But he's your best friend."

"But she told me not to." He just looks at me, eyes serious, and that's Gabe to a T, isn't it? Steadfast. Unwavering. All of a sudden I think of Bree's voice at that very first party: *You stepped in for freaking Gabe Fuller*, full of awe like that meant something. Like what I had done actually *meant* something. And it did, I guess, in a way. I wasn't noble like Gabe. But he's the kind of person you hope to be noble like.

"Even if she hadn't," he continues, "what would I even say? And how would it be my place to say it?"

"I thought there was some kind of . . . bro code, or something."

He makes a face and then digs back into his cereal. "Are you going to tell him, then?"

He's right, and I hate to admit it. I hadn't given much thought to it. How would I tell Remy? What's more, did I even have a right to?

Gabe seems to know what I'm thinking. So I just deflect: "Alice seems nice."

He raises an eyebrow, looking down at his bowl. "She is nice."

"Very nice."

"Yes. That we have established."

"You guys are a cute couple."

"We're not a couple."

"Well, you should be," I say, in one of those moments where my mouth and my brain seem to disconnect from each other. "You seem good together."

No, but like what in the actual fuck are you doing? part of me says.

LOOK HOW CHILL I AM, the part in control replies.

His tone doesn't change, but his expression darkens slightly. "Yeah, glad to know you approve." Then he gets up and heads back inside. The door snaps shut behind him.

A few moments later, Vera comes out.

"Is Gabe in the kitchen?" I ask.

"He went upstairs to shower."

"Alice from Jade Coast Christian is real," I say.

Vera gives me a look, sinking down into Gabe's spot. "Of course she's real," she says.

"I . . . thought she might not be."

She frowns. "Why would she not be real? You thought Gabe was having some kind of break, like that guy in *Fight Club*?"

"No, I just—"

"You thought we all collectively hallucinated Alice from Jade Coast Christian? Like she's some mass delusion that we all experienced?"

"You sound like me right now."

"I'll take that as a compliment." She settles back into the seat, drawing her knees to her chest and pulling her hoodie over them. "Do you like him?" she asks.

"No," I say.

"Because I wouldn't—it's not like I would be some deciding factor in this, you know that, right? As long as I never have to see you guys make out or hear about you doing sex stuff. I want zero knowledge of my brother and sex stuff. But otherwise . . . God, Sloane, you're two of my favorite people ever. Of course I would want you to be together."

I nod.

"No," I say again.

She looks at me, long and hard, and it's almost identical to the look Gabe gave me at Southern Grill, after I invoked *penguin party*.

"Do you want breakfast?" she says finally. "They've got all the best cereals."

"I'm good."

She heads back inside, leaving me alone with my thoughts.

forty

Vera and Gabe turn eighteen.

Aubrey's birthday is in March and mine isn't until May, so Vera rules out any celebratory activities that we can't all go to. Not that I was super keen on hitting up a strip club or a sex shop.

We end up instead at a tattoo parlor in Destin called Maxine's Ink. I'm not super keen on tattoos, either—mainly because of the large, mechanized needle component of the whole affair—but Vera insists that I don't have to watch the actual inking. My presence in the building will be enough for "moral support."

Maxine's Ink specializes in tattoos, piercings, and, curiously, tattoo removal. "Like they'll erase other people's shitty work, or they'll erase their own if you don't like it?"

"Isn't it nice to know they could do either?" Vera says with a smile as we enter. I don't know what I expected out of a tattoo parlor, but it wasn't this: Maxine's Ink is not dark or seedy. It's white-walled and lit with fluorescents, neat rows of designs attached to one wall.

Vera speaks to a woman about their appointment and gets some paperwork and pamphlets. We take a seat along the wall facing the designs.

"I've wanted this for ages," she says as she fills out the forms. Gabe has his own set of papers on a clipboard resting against one knee, but he hasn't started on them yet.

"You never mentioned," I say.

"Because Gabe and I have been fighting about it for a while."

"Why?"

Vera doesn't answer, just purses her lips as she fills out the Allergies portion of the form, so I look pointedly at Gabe.

"She's getting a design that Tash drew."

"Ah."

Vera looks up. "Don't *ah* me. You sound just like him, oh my God."

"The *ah* wasn't implying anything. It was a neutral *ah*."

"Gabe thinks that if—*if*—we break up, I'll regret getting it. But I think that's stupid and shortsighted. And anyway"—she stands—"who says it's going somewhere I'll ever even see it?"

"Ew," Gabe says. "God. Please. Don't share."

"It could be on the back of her neck," I say. "She couldn't see it if it were on the back of her neck. Where do you think she'd be getting it? How invasive do you think they can get with these things?"

The woman waves Vera back then, and she stands with her forms and grins at both of us. "It's happening. Whether you and Grumpy like it or not. Aubrey?"

Aubrey turns. She and Remy have been looking at the designs on the wall, starting from opposite ends. She follows Vera into the back—happy, I think, that she won't have to meet Remy in the middle.

Remy and I haven't really talked about our exchange at the winter formal. He still sat next to me in AP bio—when I arrived in class the Monday after the dance, I thought there might have been a chance he would've made Bree switch back with him. But he was there as usual. He asked if I had heard from Gemma Crane. I told him I was going to call again this week. It was our normal thing. Like I hadn't been a jerk at all.

And maybe I didn't say anything about it because I had no idea what to say, knowing now how Aubrey felt. I couldn't think of a way to simultaneously do right by both of them.

"Which one of us is Grumpy?" I ask Gabe, and he half-smiles down at his own forms.

"Do you really have to ask?"

"It's me?"

"Seriously? No."

"Are you sure?"

"Yeah, I'm sure. I'm Grumpy. Grumpy is me. I might as well get that tattooed."

"Are you going to get something, then? Not that, obviously, but something else?"

"Maybe. That was the plan, but . . ."

"Not sure what to get?"

"I have an idea."

"Whatever it is, you should scrap it, because I'm pretty sure I can think of a better one."

"Let's hear it."

"You should get a skull," I say. "Like a skull with a snake coming out of its mouth."

"You mean a Dark Mark," Gabe says. "From *Harry Potter*. You want me to get a tattoo saying that I serve the Dark Lord."

"That's actually not what I was thinking of, but now that you say it, it's kind of genius. If someone hasn't read the book, they'll just be like, *Oh, who's this unrepentant badass with the semiphallic skull tattoo?* And if they have read the book, they'll recognize you as a fellow *Potter* enthusiast."

"Who for some reason identifies with the wizard Nazis?"

"That is kind of bad, isn't it? Scratch the Dark Mark idea." I look at the wall across from us. "How about, I don't know, like a mountain range . . . wreathed in flames, or . . . an octopus breaking a ship in two . . . and the ship is on fire."

"These are possibly the worst tattoo ideas in all of history."

"How about I design one for you, like Vera and Tash? I can't draw, but it could be text-based, I guess? And instead of reminding you of our love, you can look at it years from now and be like, 'Hey, that's that girl that annoyed me in high school. I've forgotten her name, but thank God I have her chicken-scratch scrawl on my left bicep to remind me of that time we worked in the same place and occasionally hung out.'"

He gives me an odd look.

"I'd write something really good," I say, at the same time he says, "I wouldn't forget your name."

I look away. "Like *Eat your greens* or *Bless this mess.*"

"I couldn't forget you," he says, and it's soft.

"Maybe a solid Bible quote. Or a TV game-show catchphrase," I continue, fixing my eyes on the wall across from us. It's easier than dealing with whatever's going on in Gabe's eyes. That earnestness. That makes me want to throttle him. Or cuddle him. I'm not quite sure which.

"*I'd like to buy a vowel, Pat,* it could say, right across your chest. Backward, so you could read it in the mirror. I can write backward, you know. It's one of my myriad skills."

He doesn't answer, and when I dare to glance back over at him, he's staring at the designs on the wall. Snoopy holding a hand grenade. A busty Tinker Bell.

"Any one of those would work." I wave a hand in their direction. "Add some flames and you're good to go."

"Noted," Gabe says with a smile.

Vera and Gabe leave the tattoo shop with bandages adhered to them. Vera's is on her shoulder, and Gabe's is on his wrist, just at the base of his palm. He shows us in the parking lot; it's a set of numbers. I don't ask about what they mean, and he doesn't volunteer.

"So pretty," Vera says, peeling back her bandage and looking at the tattoo that evening. It's puffy and the skin around it is red, but it is pretty—a swirling design of circles and spirals. Abstract, but somehow fitting for Vera.

"Do you think Gabe's right?" she asks, as we get ready for bed. "That it was a bad idea?"

"No," I say, flicking on Vera's night-light like second nature. "I think if that's what you wanted, then why not?"

"Would you ever get a tattoo?" she asks, switching off the desk lamp and climbing into bed.

"I don't know what I'd get." A line of music I liked, maybe. Or a constellation from Laney's guide.

"Would your parents let you, though? Or would they not care?"

I consider it. "My mom wouldn't care. My dad might."

"That surprises me. He seems so laid-back."

"I guess they kind of balance each other out. Or at least they used to."

"What does that mean?"

I flash on an image of my parents in the hallway of our old place, standing close, almost as if they were about to kiss. But it wasn't romantic—it wasn't out of love at all—and I hear my dad's words, quiet and pleading: *What happens when you can't do the thing you're supposed to do anymore? If you're a writer who doesn't write, then what are you?*

And my mom: *I can't. I can't keep having this conversation. Over and over and over, Jesus Christ, Michael.*

"They might get divorced," I say.

It's the first time I've ever said it out loud. But here it feels . . . maybe not okay, but acceptable somehow. Safe in the glow of the night-light, the soft rise and fall of Vera's chest just a foot away.

"That sucks," she says quietly.

"Yeah." The words stick in my throat, too big to speak without some kind of roughness to them: "It does."

I used to end the scene differently. In my head I would play it out, where Mom says, *That sure was some fight, huh?* and Dad says, *Sure was*, and then they say I love you, kiss, and it's all okay again. And I don't have to think about Laney growing up in two places, her going to Banana Splits after school, having a weekend backpack for Dad's, both of my parents getting new places and neither having a room for me, because where would I even fit? What home would I go back to if the one I knew for seventeen years didn't exist anymore? It's not right. I squeeze my eyes shut and close my hands into fists, digging my fingernails into my palms.

If Vera notices, she pretends not to.

"What would happen?" she says after a pause. "If they did. Would you move back to New York?"

"I'll move back anyway for school," I say, trying to sound unaffected, though I'm not sure how successful I am. "I'm not—" I shake my head. "I don't belong here." *You didn't belong there, either*, something gross inside me says.

But Vera just glances over at me. "Do you really think that?"

I don't reply. Not to that, anyway. "What are you going to do for school?"

"Go to FSU with Tash."

"What if there was no Tash? What would you do then?"

"I don't know," she murmurs. "Maybe go wherever Gabe goes. Or come to New York with you."

It fills me with warmth, running liquid through me, but it won't thaw my mind. "Why does it have to be, like, based off someone else? Why don't you just do what you want?"

"What I want is to be around people I care about."

"Oh." I blink at the ceiling once, twice, eyelids getting heavy, eyes getting fuzzy. It makes sense when she says it like that.

forty-one

My parents take Laney to a movie on Sunday. Another entry for *My Memories.* I'm not really interested, so I stay home and practice a bit. But that's not particularly enthralling today, either, even though it probably should be, with my audition at Clark now firmly on the books. I end up abandoning my music and go to my dad's office instead.

I do a quick glance at his desk for the rest of the Kisney-stone fic. *Schrödinger's cat, the unopened box. James is neither dead nor alive until he turns him over and sees.*

But I don't see it. Sheaves of papers crowd the desk—older fics, some paperwork from his agency. One stack sits next to his computer—in the place of honor—and the first words catch my eye.

> Sam was independent, almost to the brink of loneliness.

I pick up the top sheet.

Though I don't think she knew what it was to be lonely. She told me once that she had never met anyone who made her believe that being with another person was better than being alone. I can't express the sadness I felt at hearing that leave the lips of my seventeen-year-old daughter. Sadness, and deep down, in my innermost depths—guilt. Because maybe I had failed her in some way.

But we all felt the call of the beach, of the water, and maybe Sam felt it more than anyone. It wasn't just the ocean. Maybe some part of her knew that it would bring Viv and Jake into her life.

I blink. Sink down into the chair and pull the stack of papers into my lap.

And I keep reading.

The room gets dimmer, but I don't move to turn on a lamp, and that's how my dad finds me. Sitting in his desk chair with the pages spread out around me in the dying light.

I can't imagine what my face looks like, but he knows.

"Sloane—"

I flip back to the first page and hold it up. "*She told me once that she had never met anyone who made her believe that being with another person was better than being alone.*" I struggle to keep my voice even. "I never said that to you."

"I know. Listen—"

"I never said it like that. I said it about love, and it was a question—I just wondered . . . All I did was ask. That doesn't mean—" I look up. "I thought you wanted *Were School*. Ghosts and coffeeshops and stuff. The characters that people want to get behind." The sheet of paper in my hand wavers. "Why are you writing about me?"

"It's not you."

"Viv and Jake? *The quixotic web star and her brooding brother?* If you're going to write us into your opus, at least make it better than the last twenty shitty things you've written."

He doesn't speak.

"Is that why you've been wanting to spend so much time together?" I say. "For material? That's why you've been interested, that's why you wanted to go with us to Birmingham. We're like *Were School* to you. You're writing fic about our lives."

"Listen to me," he says.

"No." I stand up. "It's not—this is so—" I take a deep breath, try-ing to sort myself. "I am not *book fodder.* And neither are they. This isn't . . . You can't publish this."

"I already showed it to Stacey," he says. "She . . . They love it."

"Well, tell them it was a mistake. Tell them you were plagiarizing."

"Sloane—"

"Were you even going to tell me?" I know suddenly how Gabe must have felt, that day in the hallway at their house, after discovering the loss of *The Dream.*

"Of course," he says. "But you have to understand, this isn't a tran-script of your life or your experiences with Vera and Gabe. I'm not saying there wasn't inspiration there, but this is something different, and I think when you read the whole thing—"

"I don't want to read the whole thing."

"I think we need to just sit down and talk this out. We can grab your mother—"

"Yeah, because that'll make it better. You guys are so great at talking things out."

"What is that supposed to mean?"

"It means that I know. About you and Mom. I know what's going on. I'm not oblivious." I can't help it. It comes out before I can think to stop it.

My dad just stares.

"I'm going to Vera's," I say.

He lets me. Just stands there, looking surprised and hurt, and I can't even bring myself to care because I'm still so angry.

I head downstairs and footsteps pound after me, but they're not my dad's. Too light, too quick.

"What did you mean?" Laney says, as I grip the knob to our front door.

"Sorry?"

"What did you mean, 'I know about you and Mom'? What do you know?"

I squeeze my eyes shut briefly and steal a couple of seconds to compose myself, but it's hard with fresh panic welling up inside me.

"You were snooping?" I say, turning around and facing Laney. She's stopped on the second-to-last stair, one hand clutching the railing. She's wearing her favorite TION shirt. A close-up of Kai's face graces the front, beaming at me, big and carefree. But above his disembodied head, Laney's expression is serious.

"Just say what you meant," she says, and it's a direct challenge to what I told Vera on the dock: *I'm a face-value kind of person. I just say what I mean.*

But that's not an all-encompassing truth, is it? I don't do that all the time. I certainly can't do it now.

"It's not nice to eavesdrop" is all I reply.

The resulting Mr. Yuck face is impressive. I think she's leveled up.

"I'm going out," I say. "I'll be back soon." With that, I leave.

forty-two

"It's like we're characters to him," I tell Vera when I get to her house. I've been pacing her room wildly, and now I stop and grab one of my dad's books off her bookshelf, waving it around for emphasis. "It's like we're the kids from fucking *Were School,* and he can just . . . adapt us like that, and it's not right, it's—"

The door cracks open. "Hey, Dad said—"

"Knock please," Vera says.

Gabe looks in and sees me standing, hunched in my anger. I hate being angry. Part of any experience of it I've ever had is fueled by me being mad at the fact that I have to be mad. A train running on a circular track. "What's wrong?"

Too many things to enumerate. The book, my parents, Laney's expression as she stood on the stairs . . . I don't know what to do about that. About any of it.

"Her dad wants to write a book about us," Vera answers for me, picking the biggest and most obvious one, the anger-inducing one, the only one I had composure enough to tell her about when I arrived.

"You and me?" He steps into the room. "Why?"

Vera shrugs. "Apparently we're compelling."

"What did he name our characters?" Gabe asks.

"That's your first thought?" I say. "Seriously?"

"I want a good character name," he says simply.

"I'm Viv, you're Jake," Vera tells him.

"Are we hot? Who's going to play us in the movie?"

I almost smile.

"Aren't you mad?" I say.

"Mad? Why? I mean . . . it's kind of . . . weird, I guess. But also . . . flattering?" He settles down on the end of Vera's bed.

"What I don't get is why it would suddenly matter to you now," Vera says.

"What do you mean, *now*?"

"You're in all your dad's books."

"No, I'm not."

"Maybe not always so recognizable. Maybe it's not, like, a teenage girl with your hair and your eyes and whatever, but . . . Sheila, in *All Is Hope*?"

"The old lady?"

"She makes your jokes," she says. "And Austin, in *Hour by Hour?* The principal's kid? Penelope in *Sand on Our Beach?*" She pulls the book from my loose grip and flips through it until she lands on a particular page, partway through. "*Penny laughed rarely. It was irony, a sheer twist of fate, because she could draw a laugh from anyone, in almost any situation. It was a talent she elevated to an art form, the well-timed joke, but yet she rarely laughed herself. And when you were able to coax one from her—a chuckle, or a snort, or the best of all, a big, throaty, bellowing HA!—it was a victory. The ring of the championship bell at the hometown parade, a resounding win.*"

Vera looks up at me. "Did you not . . . How could you not know?"

"That's not me."

"Yes, it is," Vera says, and her expression is soft. "Of course it is. Penny is quick, she's funny as hell, she's"—she looks down at the page—"*equal parts loyalty and righteous indignation.*" She looks up at me. "Do you really not see it?"

"It's the righteous indignation that makes you so loyal," Gabe says.

I shake my head. "But what about you guys? What about your story?"

"We're not the only people in the world to lose somebody," Vera says. "And anyway"—she closes the book and presses it back into my hands—"I like his books. It would be a privilege."

Gabe's leaning forward, his hands clasped together in front of him. I can just see the small curl of numbers starting on the inside of his left wrist. He gives me a nod, and I nod back, suddenly unable to speak.

It's the reassuring looks in their eyes, combined with the residual betrayal from my dad, combined with the shock of *You're in all your dad's books.* My throat is tight, and my eyes sting.

"Mandy made pot roast for dinner," Vera says. "It was truly terrible. You want some?"

Gabe rolls his eyes. "I'm so glad you're in retail, with pitches like that. You must be the best. 'Here, try this product—it's awful.'"

"Not everyone gets a chance to try the world's worst pot roast, Gabe. It's a once-in-a-lifetime experience."

"'Do you like good food? Here's a thought: Try this terrible food instead.'"

They go on like that for a bit, until I can talk again, and I'm deeply grateful for them both.

forty-three

The semester ends, and Gemma Crane still hasn't called.

I've left three messages. I debate back and forth with Remy about leaving a fourth. He's against it—*Three is thorough. Four is desperate.*

But I can't help but want to push further. We've come too far to give up now. And with everything going on, it's a welcome distraction.

We haven't talked about the book, my dad and me. Laney hasn't asked again about what she overheard. But it feels like we're in a particularly delicate state at my house right now all the same—like one misstep could trip a wire that blows the whole thing up.

It's nice to be out on the Saturday after the last day of classes for the semester. We're hanging around Bree's living room that afternoon with a movie on in the background, basking in the freedom of Christmas break.

That's when my phone rings.

When I look at the screen, my heart leaps. It's Gemma Crane's number.

I step out onto the dock, closing the door quickly behind me. "Hello?"

"Is this Sloane Finch?"

"Yes."

"Hi, Sloane. I'm so sorry to be getting back to you so late, but this is Gemma Crane, and I'm returning your calls about the Laura Fuller painting—"

"Yes. *The Dream.* Do you have it?"

"We do," she says.

I exhale.

I text Remy, and he comes outside. It's cold out, overcast with a thickness to the air that hints of rain, but we stand on Bree's dock anyway. "You're certain?" he says. "Like completely and totally certain?"

"It's the one," I say. "She said it's in her client's public gallery, but it's going to be moved to his apartment in the city."

"That's bad, right?"

"How is that bad? Do you hear me? She has it. They have it. The actual painting."

"But is it for sale?"

That's the sticking point, but I'm not deterred. "Not . . . technically. She said she didn't think he'd want to sell, but she'd have to follow up."

"So . . . what do we do?"

I've already thought about this. "I have my audition for Clark next month. I'll go when I'm there and talk to her. Try to get it back."

"Do you really think they'll sell it, though?"

"Of course. They just have to hear the story. If I go there and tell her everything . . . they have to give it back."

Remy looks less certain.

"Why aren't you excited?" I say. "This is—it's a breakthrough!

Instead of finding a place where the painting *has* been, we've found where it *actually is* right now at this exact moment! Which means we can go and get it!"

"I just think maybe you underestimate the go-and-get-it part."

"We've come so far, though."

"Yeah, but what's to say Gemma's client is going to care how far we've come?"

"What are you guys talking about?"

I look up. Vera and Gabe are approaching.

I glance at Remy as the two of them reach us.

"Nothing," he says, and twin stares call bullshit right back at us. It's almost impressive, their coordination.

So I take a deep breath, because this is it. It's not as good as handing it right to them, but we're closer to the painting than ever before, and I'm too excited to keep it from them any longer: "We've been trying to track down the painting. That one that got sold?"

Gabe blinks. "That's . . . that's what you guys have been doing?"

"Yeah."

"But . . . why?"

"For you. For both of you. I know how much it meant to you, and it didn't seem right . . . hanging in someone else's house, or their waiting room, or whatever. It belongs with you guys."

Gabe is still staring, his lips parted slightly, looking at me with something like incredulity, but also some kind of . . . I don't even know. Fondness, maybe.

"We started here, with Meira, and then it went to this doctor's office in Mobile, but then this old guy bought it . . . It's been kind of ridiculous. But we finally tracked it down, and I'm going to go get it. It's in New York. We wanted it to be a surprise. But . . . this is okay, too, right?

Maybe we could all go together. I think my dad would get us plane tickets if you get James from *Were School* to tweet him or something."

I look to Vera for the first time, and the expression on her face is the opposite of Gabe's.

"Sloane," she says when our eyes meet, and she looks . . . sad, and weirdly forlorn. "Shit. I wish you would've told me."

"What is it?"

Vera just shakes her head. "I wish you had told me."

"What?" Gabe turns to Vera.

She takes a breath, looks out at the water, and says haltingly, "Mandy didn't sell it by accident. I put it in that pile. With the others for Meira. I knew . . . I knew she would take it. I . . . wanted her to take it."

Gabe doesn't speak.

"I couldn't look at it." Vera's eyes shine, looking between the two of us. "I didn't like it being around. Knowing that . . . knowing—"

"Knowing what?" Gabe says, his voice low.

"Don't be mad." She means it for both of us, but I'm not mad. More confused than anything, and I don't know what to say. But Gabe does.

"You knew. What it meant to her. You knew. How could you—"

"We failed," Vera says. "We did. And I couldn't look at it anymore. I didn't like knowing that it was there, okay? And you didn't even realize it was gone. You never even went in there anyway. So just . . . stop looking at me like that."

He does. He walks away a few feet and then turns back. "You're so selfish—do you know that?"

"Hey," I speak, finally. "Come on. That's not fair."

"Not fair," he says to Vera, gesturing widely to me. "See, she said 'not fair.' Not 'not true.' Because she knows it's true. We all know it."

"Don't talk for me," I say.

"Don't butt in where you have no business," he replies, and it stings. So different from that look just moments before, soft and disbelieving.

"Whoa," Remy says, "maybe we should all just chill out for a second and—"

"I have business," I say over him, even though I know it's probably not true. "You made it my business."

Gabe's not going to let me get away with that. He can spot an inconsistency from a mile away. "Really," he says. "So I asked you to look for the painting. I asked you to go to Meira's in the first place. I asked you, that first night, to take down Mason Pierce. I stood there and asked you to your face to do all that stuff. Did I? For real?" He stares, unblinking, and I feel . . . flushed, and embarrassed, in a way that I absolutely hate.

"She's not selfish" is all I say.

"What do you call it, then?" He turns to Vera. "All you care about is your girlfriend, and taking pictures of yourself, and what strangers on the Internet think about you. Those three things. You wrap yourself up in them and you pretend like it doesn't even matter that she's gone, like you don't even care, and that is fucking selfish, Vera."

I barely register when Aubrey and Bree approach. "What's going on?" Bree asks, at the same time Aubrey says, "What's wrong?" looking at Vera.

Vera is crying, big fat tears rolling down her cheeks, and I can't take it. It's not even remotely true, what Gabe's saying—it's like he doesn't even know her at all—and suddenly it's like with Mason in the kitchen, except things are flipped now. Everything is upside down, backwards. Gabe is the Mason and Vera is the Gabe and I'm still me, the hopeless, idiotic defender. I still feel that switch flip, that circuit close inside me, and I open my mouth and the words just pour out, as they so often do.

"You want to talk about selfish?" I fix Gabe with a stare. "Do you realize how hard you are to be around because nothing—no one—measures up? Nothing makes you happy—everything is fucking . . . *deficient* in some way. And it's exhausting. You know you don't have the market cornered on grief, right? You know Vera's mom died, too?"

It's quiet. Except it's not. There's the lap of the water against the dock, the creak of the boat as it bobs, and a little farther off, a car puttering down 30A. But between us, it's quiet. Gabe stares down at the boards beneath our feet, Vera cries silently, and I stand, fists clenched by my sides, my heart racing.

"You know what?" he says finally. "You know what I thought before?"

I don't speak.

"I thought, maybe you never had good friends before because no one appreciated you. Maybe they didn't *get* you, how great you are, but now I get it. It's not everyone else. It's you. You act like you care, you put on this show of being there and listening and—tucking us in, and it's . . . bullshit. You act like you're all hard on the outside but secretly, underneath, you're all fluffy and warm and caring. But that's the lie, Sloane, because underneath that, you are fucking cold. And I get why you didn't have any friends. I understand. Because what do you do with someone like that? How close can you get before you realize there's nothing to get close to?"

I look at Vera, almost involuntarily. I look at her so she can tell him he's wrong. But she won't meet my eyes.

"Great," I say finally. "Yeah. Because this is so awesome. Having friends is the best. You guys have it all figured out. It's not the least bit fucked that you keep secrets from each other or talk behind each other's backs."

"I think maybe everybody's a little riled up," Remy says calmly, ever the voice of reason, but we're way past that now. "Maybe we should all go back inside."

"Yeah, or maybe you should ask Gabe why Aubrey broke up with you. Since he knew this whole time?"

"Sloane." It's Bree who speaks, still standing at the end of the dock with Aubrey. I turn my cruel light their way, the fucking Eye of Sauron, scorching everything in its path.

"Just for the record, no one gives a shit which celebrities have talked to you on the Internet, Bree."

Not good, Cecily says in my mind. *Not good not good not good.*

And that's it. That's all I have left. Before anyone can respond, my legs jerk to life, carrying me away. Past everyone, down the dock, through the trees, around the house. I get my bike, and I pedal, hard and fast, down the road and out onto 30A.

Sam was independent, almost to the brink of loneliness. But I don't think she knew what it was to be lonely.

But she did. She did. And she liked it. Alone didn't always mean lonely, but sometimes it did, and even then, she reveled in it.

Lunches in the music room. Afternoons reading in the park. Loneliness was a kind of wanting, but it was also this incredible freedom. Not having to rely on anyone or have anyone rely on her. No one to disappoint or be disappointed by. Alone was good and comforting and dependable. Maybe Sam was a little bit broken, but maybe it was everyone else who needed fixing.

My dad would never write that. He doesn't know her like I do.

The water flies by me on either side, the wind roaring in my ears, and I flash on that night in the nursery with Gabe, telling him that he's not alone. Wanting him to believe it. How was that possible? How could I want for someone the opposite of what I wanted for myself?

I'm one big contradiction. The sky is growing darker, which couldn't be more cliché—but I guess whatever type of weather it is would have been a cliché. The beautiful sunset mocking my distress. The storm clouds mirroring my inner anguish. Nothing is new, everything is hackneyed, the cake is a lie, and I just don't have it in me to give a fuck anymore.

The rain starts, and a sob escapes me—I can't help it. The peaks of Opal's tallest houses rise above the trees in the distance as I pass the inlet, and that's when my bike skids out, I swerve, hit the guardrail, and the earth upends.

forty-four

I don't black out. That would've been too pat. People in books and movies are always conveniently blacking out. I take a real issue with *Nancy Drew* books, because Nancy sustained more head injuries than all of the NFL combined, and she never once went for a CT scan.

I'm in a patch of gravel, in an embankment off the road leading down to the water. I can see my bike out of the corner of my eye, the back fender bent badly and the tire, held up off the ground, still spinning.

My phone flew out of my pocket. I spot it a few feet down the embankment. The screen is cracked.

I shift to a sitting position. My whole left side hurts. It takes time, but eventually I pull myself to my feet and pick up my phone. It doesn't light up.

It's three more miles home, and it's raining, and I think perhaps that this is what I deserve. So I do all I can do. I leave the bike, and I start to walk home.

★ ★ ★

"If you really love Sarah," Ruthie said, looking up at her father, her brown eyes wide and trusting, "how could you say those things?"

Jack wrapped his arms around his daughter, resting his chin in the crook of her neck for a moment. It couldn't stay this way forever; he knew that. She wouldn't be a little girl forever, and there was a time on the horizon when he would have to stand on the sidelines and watch as someone else held her close. When someone else would be her comfort, and she would be theirs in turn.

"I didn't mean what I said," he said after a long moment. "Sometimes . . . sometimes when people are angry, they say things they don't mean."

"You were angry at Sarah?"

"Yes." A beat. "No."

He turned Ruthie around in his arms. Together, they stared out over the water.

"I was angry at myself," he said. The painful truth.

"What are you reading?" Laney says from the doorway of my room.

I hold up the book so she can see the cover.

"I liked that movie," she says. " 'Cept for the dead dog."

"Gotta have a dead dog." I turn down the corner of the page. "Or else it's not a proper novel."

She steps into my room. "Which stuffie do you want?"

I only have two, sitting on the shelf above my desk. "I don't need one."

She just stares.

"Teddy," I say. She crosses the room and plucks the bear down.

"You could've named him something original," she says, tucking Teddy by my side under the blankets and then lying across the bottom of my bed. She pillows her head on her arms and just looks at me, expectantly.

"What?"

"Just waiting."

"For what?"

"For you to say why you're sad."

I don't even know where to start. *Sad* is just the tip of the iceberg.

I didn't tell my parents about the fight when I got home that afternoon. I came through the door, soaking wet, clutching my arm and crying, and instead of saying "I exploded my friend group," I sobbed, "I fell off my bike," since it was the more immediate and fixable of the two problems.

They took me to urgent care, and I got bandaged, wrapped up, and sent home with an order for rest and Tylenol.

And now here I am in bed, with Laney's wide eyes turned on me, questioning.

"I fell off my bike," I say.

Laney isn't buying it for one second. "You're mopey," she says. "And not just wrecked-bike mopey, but like legit mopey." She blinks up at me. "Don't say you're not. Just say why."

"My friends are mad at me."

"Why?"

"Because I was mean to them."

"So say you're sorry."

"I don't . . . I don't think they'll forgive me."

"Beg them," she says, and then snorts. "Never mind. You'd be terrible at that."

"What would you do?" I ask, even though I'm nearly twice as old as she is, and it should be the other way around; I should be the one dispensing advice to her. Maybe when she's my age, and I'm an adult. But even then, I have a feeling Laney will still be the wiser of us two.

"I would say sorry," she says simply. "A for-real sorry. We learned that in class. Not like 'I'm sorry your feelings were hurt,' because that's a fake sorry. Say, 'I'm sorry *I* hurt your feelings,' because that's for real. Mrs. Hutchens calls it 'taking ownership.'"

"Mrs. Hutchens sounds smart."

"She is." Laney pokes my leg. "So am I."

"Well, I already knew that, didn't I?"

Laney scoots up the bed, lying down next to me. "You should read to me," she says, and rests her head on the pillow next to mine. I kiss her temple. Then I open the book back up and begin to read.

forty-five

Laney falls asleep in my room that evening. I don't bother moving her, but I'm not tired yet, so I cover her with a blanket, switch off the light, and head downstairs. My mom has the TV on low in the living room. I settle out on the front porch and consider finishing *Sand on Our Beach*, but I can't bring myself to crack the cover again. Laney dropped off right before our least favorite part—the death of Avery the puppy.

So I just gaze out at the trees across the street, the little house tucked back behind them, and after a while my dad comes outside.

He picks up the book from the chair next to mine and looks at the cover. It's the movie tie-in version, with Dex Finnegan and a beautiful actress on the cover, foreheads touching, backlit and glowing.

"Can I ask you something?" I say.

"You can ask me whatever you want, Sloane."

"Why did Avery have to die?" I look up at him. "And don't say tragic irony."

My dad takes a deep breath. "Well, I guess Avery had to die," he says, "because Sarah didn't."

"So death has to be in there somehow. Can't leave an Everett Finch novel unscathed. Someone has to bite the big one."

"No." He pauses. "No." I think he is going to say more, but instead he just sits down next to me.

"So why, then? Why couldn't they both make it?"

He settles back into his chair. "I guess I was trying to demonstrate the idea that something perfect can end, and something broken can endure. There are no guarantees. None."

"Sarah's not broken," I mumble. "Being sick doesn't make you broken."

"I know that," he says. "Do you see what I mean, though?"

I nod.

"I would've liked it better if the puppy didn't die," I say. "Sometimes . . . maybe sometimes people would rather have the puppy live than have something deep, you know?"

Now he nods. "The majority of fics have happy endings. Did you know that? It fascinates me. They can nominate the darkest and the bleakest and the saddest stuff for awards, and maybe it's the best, but deep down I feel like something of that supposed quality doesn't hold a candle to the feeling you get when everything works out in the end. You feel that click in your chest; you feel something settle in you. That's worth a thousand tragedies to me. That's . . . that's something I've learned recently."

He looks over at me.

"This story means a lot to me. This new one? I need it. More than I've ever . . ." He shakes his head. "I've been having a tough time of it lately, in case you couldn't tell." He says this without a hint of irony. It's not a joke. It's the way my dad thinks. That his suffering is his own, that he is heroically stoic. "This is the one. This is going to turn things around."

I think about seeing them in the hallway, my mom and dad, standing close, not out of love but out of sheer frustration: *If you're a writer who doesn't write, then what are you?*

A human being. A law-abiding citizen. An excellent cook but a terrible driver, a three-time winner of the Bishop Dubourg homecoming weekend chili cook-off (and don't you forget it). A Jickey shipper. A father. Sloane and Laney's dad.

It's quiet. Finally he says, "What happened today? Besides your spill. Would you . . . tell me if something else happened?"

"No."

"Because you're mad at me? Because of the book?"

"Are you going to publish it?"

He doesn't speak, which is his way of saying yes.

I shut my eyes. I don't know what to say. How to say it. I love him so much, but I don't understand how to reach him. Like Gabe standing on the dock, the shutters closing across his eyes. Like Vera, crying silently. Close enough to touch, but I couldn't *reach* them, any of them, and maybe the distance isn't them at all. Maybe it's me. I think of Ella from elementary school, of our after-school good-bye ritual that eventually ended, so gradually that I couldn't even tell you when. We just . . . stopped doing it. And then we stopped hanging out. I always thought she had drifted away. But what if it was me? What if I was the one responsible for the distance?

"I'm not mad at you," I say after a while, because what else is there to say?

He nods. "You know how much I love you. Right?"

"Yeah." It comes out rough.

"Good." He stands and puts the book down next to me. Leans in and kisses the top of my head. Then he goes back inside.

forty-six

I read a lot of fic the following day.

I can't help but dive into one particular subset: soul-mate AUs. My dad is against them: *It takes away their autonomy. It lessens the impact of them choosing each other, because they never really had a choice.* But I disagree. I want that automatic lightning bolt or realignment of the world when they see each other for the first time, or when their corresponding marks match up, when they realize that they're meant for each other. I want that guarantee. The road might be rocky, but ultimately, no one's going to change their mind; no one's going to mess it up irreparably. They can't. It's laced into their DNA.

I read fic. I lie around. And I try to reconcile myself to the fact that I effectively squashed all of my friendships in one spectacular go.

I don't take Laney's advice. I can't. I don't know how to do it, which makes me feel even worse. Maybe I'm not capable of taking ownership.

It's late in the afternoon when there's a knock at the door. Laney gets it, since I'm huddled up in a blanket nest on the couch.

"Is Sloane here?" I hear Vera ask, and she's already pushing through the door, ducking around Laney. She sees me on the couch, and her eyes widen and very quickly get shiny. "You didn't text me back."

"What are you doing here?"

"You didn't text me back," she repeats. "You weren't answering your phone, and then *I saw your fucking bike.*"

She flings herself at me, hugging me fiercely, though favoring my right side. "God, Sloane," she says into my hair. "You could've been dead."

"I'm sorry. I would've—my phone died, and I . . . I just . . ." I shake my head.

"What?"

"I wasn't sure . . . if you guys would even want to talk to me."

"There's not a universe in which I wouldn't want to talk to you."

"Serial-killer universe?"

"We would both be serial killers. We would meet on the job and team up."

She says it with such sureness, looking at me with this ferocious loyalty and unshed tears in her eyes. It breaks something open in me.

I lean against her. Hide my face in her shoulder so maybe she can't tell that I'm crying.

"I'm sorry," I say, muffled, and I could go on forever. *I'm the worst. I don't know what I'm doing half the time. I don't know what I'm saying most of the time. You were all better off without me but I can't go back to how it was without you.*

That's it, really. Once the dust settled, once I inadvertently threw myself in a pile of gravel, I saw it for how it really was: It was fine enough to convince myself that I was fine enough alone. But it was a lie. I need Vera. She's my best friend.

"It's okay," she says, shifting to wrap her arms around me.

"It's not," I mumble. "I exploded the group."

"You didn't."

I did. At least, I exploded my relationships with them. It was almost impressive. There has to be some kind of an award for alienating that many people you care about in one outing.

"I'm sorry, too," she says.

"For what?"

"I just stood there. I didn't say anything, and I should have."

I pull back and wipe my eyes on the back of my arm. "How could he say that stuff to you, though?"

"It's different with a sibling."

"I have a sibling."

"Laney's so much younger, though. It's not the same."

It isn't, I guess. I still remember being a little kid by the shore, jumping shallow swells alone. Looking back to see Mom and Dad under the umbrella, two pairs of sunglasses, two sets of watchful eyes—though I always just assumed their eyes were on me. Maybe they were on each other.

Then Laney came, and suddenly I had a friend at the shoreline, a tiny fist to clutch as we were gently knocked by the breaking waves. *Don't you let her go*, my mother would say when Laney was a toddler—*Do not let go of her hand*—but one time I did, not on purpose, but it still wells up in me every now and then, the surprise and fear seeing one of those swells crash over her. My mom, rushing to the shoreline, wrenching her up, Laney sputtering and then crying.

I told you not to let go! my mom cried, but she was more scared than mad, and I didn't know which one of us she was addressing. Laney threw up in the sand by our umbrella, and my mom made me bury it with a plastic shovel.

I still flash on it sometimes: jumping that wave, Laney's slick hand slipping through my grasp. She doesn't even remember it. It seems strange sometimes that that's even possible, how something that was big to me—huge to me—doesn't even exist in her memory. I wonder if my parents feel that way, about all the stuff that happened to them before we were around.

But Vera and Gabe were always together. Bound up in utero, out in the world at the same time. Vera is right—I don't know what that's like. To have someone with that kind of shared history, that kind of closeness. Maybe it makes you understand each other better. Even in the bad times. Where to hit hardest. What will hurt most. But also how to fix it, maybe.

"I don't know what to say to him," I say. "I'm not his sibling."

Vera's gaze slides toward the front door, like she already knows, and when Gabe bursts through it a second later, she just smiles.

"What the hell," he says, and he's out of breath. He waves his phone around. "You can't just text me and say something bad happened to Sloane and then not follow up on that."

"She's okay," Vera says, though I'm sure in this moment I don't look especially okay. Bruised and puffy and red-eyed. Maybe just medium okay.

He looks at me, assessing. I hold up my hand. "Sprained wrist. Otherwise intact."

"What happened?"

259

"She hit a guardrail and flew through the air," Laney says, sticking her head into the room. "Papa took her to the hospital."

"Don't snoop," I say.

"Okay." She comes into the room and sits down in my dad's recliner.

Vera is clearly amused, but when I look back at Gabe, his expression is serious.

"Are you okay?"

"Laney, let's get snacks," Vera says.

"I'm not hungry."

"I am. Why don't you show me what you've got?"

Laney looks as if she knows exactly what Vera is doing, but she resigns herself to it. "We have Dunkaroos," she offers, and stands.

"I love Dunkaroos." Vera winks at me and then follows Laney into the kitchen.

"I thought you were mad," Gabe says when they're gone, shaking his head, his eyes bright. "We—Vera texted you, and I thought you weren't answering because you were mad, not because you were in the fucking hospital."

"I fell off my bike," I say. "It wasn't serious."

"Laney just said you hit a guardrail and flew through the air!"

"Laney is prone to gross exaggeration."

"You have a splinty thing! On your wrist!"

"It's just a precaution; I don't even have to wear it for that long."

If I had to catalog Gabe's expression at this precise moment, I would say it was something between fear and exasperation. But there's also . . . there's still a fondness to it, I think. Or maybe that's just wishful thinking.

"Why are you even talking to me?" I say.

And now he looks . . . hurt?

"Not—not like that. I just mean . . . I was like the world's biggest dick to you."

"I thought bigger was better."

"I was like the world's smallest dick to you."

He shakes his head. "I was a smaller dick. I was a micropenis."

I smile—I can't help it. "Yeah, no. Everything I said was . . ." I shake my head. "I'm sorry."

"Me too."

I want to say that I didn't mean what I said, but I think that's a cop-out. I meant it in the moment; I meant it to hurt. And it was selfish and mean. So I just tell Gabe the truth: "It's not true, what I said. You know that, right?"

He just looks at me, and he's about to speak when—

"Do you guys want some Dunkaroos?" Laney asks, and Vera appears behind her, mouthing *Sorry!*

"Sure," I say. Laney brings me a package, and the moment is over.

forty-seven

It's not until late into the evening that I bother to plug my phone in. It actually lights up when I do, the wallpaper image fractured but present all the same. It buzzes instantly with messages, a number in quick succession from Vera, shortly after I left their house.

> will you come back so we can talk?
> I'm sorry I just stood there like an idiot
> Gabe didn't mean what he said
> please answer

One missed call later that afternoon. And a voice mail that evening:

"Hey, so I know you're not answering, and maybe you're mad . . . Okay, I know you're mad. But can we just talk? I'm sorry . . . I'm sorry about the painting, and Gabe, and everything. He's sorry, too. Will you just answer?"

Then another text from this afternoon: Screw it I'm coming over

I stare at the messages for a while. Vera, being a better friend than me. Leading by example.

So I sit, and I look, and then I send out some messages of my own.
Bree answers first:

> It's all good
>
> Guess the drama gets to everyone eventually lololol

I don't hear from Remy or Aubrey, though. I consider sending apology messages again, but I figure it's best not to be aggressive in your apologizing. Gabe mentioned earlier that he and Remy had talked, and that things were okay between them . . . but maybe they aren't quite as okay between the two of us yet.

Then the holidays come, and it's easy to get swept up in family stuff—shopping and traditions and whatnot. I hardly even see Vera, who's all wrapped up in Tash while she's home. Without Vera and with Dodge's closed for the holidays, I don't see Gabe. I don't get any texts from him, either. My in-box hasn't been this quiet since I moved here.

But then, a couple of days before New Year's, there's a knock at the door. To my surprise, it's Remy.

"Hey," I say, instead of *What are you doing here?*—but I suppose that part is implied.

"*Were School* season five starts tonight" is his reply.

Of course it does. My dad had only mentioned it a dozen or so times in the past week.

"Are you . . . Did you get my message?"

"Yeah," he says. "Sorry I didn't answer. I just . . ." He shakes his head. "I was thinking. And I realized I shouldn't have asked you to get involved with the Aubrey thing. Because you were right. It's not a thing anymore, and I need to let it go."

"Did you guys talk?"

He nods.

I want to ask if they're good. But I'm not sure if it's any of my business. So I just nod back.

"*Were School* time?" he asks, and I have the incredible urge to hug him, but instead I just raise one hand up for a high five.

"Let's do this."

Frank hosts a party for New Year's Eve, but I don't go. I stay in with my family instead, and we watch the ball drop on TV.

Vera posts a picture of her and Tash kissing while wearing shiny cardboard New Year's hats, and then she sends me a version that must've been taken right after, where they're both making funny faces at the camera.

Before I can answer, she sends another picture. It's just the side of Gabe's face, looking away.

Grumpy refused to wear a hat, she says.

I don't know what to say to that, but my phone buzzes again a few minutes later.

I think he misses you.

I'm right here is all I say.

I know, and we're here. Hence the missing.

They're playing "New York, New York" on TV. Laney has fallen asleep, leaning against my mom on the couch.

I hover over Gabe's name for a moment in my phone. And then I type a new message: Happy New Year.

Did you just text him? He just smiled.

How do you know the two things are related? I reply.

Oh my god, you did. He's answering now.

Vera I don't need a play-by-play, I say.

I think he just hit send.

I can't help but smile as a new message comes in from Gabe: Happy New Year.

And then from Vera: What did he say? Was it lame? Was it just 'happy new year'?

Why are you so invested in this? I ask.

Because I am.

Go kiss your girlfriend, I say.

Gladly, she replies, and then sends me a picture of her planting one on Tash.

forty-eight

Auditions come before I know it.

My parents take me to the airport and stand at security, watching me go through. I wave at them over my shoulder and then head to the gate.

I'll take a flight to Atlanta and go from there to New York, where I'll stay with my aunt Brenda. Dad's sister. Aunt Brenda works downtown for an insurance company and lives on the East Side. She's divorced with no kids and has been seeing a guy from work for the past couple of years, who she refers to as her *beau*. Every time I see her, she asks me, without fail, if I have any new *beaux* myself.

I'm waiting at the gate, and I'm bored enough to consider starting a Heartmark account, just so I can winkydink Vera, or whatever they call it, when someone asks, "Is anybody sitting there?"

My head snaps up.

Vera and Gabe grin at me. Double-time twin magic.

"What are you doing here?" They both have backpacks, and Vera's holding one of those puffy neck pillows.

"What does it look like?" She sits down next to me. "We're going with you."

"How?"

"Well, we were planning on taking the airplane that's about to arrive," Gabe says.

I roll my eyes. "No, but I mean like, how?"

"We have jobs," Vera says. "We bought tickets. Your dad told us what flight you'd be on. And he booked us a hotel room, because apparently sending Brenda three teenagers was 'unconscionable.' He already called her to tell her the change of plans. And he told me to tell you"—she looks up at the ceiling, as if trying to remember exactly—" 'No funny business. Well, maybe a little. But use your judgment when it comes to funny business.' "

This is a lot of information all at once, and all I can come up with is "You're coming with me," even though that's already been established.

"I think your dad wanted a good ending for his book," Vera says, smiling big.

I audition at the Clark School of Music on Friday.

It's a beautiful little school—you could barely call it a campus, just a couple of buildings strung together on the Upper East Side. It feels cozy. Lived-in. And also undeniably . . . artistic.

After a morning spent touring the place, meeting with a financial-aid officer, and chatting with a couple of the voice faculty members, I wait in the hallway for the audition coordinator to summon me. I stand and hold my music against my chest, looking at a big bulletin board full of lesson schedules and fliers for conferences and master classes. A duo is practicing in the room nearest to me, and I can hear their scales—violin and piano, up and down. They warm up and then begin a chamber piece.

It all seems . . . like a wonderful little music bubble, warm and inviting, and all at once, I realize what hangs in the balance.

I try not to care. I really do. I am impartial. I'm the Switzerland of college auditions, because it doesn't matter to me one way or another. It doesn't.

I rub my hands against my pants. They're suddenly sweaty.

The coordinator comes for me, takes my music, and leads me into the room.

It's not huge, just a studio with a grand piano, where the accompanist is seated. Five professors sit in seats lining the wall by the door. Among them is a woman with cropped hair and wire-rimmed glasses who I met with this morning. She smiles at me and gestures for me to join the accompanist. And the audition process begins.

It does not start well.

The accompanist has to start over. We barely make it six bars. Because my tempo is off, I'm ahead of the music—

"Just give it another try," the woman with the glasses says kindly.

But this has rattled me. I'm rattled.

I make it partway through the piece. They stop me and ask me to move on to the next. My hands are shaking now, my throat sticking—the words feel like cotton in my mouth—

But I hold one trembling hand in the other, and I smile at them when I finish, and the page of sight-reading exercises they hand me only rattles a little as I hold it and attempt to work my way through. I manage to respond when they ask me what my goals are as a musician, what I hope to achieve in my undergraduate career—though for the life of me I wouldn't be able to repeat what I said. I probably wouldn't be able to recall a single word.

They thank me when it's done, and I thank them and exit the little studio—the tiny, perfect jewel of a studio—with my music clutched to my chest, and all I want to do is get away, far, far away . . .

Gabe is waiting downstairs, sitting on a bench in the lobby surrounded by four or five shopping bags that are definitely Vera's, but she's nowhere in sight. He stands when he sees me.

"How'd it go?" he says.

"I have to pee," I blurt.

I duck into the restroom off the lobby, and as soon as I push through the door, I think maybe I've made a mistake—Vera could be in here—but it's blessedly empty. So I wait an amount of time that is long enough for me to get it together but also short enough to be socially acceptable in terms of time spent in a bathroom. A few hot, stinging tears, a few deep breaths. I wash my face, and then I emerge.

Gabe is leaning against the wall across from the door. He straightens up, grasping the array of shopping bags.

I almost turn back into the bathroom, but he stops me with a step forward.

"What happened?"

"I don't know," I say, because it's the truth. How could I have blown it like that? After all that practice, all those times before when I did it effortlessly, without even thinking—pure, beautiful, bright, *automatic*—why did it fail me now when it mattered? Because it does matter. I look at the poster on the wall behind Gabe's head, advertising this semester's opera scenes: a gorgeous girl in an eighteenth century–style dress, gesturing artfully, her expression coy.

It does matter.

"Where's Vera?"

"She went back to the last store. Grabbed the wrong size or something. Are you . . . Do you want to sit down?"

I want him to stop looking at me like that. That open concern. And I want to stop the words from bubbling up, but I can't.

"Maybe you were right," I say.

"About what?"

I mean, no one loves anyone that much. Right? No one . . . feels it like that.

People absolutely feel it like that. Jesus, Sloane. Of course they do.

I blink against the tears gathering in my eyes.

"Maybe I am cold."

"Do you want my jacket?"

"That's not—not like that. Like what you said at Bree's, that underneath, maybe I'm—" The words catch in my throat.

Gabe grimaces. "Sloane, I was being a jerk—"

"No, maybe I am. But maybe underneath that is another layer, like a . . . parfait, or the chocolate bit at the bottom of a Drumstick. Maybe that bit is the fact that I don't know how to care about something without caring too much. And that could be a good thing, right, but what if it's not? What if it cuts you off from other things? What if you're afraid to—" To commit to the thing that you love. To the detriment of everything else. *It scared me*, Aubrey had said at the winter formal, and I understand that now.

Gabe doesn't speak. He is the same boy who stared down Mason Pierce in the kitchen what feels like ages ago. Although the situation is vastly different, I know that same patience can be wielded against me. I know that he can wait me out.

But the moisture in my eyes is at maximum capacity—one blink or less will see its fall—and I don't want Gabe to see that.

"Would you just turn around?" I say.

He looks at me one beat more. But he doesn't ask why. He just turns around and faces the poster girl, still artfully frozen mid-recitative.

I mash my palms against my eyes. "It didn't go great," I say after a moment.

He laughs—not unkindly, just a gentle huff. "I kind of figured."

"Don't tell Vera."

"Why not?"

"I'm trying to divide my problems between you. Vera gets personal and you get professional."

He doesn't reply, but I can imagine his brow furrowing.

"I just don't want to make it a thing," I say.

"You can make it a thing. You're allowed."

I shake my head, even though he can't see me.

"There'll be more auditions," he says quietly.

"Maybe."

"There will."

"How do you know?"

"I just do."

It's almost too much. The blind faith in my abilities. It threatens another wave of tears. But luckily, Gabe's phone dings then, and mine buzzes in my coat pocket right after.

It's Vera: Where are you guys???

I peer around the corner. Vera's standing by the lobby entrance, but her eyes are on her phone.

"Shall we?" I say to Gabe, giving my eyes a final swipe.

"Are you sure you're—"

"Yeah. Let's go."

Vera is wearing puffy earmuffs and a big scarf wrapped around her neck, and she's holding yet another shopping bag.

"You guys go shopping?" I ask, winding my own scarf around my neck.

"How did it go? How do you feel?" Vera says, grabbing my arm.

"Yes," Gabe replies. "We went to a few different stores."

"Gabe, no one cares where we went," Vera says as we exit the building.

"I care deeply," I say. "I'd like to hear a list of these stores in alphabetical order. Along with the items tried on at each store."

"Sloane, I swear to God." Vera hangs on my arm as we start down the street. "Tell me how it went."

"It went well." It comes out perfectly even.

"Of course it went well. I knew it would. Didn't I say it would?"

"Only twelve or thirteen hundred times," Gabe says. "Would the Gap be under *G* for *Gap* or *T* for *the*?"

"*G*," I say. "Gap comma the."

"Sometimes I want to punch you both," Vera says, but she's barely containing a smile.

forty-nine

We go to see Gemma Crane.

Her gallery—or her client's gallery, I guess—is down in Chelsea. It's a big white room with a tall ceiling and shiny wood floors. High dormer windows run along one side, and a big stand-alone wall that doesn't reach the ceiling divides the space.

And there's art, of course. A series of abstract black-and-white paper cuttings. A large sculpture of a girl in a flowered dress, posing as *The Thinker*. A huge photograph—must've been six feet by six feet—a full-color close-up of two tongues touching. They are extended, clearly emerging from a pair of mouths, but the mouths themselves have been whited out, so the tongues stand alone, independent of their owners.

"Eclectic," I say, and Gabe snorts. Vera takes a picture of the tongues, which I know is either going to Tash or onto the Internet, or both.

Gabe glances at me while Vera types away. He has been shooting me these looks since we left Clark, and it's simultaneously annoying and endearing. I want to tell him I'm not going to break in two, but at the same time, I don't want to talk about it ever again.

"Okay, we have to pick out which piece we'd be if we were a piece of art," Vera says after disseminating the photo. She slips her phone into her pocket and turns in a circle, taking in the room.

"You," I say, pointing to the *Thinker* girl. Vera makes a face and looks to Gabe.

"You," he agrees.

Vera considers it for a moment, and then nods. "Okay. I can see it."

Next we look for me.

"This one," Vera says. It's on the other side of the freestanding wall. A series of four canvases hang in a row, evenly spaced. Each is a shade of blue, getting progressively lighter. A single white chalk line runs across them. It's not a straight line: It slopes up a little, down, wavers, and ends flat across the middle of the last canvas, which is a blue so light that the line just barely stands out against it.

"This is you," Vera says.

"A wavering line."

"It's not, though," Gabe says. "It doesn't break from canvas to canvas. Even when you can barely see it, you know it's still there."

Vera nods. "It's perfect."

We all contemplate the canvases.

"I don't know, I think I'm the tongues," I say.

Vera laughs and then leads us over to a chair near the exit. "This one is Gabe."

"That's not art," he says. "That's a plastic folding chair. A security person probably sits there."

Vera squeezes his arm. "You help people."

"Like this humble folding chair helps ease people's foot pain," I add.

"Not fair, though, why do you guys get to be art and I have to be a chair that's not art?"

"Anything can be art," Vera says.

The click of heels against the hardwood floors interrupts us. I turn as a young woman approaches. She's "smartly dressed," as Aunt Brenda would say, and very pretty. I wonder briefly if she has many *beaux*.

"Can I help you?"

"Yeah, is that chair secretly art?" Gabe says.

The woman doesn't smile, but there's something alight in her eyes. "I'm sorry, no."

"See?" Gabe says to us, indignant.

"Is there anything else I can do for you today?" the woman asks.

Vera and Gabe both look to me, and I realize that I'm in charge of this expedition.

"Um, we're here to see Gemma Crane—are you her?"

"I am. What can I help you with?"

I felt okay, felt in charge when we were in pursuit of this. At Dr. Mark's. In the wilderness in Alabama. But suddenly, now, here, in the middle of this gallery, I feel . . . seventeen. "I'm Sloane Finch," I say. "We talked on the phone?" Gemma just blinks. "About the Laura Fuller painting?"

"Yes," she says, comprehension dawning. "Yes, we did."

"Is it here?"

She purses her lips. "I—no, I'm sorry. I mentioned on the phone that—"

"That it was going to be moved, yeah, but we were hoping that we could have a look at it. And we . . ." We're so close; it's almost in our reach. I just have to go for it. "We want to buy it," I say.

"I mentioned to you, I didn't think my client was interested in selling—"

"It's an important piece, though, to Vera and Gabe. Laura Fuller is their mom. She's . . . She passed away. This was one of her last paintings."

"Oh," she says, and looks at us for a moment. I think she's going to say more, but she just says it again, softer: "Oh."

"It shouldn't have been sold—it was a mistake," I continue. "We'd like to get it back."

Gemma's brow furrows, and she looks to the left, where unfortunately, the portrait of the tongues is hanging. Then she clasps her hands together. "I'm so sorry, I don't think . . ." I can tell she's trying to look neutral, to stay professional. I appreciate her respecting us—not laughing straight in our faces like she so easily could—but her expression says it before the words leave her lips. "Even if my employer was interested in selling, I don't know if it would be within your budget."

"Look, I know how much you bought it from Mr. Quarrells for, and I'll match it," I say.

Gabe opens his mouth to speak, but Vera beats him to it.

"Sloane—"

"I can write you a check," I say. My Dodge's money, my birthday and Christmas money for the past five years or so. I could do it. And I would. Without a second thought.

"I'm not sure how eager my client is to part with it right now," Gemma says, ever diplomatic.

"Can you at least find out?"

She evaluates us for a moment before nodding, and then those heels click away across the floor.

I studiously refuse to meet Vera's and Gabe's gaze. Instead I focus on the piece across from us, a photo-realistic painting of a fire hydrant.

"That one's Remy," I say.

Gemma returns after a while.

"I wasn't able to get ahold of him, but I left a message with his assistant," she says.

"He has an *assistant*," Vera whispers to me.

"I'm not sure when I'll hear back," Gemma says, "but I can certainly give you a call."

"Do you think it would be today or tomorrow?"

"I can't say." A pause. "There's a lot to see in this area, though," she says. "Have you been to the High Line?"

I have, but we came all the way here, so Vera and Gabe might as well see it, too.

We all thank Gemma, and she promises to let us know if she hears something. When we leave the redbrick building, I'm not sure if I'll ever hear from her again.

"She was nice, though," Vera says, looping her arm through mine. "Wasn't she?"

I *hmm* in agreement, and we head down the street.

We go to the High Line and walk down to Fourteenth Street. We stand at the railing, looking out over the patchwork buildings below us, and just farther, the West Side Highway, the piers, and the river.

"What are those?" Vera asks, pointing to a clump of logs sticking up out of the water.

"I don't know," I say. She slants me a look. "I'm not a guidebook."

"That aggressive guy with the bus-tour sign probably would've known," Gabe murmurs. "We should've gone with him."

We walk awhile, away from the High Line and into the neighborhoods around there. We're passing down a tree-lined street—the trees long having shed their leaves, stark against the winter sky—when my phone rings.

I move a little ways away from Vera and Gabe to answer.

"I was able to get in touch with my client," Gemma says, after the hellos. "Unfortunately, he doesn't . . ."A pause. "I'm sorry, but he's not interested in selling at this time."

"Did you tell him the story, though? Did you explain about their mom?"

"Yes," Gemma says.

"Did you tell him my offer? I'd pay what he paid for it."

"He said if he were to sell . . . he'd be asking a lot more."

"How much more?"

Gemma says a number that sounds like "fifty thousand," but that has to be wrong.

"Sorry?"

She says it again, and it sounds the same.

"Fifty," I repeat. "Five-zero."

"That's right."

"That's almost ten times what he paid for it."

"He thinks it's a truly remarkable piece."

"Then he should hang it in a museum, not his fucking house."

278

"I'm sorry," Gemma says, and through my anger I feel a pang, knowing that it's just like when people get mad at us at the deli counter because we don't have the kind of sandwiches we had yesterday. It's not her fault. She's just the messenger.

"It's fine," I say, even though it's not. "Thanks . . . thanks anyway."

"Anytime," she says, and hangs up.

I look back at Vera and Gabe. She's on her phone, but he catches my gaze and grabs Vera's sleeve, coming to meet me.

"What'd she say?"

I shake my head, some mixture of embarrassment and panic welling up in me because I might actually cry. I glare off down the street instead, and my voice comes out harsh, like I'm mad at Gabe somehow: "They're asking a ridiculous amount of money."

"How much?"

Vera's jaw drops when I tell them. But Gabe—Gabe just lets out one loud bark of laughter.

"Sorry," he says, when he sees my expression, and he's grinning somehow. It doesn't make any sense. "I'm sorry. It's just, if you had told our mom that one day someone would charge fifty thousand dollars for one of her paintings, she'd have flipped her shit."

"I can't believe it," Vera says.

"But it's arbitrary," I reply. "He's just charging that because he doesn't want us to have it. It doesn't mean anything to him. I don't understand—I don't—"

I look down the street, and it's quiet. Well, we're quiet. The city continues inexorably around us. Outside the bounds of this street are cabs and bikes and traffic lights and people, too many people to care about.

All I feel is disappointed. A crushing disappointment, the likes of which I've never felt before. That speaks to how great my life is, but I'm not in a glass-half-full state—I'm in an empty, end-of-the-line, end-of-the-journey state of thorough failure.

"Sloane, what's wrong?" Vera says.

I just shake my head.

We go to Rockefeller Center. Vera wants to see the rink, and even though I have zero percent interest in that, I can't deny her.

While they watch the skaters, I go inside, ostensibly to use the restroom, but I don't. Instead I stand in the shiny black-and-gold lobby and call Frank Sanger.

"I need you to be frank, Frank," I say, by way of a greeting.

"Hello to you, too, dollface."

"Frank."

"What is it?"

There's a lump in my throat at least the size of a plum. "We were supposed to get it back," I say, trying to swallow around it, trying not to sound plaintive, but that's how it comes out, whiny and frustrated and a little heartbroken. "That's what was gonna happen—he was supposed to say yes, because we were supposed to get it back."

"Hey." Frank's voice is soft, and I feel foolish, and childish, and I can't help but squeeze the phone tighter like it's his hand, like he's here. "What happened?"

I tell him, in a halted, broken-down, halfway-crying kind of way, that I've failed. We came this far and I failed.

"I know I'm being stupid," I say, after I tell him everything. "I don't mean to make it about me because it's not, it's about them, but I just . . . I just really wanted to do this for them. I thought I could. I know nothing can fill the space she left behind but I thought maybe—maybe this would make it hurt less, if we . . . if we got some little piece of her back. No one deserves what they've been through, but they especially don't deserve it, they're the best people I know and I just thought . . . I just wanted to . . . try to make it better." I swallow hard. "So what do I do now? What am I going to tell them?"

"You really wanna know?"

"Yes."

"You want me to be frank Frank?"

"Yes."

"Why don't you just tell them that you love them?"

"Sorry?"

"That's why you're doing all this, right? Because you love them? I mean . . . you do, don't you?"

I don't speak, but Frank knows.

"So maybe you don't need the thing. The painting . . . it's just a thing. Maybe you can say it without it."

I shake my head. "You don't get it. What it means to them."

"Honestly, Sloinbee? It seems like it means more to you."

It's quiet.

"Someone's calling me," Frank says after a while.

"Really?"

"No. I just didn't know how to end this conversation."

I let out a breath of laughter. "Cold grits."

"What now?"

I shake my head, even though he can't see. "Bye, Frank."

"Stay gold, sweetie pie."

I don't have time to tell Frank how much I appreciate him. How much he means to me. He has already hung up.

fifty

"She's so pretty, though," Vera says at the hotel that night.

"Who?"

"Gemma. She could be a model. I'm gonna google her."

I hum absentmindedly. Gabe is on the other bed, flipping through the channels. Our flight is leaving tomorrow afternoon, we've got no painting, and I don't know what to do.

"Holy shit," Vera says suddenly, sitting up.

"What?"

"Holy effing shit," she says, in perfect imitation of Frank, and then thrusts the phone in my direction.

There, on the screen, is a paparazzi picture of Gemma and none other than Dex Finnegan exiting a building together. He's holding the door for her but glancing toward the camera. Her head is bent away, and she's holding a coat over one arm, stepping carefully onto the sidewalk in precarious heels.

"Keep scrolling," she says, and there are more pictures of Dex and Gemma, standing outside a bar, leaving a club. Sometimes he casts a little smile at the camera, but her face is always at least partially turned away. There's no denying it, though—this is Gemma Crane.

"Oh my God," Vera says, and bounces up and down on the bed a little. "Oh my God."

"What are you guys even looking at?" Gabe says, sounding half asleep. It's only nine, but it's the walking, I think. New York will get you with all the walking.

"Do you know what this means?" Vera says.

"Gemma and Dex Finnegan are doing the do? It makes sense. Evolutionarily. She's found someone as attractive as her, and so has he."

"Dex Finnegan was shooting some Civil War movie in Alabama a few months ago. I remember because Bree and Jenny wanted to go see them shooting."

"So that's why she was there. That's when she got the painting."

"Maybe he's the mysterious art collector!"

"But that would mean she worked for him."

"So? That kind of stuff happens. Couples can work together. Maybe that's how they got together in the first place! He hired her to collect art for him"—her voice lowers dramatically—"but instead . . . she collected . . . *his heart.*"

"Oh my God, you sound like my dad."

Her eyes widen. "Sloane, we have to go see him."

"My dad?"

"Dex!"

"Where are we gonna see Dex Finnegan?"

"At the theater! Frank said he was on Broadway right now! We have

283

to go try to catch him at the stage door!" She stands up on the bed and then jumps to Gabe's bed. I'm pretty certain he's asleep at this point. "Gabe! Wake up, get up, we're going out!"

We go out. Vera's a force of nature, after all.

I don't truly believe there is any way this is going to work or help, but we go to the Al Hirschfeld Theatre, and we're early enough to elbow our way to the front, right behind the sawhorses at the stage door.

When the first actors emerge, squeals pass through the gathered crowd, but it's just the supporting cast. The play has been out awhile before Dex Finnegan emerges.

He flashes a big smile and starts signing programs. We're a little bit farther down, but I speak when he's near enough. "Dex?"

He smiles at me, kind but unrecognizing, and reaches out to grab the magazine with his face on it that Vera bought on the way over.

"You probably don't remember me, but I'm Sloane Finch . . . Everett Finch's daughter?"

He looks up as he's signing, and it flashes across his face: "Oh wow, Sloane, of course." He pulls me into a one-armed hug as he hands the magazine back to Vera. "Look at you. You're all grown up. How's your dad?" He reaches for the program of the girl next to us.

"He's good," I say, watching as Dex leans into the frame of the girl's camera and smiles. "Thank you," the girl says after they take the picture. Her hands are shaking a bit as she takes the program back from Dex.

"Hey, thank *you*. I hope you liked the show."

Another person is edging in to our left, so I go ahead: "Listen,

I know it's asking a lot, but we were hoping we could talk to you for a minute. It's . . ." I almost add *about something important*, but then I remember that in the grand scheme of things, us retrieving a painting is probably not particularly important to Dex Finnegan.

But he just nods and says, "Of course," and then he's signing another program, leaning in for another picture. "Look, go up a few blocks. Say . . . Fiftieth and Tenth. I'll come meet you there."

"Really?" Gabe says, the first time he's spoken since the stage doors opened.

"Of course. Any friend of Everett's—" he starts, but doesn't finish, as a woman near us starts telling Dex how much she loved him in the show.

We walk up and over, and we wait outside a discount tech store. One of those ones with the brightly lit clear-plastic window displays housing discount early-generation iPads and cameras from several years back.

Twenty minutes later, I've almost got the display memorized (32 GB IPHONE, $1!!!!!), and Vera finally speaks. "Do you think he meant it?" she asks, stomping her feet and inching closer to me for warmth.

"I have no idea. I've only met him twice."

"You said he came to Thanksgiving!"

"Yeah, but just because someone likes your mom's pecan pie doesn't mean they're true to their word, does it?"

"He's coming," Gabe says definitively.

I glance over at him. "How do you know?"

"He wouldn't leave a bunch of kids stranded."

"We're not stranded. This mission was voluntary."

"Yeah, but he doesn't know that. He's coming," Gabe says.

And he's right—a black SUV with tinted windows rolls up ten minutes later, and the back door swings open.

"I'm sorry," Dex says. "So sorry, should've warned you, I try to get to everyone at the stage door. It can take a while sometimes. Come in, Christ, it's cold, get in here. I'm really sorry."

"Are you serious?" Vera says, piling in. "You're doing us the favor."

"Yeah, what's up? Do you guys need a ride somewhere? We can talk on the way. Or we could—well, okay, so where could we go that's not weird?"

"Weird how?" I say.

"'Dex Finnegan Takes High School Kids to Party Hard'?" Gabe murmurs next to me, and I nearly smack him. But Dex just grins.

"Exactly." The car has already eased back into traffic, heading uptown. Dex thinks a moment, and then snaps his fingers. "Got it."

"Papaya Town?" I'd been to Gray's Papaya on the West Side and Papaya King on the East Side. Hot dogs that you eat while standing at a counter, complemented by an aggressively orange fruit beverage, are kind of a New York staple.

But I have never heard of Papaya Town.

Dex points to the sign. "This is it. This is the pinnacle of the New York hot-dog experience."

"Off-brand Gray's Papaya?" I say.

"Papaya Town came first. Don't compare it to those fakes. This is the one and only, the true original."

"Do they pay you to endorse them?"

"Nope. I do it 'cause I love it."

★ ★ ★

"So what's up?"

We've acquired hot dogs, papaya drinks, and prime standing spots at the counter by the window. "We wanted to talk to you about a painting," I say, chasing some mustard dripping down my wrist.

"A painting?"

"Yeah. We met with Gemma Crane, and the price they set for it is ridiculously high, but we sort of thought—"

"Wait, what?"

We backtrack a bit, and when we're done filling him in, Dex just blinks at us.

"Gemma said . . . why would she . . ."

"I mean, she didn't say you explicitly, but we saw the pictures of you two together, and we know that she was in Alabama when you were shooting that war movie, so we sort of just . . . extrapolated." I pause. "Did we extrapolate . . . wrong?"

"Kind of," he says, and then takes a bite of his hot dog. It isn't until he's washed it down with some papaya drink that he speaks again. "She's not my art dealer, anyway."

"Wait, really?" Vera asks.

"We were dating, though," he says. "But she didn't like the attention . . . the scrutiny, you know. She didn't want any of that. It's probably why . . ." He takes another drink, a long one, and I get the feeling he doesn't want to elaborate. "So she's not my art dealer. But she does work for someone I know. A producer. Jack Fine?"

I look at Vera, and then at Gabe, and I can't help but feel it: a little flutter of hope.

"So tell me about this painting," Dex says.

287

fifty-one

"It's the best I could do," Dex says on the phone the next morning, and I shake my head even though he can't see me.

"This is great, thank you so much."

"Anytime. Tell your dad hey. Tell him he better write a new book so we can hang out again."

"Will do."

"I love Dex Finnegan," Vera says when I hang up the phone. "I want Frank to marry him so he's in our lives forever."

We're standing outside the address Dex texted me, a building on Madison Square Park. It's raining—a light rain, more of a mist—and the wet bark of the trees is stark against the pale gray sky. Vera's hair is frizzing out a bit, and so is Gabe's, little tendrils twisting around their foreheads. I pat my own hair to see what it's doing, and as I do, I see Gemma Crane approach from down the street.

She's holding a black umbrella and wearing a stylish trench. She smiles a little when she nears.

"You guys are remarkably well connected."

"Thank you for doing this," I say.

"Thank Dex. He called Mr. Fine." She ushers us into the building. A doorman sits at the front desk. Gemma speaks to him briefly and then proceeds to the elevator. We get in, and she presses the PH button.

Vera looks at me, eyes wide. I bite my lip to suppress a smile.

The elevator opens right into the apartment. I've heard of places like that but never seen one in real life. The doors slide apart and here we are, stepping into Jack Fine's penthouse.

It's modern, mostly, but in a warm sort of way, with rich colors and clean lines. There's art everywhere—to be expected. Right next to the elevator is a framed painting. Vera steps up to inspect it, and her eyes widen.

"Is this real? A Picasso? For real?" She gets closer, squinting at the smudgy signature at the bottom.

"No, I'm pretty sure this guy collects posters," Gabe says.

"Well, you never know," Vera says defensively. "Some people think the prints are just as good."

"If the prints were just as good, we wouldn't be here, would we?"

"Mom never did prints," she replies.

Gemma leads us into a large room with windows stretching all along one wall, a panoramic view spread out before us.

We all gravitate toward the windows, looking out at the city below.

But then Gemma clears her throat. I turn, and there, on the wall opposite the windows, is *The Dream*.

According to *Laura Fuller: A Retrospective*, Laura Fuller painted five paintings in the last month of her life. They weren't like any of the others. They were . . . frantic, almost. Wild. And this one—God, this one is a sight to see. It's not realism, not even impressionism like some of her other pieces. Swirls of blues and blacks outline three figures, central to the piece, and above them a radiant skyscape—purple and yellow and white—spreads across the open expanse like wings. Like arms, embracing them.

"Fuck," I murmur.

When I look over at Vera, she's crying.

"I shouldn't have gotten rid of it," she says softly. "But I couldn't . . . Do you see why I couldn't . . ."

I nod.

"*The Dream*," she says. "Her dream. For us."

We look at the painting for a long time. I shift back after a while, and Vera and Gabe look at it still.

Finally, Vera turns, her eyes wet, and smiles at Gemma, one of those devastating Vera smiles that makes you want to give her the world.

"Could we look at the back? Please? Sometimes she would write on the back."

"We'll be careful," Gabe says, and Gemma nods.

They gently lift the painting from the wall and turn it around. The frame is handmade, the canvas hand-stretched, and when Vera pulls back the flap along the bottom, it reveals a scrawl of words:

To my darling girl and boy, Vera and Gabriel, with all my love.

Vera runs her fingertips lightly over the words. I glance at Gemma to see if she'll protest, but she doesn't say anything.

"I'm sorry," Vera says, looking at Gabe.

"Don't be." His voice is rough. He still manages a crooked smile, though: "It's not that great."

Vera gives a sputtery laugh. "Shut up. It's—"

"I know." He leans in and bumps his shoulder against hers. "Don't be," he says again quietly, and runs his fingertips over the words, too.

They hang the painting back up, and Vera takes several dozen pictures of it and makes Gabe do the same, just in case. I take a few of the two of them in front of it, and then Gemma steps up, hand outstretched for the phone.

"Why don't you jump in one, too?" she says.

"Yes." Vera reaches out for me, and I join them. Then Vera makes Gemma join, too, a selfie with all of us and the painting, and when Gemma smiles, it's strikingly beautiful, almost as powerful as Vera's.

And then it's time to go.

Gemma pauses in the foyer of the building, fumbling with something in her purse.

"My information," she says, and holds out a black business card, the same black rectangle with embossed white writing that Mr. Quarrells presented to us at Wilderness Art and Antiques. "My cell is on the back. If you're ever in the city and you'd like to come see the painting, please, don't hesitate to call. I could try to arrange another viewing for you—"

It's little consolation. But Vera just takes the card from her outstretched hand and smiles. "Thank you so much." She nudges me. "Maybe you can come visit it, when you're back for school."

Maybe. Yeah. I try to smile at Gemma. Gemma, who would probably move on from this job before we're even back again. It's little consolation indeed.

It's still misting when we get outside. All the benches in the park are wet, so we just stand to the side of a footpath, near a dormant garden bed.

"Do that thing," Gabe says finally, "where you say something funny and distract us."

"I thought you hated that."

"It's one of my favorite things about you," he says, and it's honest, earnest. I blink.

"Well, it's not funny, exactly, but I read this thing . . . I read this thing that said maybe fingerprints are formed when a fetus pushes their hands up against the inside of the womb. So if that's true, it means you're actually walking around with the blueprints to your mom's uterus on your hands."

It's random enough that Vera stops crying for a moment. "That's really weird, Sloane," she says, before her eyes flood again.

"Don't cry," I say.

She blinks at me. "Why not?"

I hadn't really thought about it before. But it is a pretty dickish thing to say, isn't it? Why shouldn't people cry? What's so bad about it, except its capacity to make an outside party feel uncomfortable? If I said "Because I don't want to see you sad," it would be making it about me.

So I just open up my arms and Vera leans against me, and Gabe steps closer, putting one hand on her hair and petting it absently. None of us say anything. The city pulses on around us, and I'm not sure which one of us is anchoring the others, but I've never felt less adrift.

fifty-two

Vera makes me sit between her and Gabe on the flight home. Even though I hate the middle, I oblige.

A hush sets in as the plane takes off. A baby grouses somewhere toward the back, but it's quiet here, between us.

I thought that I could do it. That it would be coming back with us. But I didn't, and maybe that's okay. Maybe it was enough just to see it again. I glance at Vera, scrolling away on her phone, and at Gabe, flipping through one of those airline travel magazines, and I hope so.

I watch the screen on the back of the seat in front of me, charting our journey. A little airplane avatar inches along a thin orange line from New York to Atlanta.

I look over at Gabe and the flash of his wrist as he turns the page.

"Coordinates," I say. "Right?"

He wrinkles his brow but then follows my gaze to the string of numbers below his palm.

"Yeah," he says. "For the beach at Grayson. It's, uh, it's where we scattered our mom's ashes."

"Gabe's a sap," Vera says.

"It's not sappy," I reply automatically, but Vera just smiles.

"I know. I'm just making fun. It's my job because I'm older."

"Are you?"

"Yup. I existed in the world without him for nine whole minutes." It starts light, joking, but her voice is soft by the end: "I never want to go through that again."

Gabe doesn't speak, just looks down at the magazine in his lap.

"Can I ask you something?" I say, when I can't keep it in any longer. I ask it of the seatback in front of me, rather than either of them specifically, because I'm not sure who would answer.

"Anything," Vera says.

"Why didn't she dedicate it to him, too? The painting. Why didn't she dedicate it to your dad? He's in it, too."

Gabe's voice is quiet when he speaks: "Maybe she knew he'd fuck up."

"He didn't fuck up," Vera says. "He just . . . moved on."

Gabe's mouth twists.

And I don't like it, the downcast eyes, the furrow in his brow. So I speak. "Maybe there are people who love someone so much that when they lose them, they never want to be with anyone else again. But maybe there are people who love someone so much that it makes them want to find that kind of love again. Maybe they loved them so much, they can't live without that kind of love in their life. And maybe . . . it's a kind of love where you don't have to say it. Where they're such a part of you and you're such a part of them that it doesn't need to be said. Because you already know."

When I glance up at Gabe again, he has his eyes on me.

"Yeah," he says. "Maybe."

"I like that," Vera says with a small smile. "I think it must be like that."

I think about that kind of love as we increase in altitude. How maybe it doesn't just stand for romance—maybe it works for friendship, too. Maybe there's a kind of friend love that opens you up . . . Maybe you didn't have a place for it within you before, but once it finds you out, crawls inside, and makes space for itself, you can't live without it ever again.

I look over at Vera, and I think about what she said to me the first day we had lunch together: *They never really say that they love each other, but it's so freaking obvious. Like, Sherlock would straight-up kill for Watson.*

"Just so you know," I say, "I would straight-up kill for you."

Vera just smiles. Wraps one arm around me and pulls me closer. I rest my head on her shoulder, and she presses her mouth against my hair.

"Ditto," she says, and it warms and soothes.

fifty-three

I arrive home in time for a late dinner and for Laney's pleading with my mom to go out and see the "winter constellations."

"It's peak conditions!" Laney says, waving *A Comprehensive Guide to the Stars* around for emphasis. "Crisp and clear! That's supposed to be the best! And it's *Saturday*, Mama. We can stay up on Saturday."

"I'll take her," I say, finishing up my food.

"Just a quick walk down to the beach and back," Mom says. "And not down the stairs to the water. Just stand at the top and look."

"Got it."

"And then right back."

"We got it!" Laney says, and grabs my hand, pulling me up out of my chair. "Let's go!"

We take the short walk to the beach access closest to our house, just through the neighborhood and across 30A. Laney's flashlight bobs in the darkness as we walk.

"Papa said you couldn't get the painting for Vera," Laney says, after a few moments of silence. Just the scuff of our sneakers against the sand-packed road.

As we were waiting for our flight, I had texted my parents with just the essentials—that we got to see the painting, but it wasn't for sale. I was still too disappointed to deliver the news in person.

"Yeah," I say. "I couldn't."

"Bummer," Laney says, in such a way that indicates she truly thinks it's a bummer. I can't help but smile.

"It is. It was a really beautiful painting. It was . . . I think it was really important to their mom."

"It's too bad she didn't have a *My Memories*," Laney says. "Then at least you could see everything she was thinking when she painted it."

I blink.

I text them both that night: *Did your mom have sketchbooks?*

fifty-four

Vera comes over on Sunday afternoon and pulls a black, cloth-bound book out of her backpack. We settle on my bed, and she turns the pages slowly. They're covered with drawings, some in pen, some in colored pencil. Some of the pages have writing on them, but Vera turns them before I get the chance to read too closely.

"We spent all morning looking at them," she says. "Me and Gabe. Mandy even looked, too, for a little bit. It was . . . it was nice. We haven't . . . All that stuff was boxed up, after she died. We hadn't gone through them. But look."

She stops on one page, toward the middle of the book. It's a pencil sketch of three figures, with lines swirling around and above, radiating away from them but also somehow radiating toward them.

It's stark and so rough. But it's *The Dream*.

Vera smiles at me and turns the page. Another iteration is there, and on the page opposite, yet another. The fourth has some color added, and the fifth even more.

It's Laura Fuller's thought process. It's her plan for the painting.

I swallow.

"It's awesome," I say, a pathetic understatement, but Vera understands. She keeps flipping, more life spilling into the painting with each page, until she stops on one that almost depicts the real thing.

"This is the last one," she says. "There are a few pages of other stuff after, but . . ."

We're just over halfway through the book. The rest of the pages are empty.

It's not like I have some brilliant revelation. It's not like I understand death intrinsically now. But I don't think I ever understood it as clearly as I do seeing the empty pages, the ones that Vera's mom will never fill.

"We should've looked before," Vera says, her voice soft. "We could've saved you the trouble."

"Are you kidding? The trouble was the best part."

She smiles.

We hang out after that, just watching videos online and talking about nothing much. It's late in the afternoon when Vera's phone buzzes.

"Ah," she says. "Gotta get going. Walk me out?"

I walk with her downstairs and out onto the porch, hugging myself against the cold.

To my surprise, Gabe is getting out of their car in front of our house.

Vera heads down the steps and takes the keys out of his hand. "You can ride my bike back," she says to Gabe, then blows me a kiss. "Call me later, okay?"

"Did you guys plan this?" I say.

"Wait, wait, wait." Gabe ducks around to the back of the car and pulls something large and rectangular out of the trunk. "Okay, now get lost."

Vera grins at me, shuts the door, and drives away.

"What are you doing here? What's that?" I'm still on the porch, but Gabe doesn't climb the steps to meet me. He just stands out front, awkwardly holding what's clearly a canvas, the front of it facing away from me.

"Remy told me," he says. "How you saw the mom with the day care. I thought maybe . . . He said Day Care Mom wasn't happy with this one. So I thought maybe you could give it a home."

He turns the painting around. It's the red dock, jutting out into the water, with the bright sun beating down, warming it from the inside out. If you squint, it almost looks like Bree's dock.

"How did you get it?"

"Remy went back with me," he says. "She really wanted to get rid of it. It was a bargain. She was asking almost fifty grand less than Jack Fine."

"You didn't have to do that."

"You didn't have to do what you did. Any of it. But you did."

"Yeah, well. You know. It was . . . for a good cause."

"What cause?"

"You."

We look at each other for a moment, and it's Gabe who looks away first.

"I don't like Remy," I blurt.

He looks back quickly.

"I mean, I like him. But not like that. Just in case . . . you thought

300

that. I mean, Aubrey thought that. I don't know who else was under that . . . misconception . . ."

He nods. "I'm not with Alice," he says.

"I can see that. Unless she's gone invisible."

That brings a small smile to his lips. "You know what I mean." A pause. "We weren't ever . . . We just hung out, really. She liked having someone to go with her to the Jade Coast parties and stuff. And I liked . . ." He looks away. "I didn't know her before my mom passed away. So. I guess I kind of liked hanging out with someone who wouldn't . . . look at me the way everyone else does sometimes."

I nod. And I can't help it, but it just slips out—"Is that why you hang out with me?"

"No," he says, fast enough to dispel any doubts. "God. No."

"So . . ."

So what is it? If it's not because of Remy, or Alice, if there's no barrier, no obstacle, no mistaken anything, why is there still distance between us? But maybe that was never the reason. Maybe he just doesn't . . .

When he looks at me again, it's with uncertainty.

"I thought maybe you just didn't . . . you know."

"Lust after you with the heat of a thousand suns?"

"Maybe not a thousand," he says, eyes shining. "Maybe just one. One really big sun. And maybe not just lust, specifically, but like lust and all the other stuff."

"With, like, the brightness of a star and the speeding intensity of a meteorite and the . . . diffuse energy . . . of a gas giant?"

"Yes."

It's not a thunderclap. Or a lightning bolt straight to the chest. It's

301

not a magnetic pull toward my heart's true north. It's just . . . natural, to step off the porch and step up to him, the painting still between us. It's a little bit like breathing, like what Remy was saying—something you just do without conscious thought. Something that is because it is; it exists because there's no other way than it existing.

The realization is all at once stunning and at the same time, somehow, not a surprise at all. I must've loved him all along. I just didn't realize it.

"I gas-giant the shit out of you, Gabe," I say, and I kiss him.

I kiss him very briefly but with great feeling, and then I pull back a little and look at him, his eyes wide, lips parted, and when he gives me the most radiant smile, I can't help it—I go back twice as hard, pulling him closer and kissing him like I mean it, because God, do I mean it. And as he threads one hand through my hair and kisses back with just as much feeling, I send a silent thanks up to Frank for not letting me kiss him that night on the porch, because he was right—this is so much better. That kiss would've been fun, no doubt. But this is one to cherish.

"Really?" Gabe says, when we break apart for a moment. I can't help but snort.

"No, you're right, I changed my mind."

"Wait, really?" he says, and I take his face between my hands.

"I like you," I say. "I lustful-sun like you, I meteorite like you, you are the fucking pink Starburst to me."

He grins. And kisses me again but then eases up, shifts the painting to one side, wraps an arm around me, and just hugs me, and I think I like that just as much. It's at the very least an incredibly close second.

"You said no, though," he says, slightly muffled. "When I asked you out. That one time."

"Wait, what?"

"That time at work? I asked you to the movies, and you said you would invite Vera?"

I pull back a bit. "That wasn't—you weren't *asking me out*. You said I could come, too, if I wanted. That's not asking someone out."

"It was to me," he says, sheepish, and I want to poke him, but I also kind of want to hug him forever.

"Next time you want to ask someone out, maybe be less subtle. Maybe try to use the word *date* or *together*. Maybe phrase it as an actual question, you know, get some upward inflection going at the end of the sentence?"

He just looks at me, a little bit like he wants to poke me, but maybe also hug me forever. Instead he just kisses me, and it's a long time before we break apart again.

"Geez," he says finally. "I would've stood farther away from the trash cans if I knew you were gonna kiss me." I smile, up close, almost against his lips.

"Don't worry. My dad'll write it better in his book."

He shakes his head.

"Not possible."

fifty-five

"We saw you kissing outside!" Laney crows when I step back into the house holding the painting. Gabe has headed off on Vera's bike. "I saw it! I saw you! Kissing! You were kissing!"

"Mom."

"She's right, we did. See you. Kissing," my mom says, barely suppressing a grin. "What do you have? What did he give you?"

"Besides *the tongue*," Laney says with glee.

"Mom! Make her stop!"

"What do you know about the tongue?" my mom says to Laney. She comes over and takes the painting from my hands. "Oh, wow. He gave this to you?"

"Yes," I say. "Along with the tongue." My mom makes a face at me, but it softens when she looks back at the canvas. "Their mom painted it."

"What an incredible gift," she says, and it's true. It is.

I find my dad in his office that evening, typing away. He stops when he sees me in the doorway.

"More fic?"

"Not tonight." He pulls his glasses up and rests them on the top of his head. "What's the word?"

I shrug, leaning against the doorframe. "Am I Penny?" I say. "From *Sand on Our Beach*? And Austin, and Sheila. . . . Am I them? Are they me?"

He pauses, and then: "They're them. And you're you. But I wouldn't have them if I didn't have you." A beat. "You know, the thing about fic is that it comes from love. Characters you love so much, that you feel so deeply for, you'll watch them fall in love a thousand different ways, over and over.

"I've never loved any of my characters that much," he says. "But I love you that much. So maybe . . . so that's where I went. That's what I went with."

I nod. "I love you, too. I mean, I don't want to write a book about you, but I love you, too."

"Maybe someday you will," he says. "A bestseller. Dex Finnegan can play me in the movie."

I smile. "You wish."

He smiles back, but it slips after a moment, and he looks down. "Sloane . . . listen. Your mom and I, we—"

"It's okay. We don't have to talk about it."

"We're a work in progress."

"You're never supposed to read a work in progress," I murmur, and he shakes his head.

"No. I think I was wrong about that. I think . . . I think there's some joy in seeing where it goes. There's struggle, too, and the chance that you may not finish or it may not end the way you expected it to . . . but there's joy to it, as well."

I don't know if I believe him. But I think at least he believes himself. So that's something.

fifty-six

Aubrey sits down next to me in concert choir the next week.

"How did the audition go?" she asks.

"Okay."

She raises one eyebrow. "Just okay?"

Everyone should have punched-in-the-face-for kinds of friends, Gabe had said that night outside the party. I'd never had that kind of friendship before. But maybe it's because I'd never been that kind of friend.

And maybe Aubrey and I would never be particularly chummy. But I could put the effort in, at least.

"It wasn't great," I say. "But . . . if I'm lucky, maybe I'll get another shot at a different school."

She nods. "I hope it works out."

"Me too."

It's unseasonably warm this week, and Vera suggests a trip to the beach after school.

I stay back with Gabe while the others run ahead. Vera jumps on

Frank's back, and he carries her, piggyback-style, while Bree skips along in front of them. Remy and Aubrey follow, slower. The sun hangs low in the sky, and that midwinter light dances over all of them, golden, making their shadows impossibly long.

"What do you think about them?" Gabe nods in Remy and Aubrey's direction as we settle down onto a bench.

"What, are we taking bets?"

"No." He makes a face. "No, just . . . What do you think?"

"They're not back together or anything."

"No."

"But in a perfect world," I say, "they'd be great. Look at them. He's beautiful and she's beautiful and they'd grow up and have brilliant, civic-minded children who would always recycle. They'd recycle so hard, Gabe."

He smiles at me for a moment, and I can't help it—I kiss him.

"What was that for?" he murmurs when we break apart.

I shrug. "You smell good to me." And it's the truth. I drop down to a whisper: "You smell like a thousand babies planking for a thousand years."

"They wouldn't be babies anymore after a thousand years," he whispers back.

"They're Forever Babies. They've been genetically engineered."

"Why would someone want a baby forever? What's more, why do the babies want such tight abs?"

I grin and kiss him again.

When we both look back out at the beach, Vera has abandoned Frank, who is now down at the water's edge with Bree and Aubrey. Vera looks up at us. When she catches our gaze, she smiles, bright in the setting sun. She presses a kiss to her hand and then holds it to her heart.

I glance at Gabe, who does it back.

"Not you!" Vera yells. "Sloane!"

I laugh and do the same, and it reminds me of the elementary-school ritual from back in the day. A promise. An oath. And maybe it's a little bit like mine and Ella's—*See you tomorrow*—but maybe it's deeper than that. Maybe it's also *I love you.*

Then Gabe flips her the bird, and Vera makes a face at us both.

She turns and skips to the waterline, coming up behind Frank and wrapping her arms around his waist. He does a little shimmy and she holds on, laughing. That's Frank Sanger. For all people.

I glance over at Gabe. Maybe I was wrong about me. About being for no one. I don't know what the future holds. My dad is right—there are no guarantees. None. But I pick up Gabe's hand and lace our fingers together, and that's enough in this moment.

We look out at the water, and that is more than enough for now.

acknowledgments

This book exists in large part through the magic of Kate Farrell, first-rate editor, and Bridget Smith, top-notch agent—sincerest thanks to you both! Thank you also to the talented people at Macmillan/Henry Holt, with particular thanks to Brittany Pearlman for her publicity wizardry, to the Fierce Reads team for their ongoing awesomeness, and to Liz Dresner for the gorgeous cover design.

Additional thanks to my Mama, Papa, Hannie, and Cappy for all the love. To Pei-Ciao, Rachel, Shawn, and Lakshmi for the fun times. To Rochelle, for the insightful and ever-helpful beta read. To Wintaye, for Frank Sanger and fandom discourse. To Sara, for surprising me in the signing line! To Mike and Sarah, for never forgetting to be awesome. To the members of the Elmify and How to Adult communities, thank you so much for your kindness and support.

I did not discover fan-fiction until the age of twenty-four, and it was a revelation. I have found comfort and joy in fandom ever since. Thank you to fic writers everywhere, for all that you do. A million "kudos" could not be enough.